Murder Behind
the Screen

D1806468

Murder Behind the Screen

IAN RICHARDSON

THE CHOIR PRESS

First published in the United Kingdom in 2021 by
The Choir Press

ISBN 978-1-78963-165-4

Murder behind the Screen is a work of fiction. Names, characters,
businesses, events and incidents are the products of the author's
imagination. Any resemblance to actual persons, living or dead, or
actual events and places is unintentional and purely coincidental.
Some long-standing institutions, agencies and public offices may be
mentioned to create scenery for the purposes of the story but the
characters and events involved are wholly imaginary.

PART I

RUN-UP TO THE FIRST MURDER

Chapter 1

Outside a studio in the unfashionable end of Hollywood, close to Hollywood Boulevard but far away from the main tourist sights, a few Japanese tourists were taking photos of the featureless building, hoping some of the imagined glamour would rub off on them. It was close to Christmas, and the temperature was as cold as it ever is in southern California.

Inside the studio, an artificially blonde young starlet reclined on a bed, beneath the hot lights. She altered her transparent negligee, as the director told her, to give the paying customers what they wanted.

Suzy Flanagan shuddered with embarrassment when she thought back to the ambitions of stardom that had brought her here. Her family back home in Georgia fondly imagined she had a steady role in an afternoon soap opera. At times like this, she told herself she was glad she had adopted a stage name, so that they should never see the type of film in which she appeared.

Suzy forced herself to smile welcomingly as the leading man with bad breath lay beside her. She was practised enough to feign enjoyment as the two had sex with cameras focussed on their bodies. Once the performance was finished, the male porn star was ushered out immediately, as he had other films to appear in.

In the next scene in her script, the door was to burst open and a famous actor playing her husband was to enter with a gun in his hand. Her character was to be killed at this point. This was the end of her appearance in the picture and she wanted to make as good an impression as possible. She told herself that, by some chance, a mainstream casting director might spot her and book her for something better, even though she knew how hopeless her dream was.

As the script demanded, the starlet smoked a cigarette in bed.

The door on the set burst open as the director entered with a gun. Suzy had seen no sign of the famous actor and had been told his appearance would be cut in later. She had the feeling his name had only been mentioned to persuade her to appear in this film.

Suzy put on a startled expression as the director pulled the trigger. She told herself it was a relief to finally do some genuine acting.

Suzy faked a horrified scream, but this soon became real, as live bullets tore through her flesh and into the set behind. Her blood spattered across the satin sheets on the bed. The director reflected she probably never realised the bullets were real until it was too late. Blood spurted out of the back of her head as she suddenly fell forward onto the mattress. The director yelled, 'Cut!' and the cameras stopped rolling.

The handful of men in the studio sighed with the satisfaction of connoisseurs of a particular perversion. There was a niche market for watching people die for real, and some wealthy men were happy to pay over the odds for the pleasure it gave them. Most customers had to be satisfied with buying videos to watch at home; only a select and very rich few were allowed into the studio to watch the murders taking place.

'OK, print,' shouted the director. 'Someone get rid of the body.'

Two men in overalls put the body into a large plastic body bag and took it away. Once they had gone, no speck of blood remained to reveal any clue to the murder that had recently taken place in the studio.

The director turned to one of the small group of men in suits standing at the edge of the set. 'Is that good enough for you, Sir Giles?' he asked.

A portly man, aged around sixty, stepped forward from the shadows. 'That's excellent,' he said, his English public-school accent sounding out of place in the Hollywood studio. 'It's always a pleasure to see a true artist at work. If you can print it off overnight, I'll take it back to London with me tomorrow. I have some demanding customers crying for high-class exotic material like this.'

Sir Giles Palmer shook the director's hand and prepared to leave. He climbed into his hire car and drove off to his hotel in Beverley Hills. It was close to Christmas 1993 and the plastic Father Christmases were set out on the plastic snow around the expensive houses. Sir Giles allowed himself a small smile of satisfaction as he surveyed the scene. He told himself it had been a very successful day.

*

The following evening, the video of Suzy's murder was in Sir Giles Palmer's briefcase as he sat in the first-class cabin of the British Airways flight from Los Angeles to London. As he had come to expect, the cabin staff treated him with the deference due to a regular big-spending customer. Sipping his complimentary champagne cocktail, he doubted anyone would suspect him of any criminal activity. He told himself that his inherited baronetcy was very useful from that point of view.

In the row behind Sir Giles, a crew-cut American man in a cheap suit sipped a glass of bourbon. As the American watched, Sir Giles relaxed in his seat and reflected on how successful his visit to Los Angeles had been. He planned his next steps when he would be back in his City of London office. To pass the time during the flight, he opened the latest issue of *Dirty Money*, which he had bought at Heathrow on the outward flight. He knew it was a magazine that had developed a reputation for unveiling dubious accounting practices within the City of London.

Sir Giles flipped through the first few pages, revelling in the gossip about his business rivals. Suddenly, he sat up in shock. An article about his own company, Palmer Associates, written by the editor, a man called Robin Lynch, made him put down his drink with a crash. He read the revelations in the article with mounting horror, as he knew they were largely true. He vowed to find out who had been leaking such damaging information to *Dirty Money* as soon as he returned to his office.

Once the plane landed at Heathrow, Sir Giles strode off towards his chauffeur-driven car, which drove him smoothly to his home in one of the leafier parts of Fulham.

The crew-cut American watched Sir Giles leave, then phoned his London contact to inform him of Sir Giles's imminent return home. Then the crew-cut man walked over to the airline booth to book the cheapest possible flight back to Los Angeles. He would miss the comfort of his first-class outward flight, but, as an undercover detective, he accepted the need to save the Los Angeles police department funds by economising on travel wherever possible.

Chapter 2

The next day, Sir Giles walked into the marbled entrance hall of Palmer Associates in the City of London. He always enjoyed the way the receptionist jumped to attention and rushed to hold back the door of his private lift as he arrived.

When he reached the top floor, Sir Giles entered his private room and pressed the intercom. Only Derek Ringer, the managing director of the company, knew about his profitable sideline in snuff videos, and Derek was the person he summoned first.

Derek entered immediately, carrying a locked briefcase. He had come a long way since his first job, as a clerk in one of Sir Giles's other companies, and he knew that if Sir Giles was dissatisfied with his work, he could be back where he started.

'It's great to see you, Sir Giles,' Derek said. 'I hope you had a successful trip to California. Is there anything I can do for you now you're back?' He waited patiently for Sir Giles's orders, keeping his head bowed in deference.

'We've got another video for distribution, Derek,' Sir Giles said, brushing aside Derek's sycophantic greeting. 'This one's only for our most secret customers. It's a good one. I think it should sell well.'

Derek took the video with reverence. He was proud to serve Sir Giles in his criminal activities. This responsibility was reflected in his salary, which was several times higher than expected of his level. 'I'll approach the gold customers first, shall I, Sir Giles? It sounds as if it's the sort of thing only the best people will appreciate. It's a pleasure to meet customer demand in this way. There's one contact who is a particularly good client of ours. I'll make an appointment to see him straight away.'

'Yes, yes, you know the drill,' Sir Giles said. 'I don't need to know the details. Oh, and have you seen the latest edition of this rag?' Sir Giles pulled out the edition of *Dirty Money* he had been reading on the plane and threw it at Derek. 'This man Lynch is getting too close to the truth. Someone in this office must have been talking. Look into it straight away.'

Derek picked it up and stared at the headline on the article. 'I'm sure no one in the office would leak any secrets. But I'll investigate it straight away.'

'Make sure you do,' Sir Giles said. 'I want whoever is responsible out of this company as soon as possible.' He turned away to dismiss Derek. Derek bowed out, concealing the video in his briefcase and holding the magazine in his hand.

Sir Giles started to read through the correspondence that had piled up while he had been away. He reflected that Derek's fawning could prove cloying after a while.

*

At the same time, an attractive dark-haired young woman at a desk a hundred feet from Sir Giles's office put down the computer printout she was studying.

Heather Morgan sighed as she watched Derek Ringer walk out of Sir Giles Palmer's office. It seemed that Derek was always the first person Sir Giles asked to see when he came back from his regular trips to Los Angeles. The company's business involved importing and exporting as well as providing finance to various countries around the world, but Heather could see no real benefit from Sir Giles's monthly trips to California, and wondered why he was so secretive about them.

Heather shook her head, then returned to her routine task of preparing monthly salary cheques. Each month, she was baffled by how large Derek's salary was. He was her boss and she would have expected his salary to be higher than hers, but it seemed to be more than double the market rate for someone in his type of management role. While she had been in Palmer Associates for about a year, and had a responsible job dealing with the company's accounts, there were many things about the company that she did not yet understand. She reflected that Palmer Associates was one of the many secretive companies trading in the City of London that remained obscure even to their own employees.

'Hello, Heather, love, how are you?' The voice of James Faulkner, her assistant at work, interrupted her thoughts, as he stood behind her.

She and James had been engaged for a few months. Heather supposed the cliché that he had swept her off her feet was true, but over the last few weeks, their relationship seemed to have gone flat. She was not sure whose fault it was, but perhaps it was because they had become engaged while she was still on the rebound from her relationship with David Gould, a detective chief inspector in the City of London police.

She often wondered if she had made the right decision when she had broken up with David. She shrugged to herself sadly and reminded herself that there was no way of reviving her old relationship with David, and she was going to have to live with the consequences of her decision. In this case, those consequences seemed to involve getting married to James.

Heather forced herself to smile at James. She reminded herself James was her fiancé, although there were no wedding plans yet and his Scottish breeziness was beginning to grate on her. She wondered if it might be better if the engagement came to an end soon. Inwardly she could not bear him touching her, but she smiled and dutifully kissed his right hand, which was massaging her shoulder in a proprietary way. James came from a farming family in the Scottish Highlands, and it suddenly occurred to her that his father, whom she had never met, would probably have massaged a prize heifer in exactly the same way.

'I'm all right, I suppose, thank you,' Heather answered vaguely, and tried to return her concentration to work. 'James, what do you think old Palmer does on his trips to Los Angeles?'

'I don't know,' James replied. 'Why the interest?'

'I never see any evidence of what he does helping our company at all. He could do more by staying at his desk in London. Perhaps there's something I'm missing,' Heather said, thinking aloud. She forced herself to change her mood. 'Still, that's enough about work. Are you coming around tonight?'

'Well, I'm not doing anything else,' James replied, in a vague fashion. 'I may as well come around. What will you be cooking tonight?'

Heather tried to hide her disappointment at her fiancé's lukewarm response. 'I haven't decided yet, but I'll think of something special,' she said, trying to sound cheerful. Then she changed to a more formal tone. 'By the way, have you tidied up those accounts yet?'

'Yes, ma'am. You're in your boss mode now, are you? Yes, they're ready.' James caught Heather's unforgiving glance. 'Well, they're nearly ready, anyhow. They'll be on your desk first thing tomorrow.'

'Make sure they are, James,' Heather replied. She realised she was sounding harsh. She knew she was uncomfortable with being both James's boss and his fiancée. She told herself this was another reason why breaking off the engagement might be a good idea.

'Sure thing.' James walked away, as he tried to catch Derek's attention.

Heather looked after James, wondering why her relationship with him was not working. She reminded herself of the many successful relationships she knew of between male bosses and their female staff. She could think of many cases where, say, a male doctor had married his nurse or where a boss married his secretary and the relationships worked fine. She asked herself why it did not seem to work out when the woman was in the senior position. Was it inevitable or was she just a failure at this? Was it her fault or James's? She somehow felt it was mostly his. Heather shook her head to cast her unflattering thoughts about her fiancé aside, and returned to the accounts she was trying to balance.

Just then, she heard a voice she dreaded. 'Miss Morgan, come into my office at once,' Derek Ringer said, standing close behind her. She had not heard him approaching but felt sure he had been looking at the papers on her desk.

'Yes, Mr Ringer,' she said, following him into his office.

'Close the door,' Derek said. 'Take a seat.' He raised himself to his full five foot six inches, as he prepared to berate the young woman in front of him. 'Now, can you explain this article?' he shouted, throwing the issue of *Dirty Money* at her.

'I haven't seen this, Mr Ringer,' Heather said, skimming through it. 'It seems to be about the company accounts. It makes some terrifying claims. Are any of them true?'

'No, of course not,' Derek replied in an annoyed tone. 'Our business is completely legitimate. Sir Giles wouldn't allow any of the stuff this article describes to go on. But lies like this can still be very damaging to us. I want to know where this man Lynch got his information.'

'I don't know, Mr Ringer. Perhaps someone has made it all up – if, as you say, it isn't true,' Heather said, not sure if Derek suspected her of being disloyal. 'There are some subsidiary accounts that even I'm not allowed to look into. I've said before that I need to have access to all the company accounts if I'm to do my job. I couldn't have leaked stuff to this magazine if I didn't know it.'

'I didn't say it was you, and I'm not giving you any more access,' Derek said, 'but someone in this office has been talking, and I want you to find out who. Is that clear?'

Heather opened her mouth to protest, but realised that Derek considered the conversation at an end. 'Yes, Mr Ringer,' she said, as she left the office. 'I will do what I can.'

*

At lunchtime, Heather switched off her terminal and put on her coat. She glanced at the wintry weather through the windows, and shivered. She told herself she was looking forward to a lunch break out of the office, even though there was sleet outside.

'Are you ready?' Margaret Prestwood appeared before her. Margaret was Heather's best friend at work and they often went out to lunch together.

Heather glanced at Margaret, curious as to what she was wearing. Today she was wearing hippyish clothes that would have been fashionable in California in around 1969. It often occurred to Heather how out of place her friend looked in the formal surroundings of the City, and how she did not match the image of the City executive that she in fact was. Perhaps because of this, Heather felt safe describing suspicious things she had noticed at work to Margaret at their lunches.

The two women walked through the lobby of Palmer Associates and strolled without discussion through the lunchtime crowds to the new Broadgate shopping centre. They each ordered a Caesar salad in one of the many small restaurants in the centre.

'How's your morning been?' Margaret asked, as they waited for their food to be served.

Heather sighed. 'Pretty terrible, to be honest. I'm trying to get last year's accounts to add up. There are some strange payments – I can't see what they're for.'

'What sort of payments?'

'Large sums of money with no explanation.'

Margaret shrugged, and then finished her salad before changing the subject. 'How's Ringer treating you these days?'

'Don't ask. That's another thing. Why the hell's he paid four times as much as me?'

'God knows. Didn't anyone tell you it's a man's world in the City?'

'It certainly is. And now Palmer wants me to investigate some article in the *Dirty Money* magazine – you know the one. It's always targeting City firms.'

'What does it say?'

'It says Palmer Associates haven't been investing in films the way we say we have,' Heather said. 'The trouble is I don't know if it's true or not. I'm not allowed to look into those accounts – Palmer keeps them close to his chest.'

'You poor thing, it sounds like you've had a bad morning. Let's forget about work for a while.'

The two women ate in companionable silence for a while before Margaret spoke. 'Are you looking forward to the Christmas party on Saturday night?' she asked.

'Oh, God, I'd forgotten about that,' Heather said, looking up in shock. 'I must start preparing for it. I'm not sure what to wear. Who are you going with?'

'Oh, just me. You know me – the eternal singleton. How about you?'

'Yes, well, I'm going with James, of course. It'll be great,' Heather replied, trying unsuccessfully to keep a lack of enthusiasm out of her voice.

'Is anything wrong between you and James?' Margaret asked, after a pause.

'No, of course not. I want to go with James, of course I do. We're engaged, after all. But the idea of meeting all the office people I can't stand, and making light conversation ...' Heather's voice trailed away.

'Heather, I'm your friend,' Margaret said, reaching across to touch Heather's hand. 'How are things really with James?'

'Oh, just the same, I suppose. I'm not sure I see myself as the dutiful wife. I'm glad we haven't moved in together. James wanted to; he said it would save money. He didn't realise that didn't sound very romantic.'

'Yes, well, at least you've got a man to go around with,' Margaret said.

'You're still having no luck on the men front?' Heather asked.

'None at all. I think I'm what they call an acquired taste, and no one seems keen to grab me. Never mind; I'll survive somehow. Now, tell me the choices for what you're going to wear.'

While Heather was pondering her answer, she became aware of a tall blond man approaching their table. She jumped up as she recognised her former boyfriend.

'Heather? I thought it was you. How are you?' David Gould asked, walking towards her.

'My God, David, what are you doing here?' Heather stood up, blushing. 'I haven't seen you for ages. You're looking great. Have you been looking for me? You always make me feel guilty. Do you think I've robbed a bank or something?' She tried to stop herself gabbling.

'Hello, Heather. No, don't be alarmed. I'm not on duty. Philippa and I were having lunch over there with the Commissioner – Bob Watson – and I thought I recognised you.' Detective Chief Inspector David Gould indicated a table on the other side of the restaurant, where a distinguished-looking middle-aged man was seated with a slim, attractive young woman. 'I just thought I'd see how you're doing. You're looking lovelier than ever.' He bent down to Heather and gave her cheek a kiss, then took the vacant chair at the table.

'Oh, I don't know about that, but I'm surviving,' Heather said. 'I'm not sure if you know I've changed jobs and I've joined an investment company since I saw you last. It's very stressful.' She noticed Margaret was being excluded from the conversation. 'David, I must introduce you to Margaret. Margaret, this is David Gould – I've told you about him. Margaret and I both work in the same office, David, but we're both rebels in the organisation. We're just discussing what to wear for the office Christmas party.'

'How do you do, Margaret?' Gould said, shaking hands with her. 'I'm pleased to meet you.'

'Hello, David,' Margaret said. 'I didn't know Heather had friends in the police.'

'David and I are not exactly friends any more,' Heather said, feeling herself blushing again. 'Not now I'm engaged.'

'Oh, I didn't realise you're engaged, but of course now I see the ring,' Gould said, as Heather displayed a small diamond ring on her finger. 'Please accept my congratulations. Who's the lucky man?'

'His name's James Faulkner. He works in my office. We're just planning the wedding,' Heather replied, wondering why she was blushing. She felt a ridiculous urge to apologise for her choice of fiancé, and decided she needed to change the subject. 'And how about you, David? Are you hooked up with some lucky lady? Or are you still engaged to your work, keeping the streets of the City of London safe for the rest of us?'

'Yes, I suppose you could say that. I'm still single,' Gould said, with a rueful smile. 'Police work keeps me busy.' He turned to Margaret. 'The criminals in the City wear suits rather than hoodies, Margaret, but it makes them all the more dangerous. They're cleverer and harder to catch.'

'Yes, I can imagine,' Margaret said, continuing to eat her salad.

'And how's that female detective sergeant of yours?' Heather asked Gould, indicating the young woman seated at the far table, who glanced over to Heather without warmth. 'I don't think she ever liked me.'

'I'm sure that's not true. She often asks about you,' Gould said. 'Yes, Philippa's still in my team. Like me, she's wedded to the job, I think. But I don't want to intrude.' He stood up. 'Enjoy the rest of your meal and your Christmas party. We must meet up again soon, Heather. I hope your wedding is a success. Whoever he is, he's a lucky man. I hope he appreciates you. It's nice to have met you, Margaret.' Gould touched Heather's shoulder as he walked back to his table on the other side of the restaurant.

'So that's David Gould,' Margaret said, as she and Heather

drank their coffees. 'You mentioned him, but I didn't realise he was a senior detective. He'd be quite a catch. He's very handsome. I wouldn't mind being arrested by him.'

'Oh, there was nothing serious between us,' Heather said.

'Nothing serious?' Margaret echoed, looking quizzically at her.

'Well, there was something. Quite a lot, actually,' Heather admitted, 'and it might have gone further. But it finished a long time ago.'

'So why did you break up?'

'Oh, I'm not sure. Lots of things, really. He was a bit too obsessed with his work. He was divorced before we met. I'm sure his work broke up his marriage. Then I came along. It started well, but, if we went to a pub, he'd be eyeing up the other customers, working out which ones were on the police computer, and which members of staff were looking shifty just because they hadn't a work permit. It gets offputting when you're looking forward to a romantic night out. And there were just too many times when he stood me up, while he spent all the hours God sent investigating some financial crime. Then he'd put me off my meal, talking about some particularly gruesome murder.'

'And why didn't this Philippa like you?'

'Well, she and David had had an affair before I came on the scene. I don't really know what happened between them. She broke up with him, so I was told, so she had no right to object to us getting together. She was going out with a man she'd met on one of their cases, but that seemed to fizzle out. Because of their past, I always thought Philippa working with David was a threat to us.' Heather and Margaret both looked across at Philippa Cottrell, who was talking to Gould. 'As you can see, she's very pretty in a boyish sort of way. Too pretty, really, for a detective, and she still seemed to be a bit in love with David. I suppose I was jealous of them working together. I think I'd prefer all his staff were old-fashioned policemen with size 12 boots, like Dixon of Dock Green.' She laughed. 'Perhaps I was born in the wrong era.'

Margaret looked over at Gould's table again. 'I can see what you mean. Philippa doesn't look like your typical policewoman.'

'Not at all. You expect female police officers to be butch and tough, but she isn't; not at first sight, anyway. She would fit in as a secretary in any company. In fact, she did just that undercover in some travel agency, before I met David. I think it was an argument about that case that drove them apart. David tends to break rules when he feels the need, and Philippa appears a bit gentler, but, believe me, she can be tough when she wants to be.' Heather stood up. 'Come on, we ought to be getting back to work.'

Heather and Margaret continued their chat on their way back through the sleet to Palmer Associates.

*

Later that day, after work, Heather stood in the small kitchen of her flat, cutting up steak and kidney for James's meal. She was a vegetarian and hated touching meat, but her fiancé always said he liked the type of food his Highland mother used to make. As she cut the raw meat, her fingers became stained by blood, and Heather looked at her hands with distaste. Sometimes she wondered if she was cut out for the devoted wife role. She told herself perhaps that was why she had broken up with David Gould a year before, and why her engagement with James Faulkner was not going well.

Once the meal was in the oven, Heather relaxed in an armchair, sipped a glass of wine and pondered her plans for the future. The chance meeting with David Gould that day had made her review her position. At the moment, she was heading for a marriage with a man she was not sure she loved. How had she landed in this position, at the age of twenty-eight? She knew that something had to change in her life, but wondered how she could set about it.

She went to the sideboard and took out a photo of David Gould, hidden away at the back of a drawer, and looked at it for a moment, before replacing it. She did not know why she had kept it and wondered if she was still a little bit in love with Gould. Maybe her life would have been better if she had stayed with him.

As well as being uncertain about her relationship with James, Heather was unsure about her status at work. She was qualified as an accountant, yet there were large black holes she knew nothing about in the accounts for which she was nominally responsible. Before too long, she would have to tackle the management at Palmer Associates – either Derek Ringer or Sir Giles Palmer – to find out more about how the funds were really being invested. She had no idea if the claims in the article that Derek had thrown at her that day were true, and was unsure of how to find out.

Returning to the prospect of the next few days, she shuddered at the thought of the Christmas party. She wondered if perhaps then would be a good time to tackle Sir Giles Palmer about the accounts. Just then, she heard James at the door, and she reminded herself to act the part of the carefree fiancée.

'Hello, James,' Heather said, as she opened the door and put her lips up for a dutiful kiss.

'Hello, love, how are you?' James asked in a mock-Cockney accent covering up his native Highland Scottish accent. This annoyed Heather; it always sounded phoney to her. James's background was something of a mystery. He always kept quiet about his family, and had never introduced Heather to any of them. She was hoping to meet them before she and James got married.

'That food smells good,' James said.

'Yes, I made your favourite. I know you like steak and kidney.' The word *kidney*, with its reminder that meat was once functioning parts of an animal's body, made her shudder internally, but she kept her feelings to herself. 'Can you set the table for me?'

'Yeah, sure, but can we watch the football first? Scotland are playing England tonight.'

'Oh, must we? I want to plan who's coming to the wedding.'

'Well, we can do that any time. Now, where do you keep the cutlery?'

'Same as always, James,' Heather said vaguely as she touched her engagement ring. 'But we really must plan the invitation list. We must invite the right people from your side. You're the only one who knows them.'

Heather came into the main room a few minutes later, and saw the cutlery put haphazardly on the table, with James watching the football on the television. She made a face, but silently placed the cutlery correctly on the table. She knew she would have to delay the meal until the end of the football match. She reflected she was glad they had not moved in together, and told herself the wedding plans could go on the back burner for a while.

Chapter 3

At work the next day, James Faulkner looked at the accounts in front of him. As Heather had said, they showed that Palmer Associates had invested in film production, but they did not show the names of the films. Investments were all shown in obscure subsidiary companies. The main result, as far as the investors were concerned, was that they showed a large increase over the last ten years.

But James was experienced enough to know that profits in such a volatile industry as film production did not grow as steadily as shown in the Palmer Associates accounts. When the dividends in Palmer Associates were higher than in the film industry as a whole, the investors would be happy. But when the film industry was showing fast rates of return, with many blockbusters breaking all records, as had happened in the last few years, James knew they would be much less happy.

While no one was looking, James pulled a copy of the *Dirty Money* article that he had heard Heather mention out of his drawer. He started as he realised he recognised the name on the byline. Turning around to make sure he was not being overheard, he picked up a phone and dialled the number shown on the article.

A familiar Scottish voice from his childhood answered. 'Lynch here.'

'Robin,' James began, covering the mouthpiece. 'How are things? It's James Faulkner here.'

'James, is that you?' came the reply. 'I haven't heard from you for over a year. How's your family? Are you still in London? Or have you gone back to your dad's farm?'

'No, we've both come a long way since then, haven't we?' James replied. 'Farming wasn't for me. No, I'm in the City, like you. I was interested in your article. Very interested, in fact. I work in film finance – for Palmer Associates – the company you wrote the article about.'

'Oh, I didn't know that.'

'Yes, but anyone who looks into my record and realises we came from the same town will think I've been leaking information to you.'

'I'm sorry about that, James, but I don't know what I can do.'

'Well, I've decided that if people think the worst of me anyway, I may as well be guilty. I don't think I'm going to stay here too long. I have something that might be of interest to you. I've spotted some dubious figures in the accounts.'

Lynch audibly took a deep breath on the line. 'Wait a minute. Let's make this clear. You have what sounds like a good job in Palmer Associates and you're passing confidential information to a seedy magazine like mine. Do you know what you're doing? You could lose your job if your bosses know you've been talking to me.'

'I don't care about that. I want to change my job anyway. I don't see this as a career for me. I'm not a company man. I've always been jealous of you and your career. If this comes about, I thought you might have an opening for me.'

'You want me to give you a job? God, James, you don't want much, do you? I don't have enough money for me and my secretary as it is. I can't pay you as well.'

'Yes, but the information I have is explosive, Robin.'

'James, you do realise that if they catch you leaking anything to a paper like mine, not only will your company sack you, but you'll never work in the City again? Besides, I'll need proof. Rumours aren't enough for me.'

'Well, OK, Robin. I'll keep digging. Shall we meet up for a drink sometime?'

'Let's do that. But I can't pay much for anything you give me. I find it difficult to get advertising money. All the big companies hate me. I suppose I don't blame them. Let's meet at the Bunch of Grapes in Fleet Street at six o'clock tonight. Do you know it? That should be far enough away from your office to be safe. See you then.' There was a clatter as Lynch put the phone down.

James stared at the scene outside his office, as upwardly mobile young men and women walked past to their well-paid jobs. He wondered if he was making the right decision. He had to admit that, so far, he had few facts to support his suspicions. But, as he had told his old school friend Robin Lynch, he did not see himself working for an orthodox City firm in the long term. With a little more digging, he thought he would be able to advance on a new career as an investigative journalist. He would not be paid as much, but he felt it would be more satisfying.

He told himself that he would miss Heather if he had to leave the company, of course. She might be persuaded to leave as well, and they could start a new life together somewhere else. The prospect did not thrill him, for some reason, and he doubted Heather would come with him. He was not fully convinced he was the marrying sort. Perhaps the engagement to Heather was a mistake.

Just then, Alison Coates, the secretary to both Sir Giles and Derek, came up to him. James had enjoyed going out with her not long ago, and a memory of her naked body in bed came to his mind. They had broken up once his engagement to Heather had been announced, but he still enjoyed gentle flirting with Alison, while Heather was out of the room.

Checking that Heather was not around, he looked at Alison's athletic frame and sighed aloud. 'You look ravishing today, Alison, love. Who's the lucky man you're going to the Christmas party with?'

'Linus, of course,' Alison said, referring to an executive who had arrived from the company's Los Angeles office. 'We're a couple now. Anyway, what's it to you? I thought you were happily engaged to your boss lady,' she added in her natural Cockney accent.

'Yes, we're engaged, but I don't know about *happily*. You and I had some good times together, didn't we? Perhaps we could meet up again after work?' He caught Alison's reproving glance. 'Maybe not. You're probably right. I'll do my duty and escort Heather to the party, but I'm jealous of Linus. Now, was there anything you wanted workwise or are you here to torment me with your beauty?'

'Yes, Mr Ringer wants some papers on that film company,' Alison said, trying to adopt a formal accent, but failing. 'He said you had them.'

'Yes, here they are.' James passed over some paper files. 'I'm happy to talk to Ringer if he needs to know anything,' he said, as Alison walked away. He gazed wistfully at her departing body, then saw her embrace Linus, a tall athletic-looking man, in the corner. James often wondered if it had been the right decision to drop Alison for Heather.

Out of the corner of his eye, he saw Heather arrive back at her desk. Blushing, he returned to his terminal and looked at a spreadsheet. He noticed Heather glaring at Alison and realised their flirtatious chat had upset his fiancée. He wondered how he could make amends to Heather, but then he wondered if he wanted to.

His mobile phone rang to remind him to attend a meeting. As he stood up, Linus Murray came to his desk. He realised they were on the way to the same meeting.

'Hello, Linus,' James said, as casually as he could.

'Hi, James, how are you doing? I saw you talking to Alison. I've told you before that is not a good idea.' Linus drew himself to his full height. 'Do I make myself clear?'

James looked up at Linus. 'I understand,' he said.

James walked along the corridor into the meeting room. As he entered, his heart sank. Two of the people he most disliked in the office were there ahead of him.

'How are you, Margaret?' James asked, as he saw Heather's friend.

'Fine, thank you, James, and how are the wedding preparations going?' Margaret asked.

'Very well, I think,' James replied. Inwardly, he added, *Not that it's anything to do with you,* but told himself there was no reason to antagonise Heather's friend needlessly. 'And how are you, Michael?' he asked the other person at the meeting.

'Very well, thank you,' Michael Dawson, an executive who had joined the company at the same time as Heather, replied. He had a military bearing and an innate air of authority. He made no secret of his disapproval of James, both in work terms and as a partner for Heather. James suspected Michael had been hoping to start a relationship with Heather, before her engagement to James, and was probably still keen to step in if the engagement failed for any reason. 'I see that Heather delegated this meeting to you. I'm disappointed. We were expecting someone more important. But I suppose we have to put up with the oily rag if the engineer is away.'

'Thank you, Michael,' James said. 'I can assure you I have Heather's confidence. She's pleased with all aspects of my performance,' he added, with a sly smile.

'What do you mean by that?'

Their sparring was stopped by Linus joining the meeting. 'Hi, guys, sorry I'm late.'

Only Margaret acknowledged Linus. 'That's all right, Linus. Good to have you with us. Shall we start the meeting?'

The three men nodded their agreement as the formal discussion started.

*

While the meeting was taking place, Heather was standing in the lobby of Palmer Associates, dealing with an irate, distinguished-looking gentleman wearing a pinstripe suit. Alison had called her to deal with a scene that was becoming fractious.

'I'm afraid Sir Giles Palmer and Mr Ringer are not here today, Mr Fretwell,' Heather said.

'But that's not good enough. I'm a major investor in this company,' the man said. 'I demand to see someone in charge.'

'That may be so, Mr Fretwell, but being an investor does not give you any right to enter these offices. I will tell Sir Giles you called.'

'The other day Palmer mentioned a Christmas party here on Saturday.'

'Yes, but that is only for staff.'

'Tell Sir Giles Palmer I'll be there, and I want some answers about where my money's gone.'

'Yes, Mr Fretwell, I will tell him. Now, if you would leave, the door's behind you.'

'Very well. Perhaps I will see you then.' Fretwell studied Heather's office pass. 'You're Miss Morgan, is that right?'

'Yes, that's right.'

'You're a pretty young filly, I must say. You seem very young to be a manager.'

'Please leave, Mr Fretwell. I'm sure you don't want to cause any more of a scene,' Heather said, successfully guiding Fretwell out of the glass doors and locking them afterwards.

'Thank you, Heather,' Alison said. 'I didn't know how to handle him.'

'I don't need your thanks, Miss Coates,' Heather said, walking back to her office. 'You should be able to deal with people like Mr Fretwell without my help.'

Alison made a face behind Heather's back as she left.

*

After work that day, still seething from her dressing-down from Heather, Alison Coates waited outside Blackfriars station for the 388 bus to take her to her grandfather's home in Elephant and Castle. This was not her usual journey home, but she had promised to visit her grandfather for a chat.

Alison looked around the bus shelter at the other young female office workers travelling home. She reflected that most of their grandfathers were probably kindly, respectable old gentlemen who gave them small treats when they paid duty visits. Alison's grandfather, however, was very different.

Alf Coates owned a pub with a large house where many members of his extended family lived. Most of the tourists who visited his pub were unaware of Alf's main business interest. They would have been amazed to learn that Alf Coates was one of the main old-style major villains still operating in the East End of London. Many of his contemporaries such as the famous Kray twins were long ago either locked up or dead, but Alf was more intelligent than them and, perhaps because of this, less well known, and was still free to run his criminal businesses.

Alison took a seat on the bus and looked out of the window. She always enjoyed making this trip. The contrast in simply crossing the river, between the wealth of the City of London and the Elephant and Castle area where she grew up, was stark. The glossy high-rise office blocks were behind her as the bus crossed the river and left the square mile of the City of London. Alison looked around. Canary Wharf, newly risen from the former docks, was on her left. Ahead of her lay her own stomping grounds: the council flats of Elephant and Castle.

Alison knew that many of the executive university-educated women at Palmer Associates – Heather and Margaret in particular – looked down on her appearance, on her job, her lack of education and her Cockney accent, but she pretended not to care. Still, she did resent their sense of superiority, and she looked forward to the time when she would gain the upper hand on them. She would find some way to bring Heather Morgan down a peg or two.

Alison got off the bus close to her grandfather's house and walked down the street and into the pub where she knew her grandfather would be waiting. She remembered visiting him in prison, when she was a child. He had always had a warm smile and a treat for her, despite the grim surroundings.

She walked into the saloon bar. 'Hello, Granddad,' she called.

Alf Coates stood up from his favourite stool in a corner where he could keep an eye on the clientele, and put out his arms to greet her. 'Alison, love, it's good of you to come and see your old granddad,' he said, as he kissed her cheek.

'Well, it's a change to come back to this part of London. I miss it, really. The City still seems like a foreign country to me. This area will always be the real London. How have you been? Your message said you wanted to see me, but you didn't say why.'

'I just wanted a chat, really. I wanted to know you hadn't forgotten your roots,' Alf said, signalling for a pint for himself and a glass of wine for Alison.

'No, I haven't changed. You know I'll always be a Cockney girl. I haven't forgotten where I came from, not like some of the women in the firm.' Alison looked at her grandfather with suspicion. 'I've got a good job now. I hope you don't mind me trying to better myself.'

'No, I think it's great that you want to get on. But tell me more about how things are going at that poncey firm of yours,' Alf added with a smile that was wafer-thin.

'Well, I told you I broke up with James, so I don't get as much gossip from him as I used to. He thinks he's too good for me, which he's not. He's engaged to his boss – a posh bird called Heather. She's a pain in the neck. She gave me a hard time today for no reason at all. Then there's going to be a Christmas party on Saturday night. I expect James will take Heather. Don't worry, I'll find someone to go with. I don't want to be alone all the time like that ugly cow Margaret—'

'Alison, love,' Alf interrupted, 'I meant what's happening on the work side.'

'Oh, that. Well, old Palmer's just come back from Los Angeles. No one knows what he does there, but I saw him give Ringer a package and tell him to sell it to the usual customers. Then Palmer was angry about some article about the company in *Dirty Money* – that's a magazine they read a lot in the City. It seems to have all the latest gossip, but I can't really understand it.'

'I know what *Dirty Money*, is, love. I'm not as stupid as people think, you know.'

'All right,' Alison said, surprised by her grandfather's knowledge. 'But whoever wrote this article seems to know an awful lot about what the company does. Ringer asked Heather – the one I told you about – to look into it. Someone in the company must have been leaking secrets. I hope the bosses don't start looking for them. I don't want to be around when that happens.'

'Don't worry, love. If you haven't told anyone, you don't have anything to worry about.'

'Oh, I wouldn't tell anyone outside anything. Just you, of course, but you're family.'

'You don't have to worry about me, Alison. You know I can keep secrets.'

After some other chat, Alison got up to leave. 'I hope you're proud of me getting my job in the City, Granddad. I want to get on in the world.'

'Of course I'm proud of you. You made it on your own. Aren't you going to stay here tonight?'

'No, I'm living on my own at the moment – over in Dulwich. Good night, Granddad,' Alison said, stooping down to kiss her grandfather goodbye.

As she left, she wondered why she hadn't told the old man that she was now living with Linus. Although she loved her grandfather, she felt he might not approve of her having a visiting American as a boyfriend. She promised herself she would tell the old man the truth the next time she saw him.

*

After work that evening, James Faulkner entered the Bunch of Grapes in Fleet Street, and peered through the thick tobacco smoke. As he had expected, the pub was packed with office workers on their way home. Eventually, he recognised Robin Lynch in a corner and went over to join him.

'Hello, Robin. It's good to see you again,' James said, shaking Lynch's hand.

'Yes, it's good to see you. It's a long time since our school days, isn't it?' Lynch replied. 'I've ordered a pint for you. It was a surprise to get a call from you. What have you got for me? You said you had something I'd be interested in.'

'Thanks. Well, I've been digging, and I think I'm on the edge of something big. But, first of all, what would you give me for information on Palmer Associates?'

'I told you the magazine doesn't have much money. I could either quote your name and you get publicity or keep it quiet: whichever is your choice. It depends on where you see your career going.'

'There's nothing definite yet, but there's a big Christmas party on Saturday evening. Giles Palmer always puts in an appearance. I'm hoping I can tackle him and find out something useful.' James was excited. 'I'm going with my girlfriend; my fiancée, in fact. Her name's Heather, but I'm not sure how things are going between us. I may want to move on soon.'

'And you trust me to keep your name out of it, do you?'

'Yes, sure. We're friends from way back, aren't we?'

Lynch gave a forced smile. 'Of course we are. Tell me more about this party. It sounds interesting.'

'The whole office will be there. It should be an ideal time to find out what's going on in the company. By the way, I'd love to know who gave you the information you published this week. We both know it wasn't me.'

'I'm sure you would be interested to know who it came from, and I know we're old friends. But I'm still not going to tell you.'

Lynch carried on listening to what James told him. James did not spot that Lynch was recording the conversation on a Dictaphone in his pocket. James also did not notice that by chance Lynch had chosen a pub that was a local of one of James's colleagues.

In the far corner of the pub, Michael Dawson, still unhappy with the way James had spoken to him at the recent office meeting, noticed him talking to a strange man, but put it to the back of his mind for now.

*

Soon after Alison had left her grandfather's pub, another employee of Palmer Associates entered the saloon bar. Derek Ringer looked carefully round to check he was not being followed, as he approached the man he only knew as Alf Jones.

'We spoke on the phone, Mr Jones. Could we go somewhere more private?'

Alf Coates stood up slowly and led Derek to a quiet room behind the bar. 'I'm in the snug. I don't want any interruptions,' he growled at the barman.

'I've got a high-quality video here, Mr Jones,' Derek began, once he was sure the door was firmly closed. 'I think your customers will appreciate it.'

'We'll see about that, Mr Ringer, but I think we can agree the same terms as before.'

'I was hoping for some increase . . .' Derek's voice tailed away as he saw Alf's hostile expression. 'But I'm sure I can persuade my manager to accept the status quo. That means I'll accept what we agreed before,' he clarified in response to Alf's baffled look.

'I think that would be very wise. Let's shake on it,' Alf said, as the two men shook hands. 'I've been reading a lot about your company recently, Mr Ringer. Not all of it good.'

Alf looked at the cover of the video he had just bought. He never looked at the films he handled; he regarded himself as just a businessman satisfying a customer's needs. The films were for a niche market and he accepted he operated outside the law. However, he told himself he was providing a service to the public, just as the supposedly respectable businessmen who would not let him join their clubs did all the time. He told himself that soon his day would come.

The man opposite him, Derek Ringer, was one of those who looked down on him. Alf knew that Derek was just a junior for Sir Giles Palmer, the real power behind the business. Alf had a promising plan to take over the company, but he was happy to leave Derek in ignorance for the time being. He had learnt a great deal about Palmer Associates from his granddaughter and other sources. He knew he would pounce when the time was right.

'Oh, I wouldn't believe everything you read in *Dirty Money*,' Derek said.

'No, but I might be interested in investing in a company like yours.'

'Well, we have some very loyal investors already, Mr Jones. I think we should keep things on the present basis as much as we can.'

'Yes, perhaps we will. But if you ever need new investors – say, if the present lot got cold feet when they read what's in *Dirty Money*, for instance – you can always count on me. I'm looking for a way to diversify away from my present interests.'

Derek inwardly shuddered at the thought of the man he knew as Jones taking over Palmer Associates, but replied politely. 'I'll tell Sir Giles to bear that in mind, Mr Jones. Now I must be going.'

Derek left the pub, keeping his eyes down as much as possible, to avoid being seen. He always felt unclean after these illicit trips to Elephant and Castle, and looked forward to returning to his comfortable home in Guildford.

*

Robin Lynch sat at what he liked to call his editor's chair, which, in fact, was the only usable chair in the *Dirty Money* office. He played back the tape he had made of his conversation with James Faulkner. He felt guilty betraying his old school friend, but then he looked around at the sorry state the office of *Dirty Money* was in. He knew he was in no position to have scruples and told himself he could put any money he received to good use in keeping his magazine afloat. He could salve his conscience by exposing future scandals, of which he had no doubt there would be many. Lynch drummed his fingers as he picked up the phone.

'Mr Coates? This is Robin Lynch of *Dirty Money* ... Yes, I know I promised to only phone in an emergency, but this is important ... I've had a meeting with a man named James Faulkner ... He's some sort of executive accountant at Palmer Associates, the company I'm writing about ... We knew each other from school, but that doesn't matter ... Well, he's offered to act as a source for the series of articles I'm writing – with your help, of course ... Very well.'

Robin Lynch sang happily to himself as he realised that the generous amount of money he was receiving from Alf was about to be increased. He did not feel good about betraying James Faulkner, but he put any feeling of guilt to one side. Judas had been paid thirty pieces of silver for his betrayal. Lynch wasn't sure how much that would be nowadays, but, even allowing for inflation, what he had received was a very generous fee for betraying a friend.

Chapter 4

The following evening, before the office Christmas party, Heather looked at her reflection in the full-length mirror in her bedroom, as she tried on the little black dress she had bought while shopping with Margaret. She winced as she recalled the amount of money it cost. She moved her body from side to side and noted in the mirror how the dress flowed over her body. At least she was satisfied with the way she looked. It was certainly far better than anything Margaret was likely to be wearing. Heather could not imagine how an intelligent woman like Margaret could dress so badly.

Heather was not looking forward to the party at all. She knew she would have to make small talk with people she had spent the rest of the year avoiding. Then, she predicted, James would have too much to drink and talk too loudly. He would show her off to his friends by putting his arms all over her in a proprietary manner. She shuddered at the thought.

Heather put her coat on as she heard her fiancé knocking at the door. Taking stock of how she felt about James, she made the decision she would break off the engagement that night. She did not want to hurt James's feelings, but she had no doubt the decision was right for both their sakes.

'Hello, love, you look great tonight,' James said, as Heather let him in. He leant over for a kiss. It was obvious he had already been drinking. 'Is that a new dress?'

'Thank you, James. Yes, it is. It should look good, the amount it cost,' Heather said, avoiding his lips. 'I think it would be better if I drive, don't you?'

'Sure, you can drive. Shall we go?'

Heather picked up her handbag and, after checking herself again in the hall mirror, followed James down to his car. As they drove off, James looked at her cold expression reflected in the driving mirror. He was sure he was not in her good books at the moment. Apart from that, he could tell Heather was not looking forward to the party.

'Come on, love. We'll have a good time,' he told her.

'I'm not sure about that,' she replied. 'You will behave, won't you? Don't forget we're a couple now. I don't want you chatting up other girls.'

James did not reply, but touched her hand in reassurance.

An hour later, Heather followed James into the party. In the lobby of the building, she saw a man she did not recognise, apparently a journalist, shouting questions to staff entering the party.

'Do you have anything to say in response to the latest reports about Palmer Associates' accounts?' he shouted at Derek Ringer. Getting no response, he yelled, 'Can Palmer Associates continue?' at Sir Giles Palmer, who ignored the question.

'I wonder who that man is,' Heather said as she and James followed Sir Giles and Derek into the building. 'How does he know about the party? It's supposed to be private.'

'Oh, that's Robin Lynch,' James said, in a low voice to avoid being overheard by Sir Giles and Derek. 'He's editor of *Dirty Money*.'

'Do you have anything to say to the allegations, James?' Lynch called out to James.

'Be quiet, you idiot. I'm not supposed to know who you are,' James replied, trying not to be overheard, before walking forward.

'How do you know that man?' Heather asked, holding James's elbow.

'Oh, we were at school together,' James said. 'I haven't seen him since.'

'Are you sure that's all? You don't want to be seen as a friend of his. He's an enemy of the company and I'm sure Ringer heard him call your name. He'll be wondering if you've been leaking stuff to him.'

'God, I hope not,' James replied, with a shudder. He saw Lynch walk out of the lobby, cross the road outside and bend down to talk to an elderly man in a top-of-the-range Land Rover. 'I wonder who Lynch is talking to. I didn't think he had any friends who could afford a car like that.'

'Who knows?' Heather shrugged her shoulders. 'Perhaps he isn't as pure as driven snow himself. Someone could be paying him to damage Palmer Associates. Some people would pay a lot of money to spread dirt about us.'

'You could be right,' James said. 'Come on, let's enjoy the party.'

Heather felt that he seemed uncharacteristically thoughtful.

As the two of them entered the party, Heather noticed the office had been decorated with cheap Christmas novelties. As she looked around at the decorations, she shuddered. The contrast between the dark mahogany desk in the boardroom and the childish Santa Claus decorations struck her as particularly gruesome. She saw that the boardroom had been locked, which she assumed was to keep out any alcohol-inspired misbehaviour.

Looking around the room at her colleagues, Heather recalled why she had spent much of the rest of the year avoiding them. She would need some alcohol to survive the party. She grabbed a glass of wine from the free bar and went forward. Meanwhile, James headed in a different direction to collect a pint of beer.

While James was gone, Heather stood on her own in the corner of the party and tried to make sense of her feelings towards her fiancé. She reflected she had broken up with David Gould a year before. All her friends had warned her that her engagement to James was too quick, and she needed more time to recover from her relationship with David. She had not believed them at the time, but perhaps they had been right all along. She reminded herself that tonight was definitely the night to call off the engagement with James. Heather nervously sipped more of her white wine as she pondered the best way to go about it.

'Hello, Heather,' Michael Dawson called as he came up to speak. As Michael was tall and heavily built, he had to bend down to talk to Heather. She knew he had been an officer in the special forces in the Army, and he still possessed a military bearing.

The two of them had always enjoyed a playfully flirting relationship. Heather suspected Michael was disappointed it had never developed with her any further. Sometimes, she told herself she felt the same. Michael might well be an improvement on James, but she knew she was not free of her fiancé yet.

'Hello, Michael,' Heather said with a smile. 'How nice to see you. Are you here on your own?'

'Yes, I'm on my own. I was hoping you'd be here. You look great, Heather; that's a lovely dress. You must tell me how you have been getting on since we last chatted. But I suppose you came with James.'

'Yes, of course James and I came together. We're engaged,' Heather replied, subconsciously touching her engagement ring. She told herself that it was still the truth at least for the moment, but probably not for much longer. She hoped Michael had not noticed her embarrassed expression or lined up any more questions for her.

Heather noticed Michael's eyes go towards a corner of the room, where she now saw James was chatting up Alison, who was giggling loudly and becoming extremely drunk. Heather knew that Alison was one of James's many previous girlfriends, and she wondered if any affair was still going on between them. She suspected it was, even though Heather knew that Alison was living with Linus Murray.

At that moment, Heather noticed Linus on the other side of the room, looking angrily at James and Alison. Feeling the tension in the room, Heather could tell there was going to be an argument between James and Linus, and she was worried it would develop into a fracas. She realised she could do nothing to stop them if the two men started fighting, and she looked helplessly around, wondering whether she should leave.

'Come on, Alison, let's dance,' James said in a loud voice. As the music started, Michael and Heather both saw James pull Alison onto the dance floor and hold her very close. Heather looked away and decided, despite James's behaviour, she would do her best to enjoy the party.

'Why don't we two have a dance?' Michael asked. Heather nodded acceptance, then moved gently around the dance floor with Michael for a few minutes.

After a while, Michael said quietly, 'James and you are engaged, you say. In what sense was that?'

Heather shrugged helplessly, while forcing herself not to cry. She began to relax in Michael's arms, trying to forget James. She wondered over her feelings for Michael Dawson, and made the decision she would welcome any relationship with him. She was enjoying a dance for the first time in what seemed ages; it never seemed to happen with James. She realised it would not do her reputation any good to be seen flirting with another man while she was still engaged to James, but then decided she did not care about appearances.

Just then, Heather saw Linus Murray stride over to James, who still held Alison close to him as the pair staggered around the dance floor.

'I think you've had too much to drink, James,' Linus said. 'Come with me, honey,' he added to Alison. 'We're leaving.'

'She can stay with me if she wants. Perhaps she's had enough of you,' James said, his words slurred with drink.

Linus came closer to James and towered over him. 'Now, are you going to let Alison go or shall I force you?' he asked, his American tones full of aggression.

James looked up at Linus and seemed to consider whether to hit him. It obviously drifted through his drunken mind that he would be bound to lose any such fight with the much stronger and fitter Linus. 'Very well, you can have her. I've had the best from her already.'

Linus pushed James back onto a chair, and pulled Alison away.

'What do you mean by that?' Alison shrieked, and slapped James as hard as she could across his face. James looked as if he was about to strike her back, when Linus stood in front of him.

'We'll leave it there, I think, James,' Linus said. Turning to Alison, he ushered her away, saying, 'Let's go, honey.'

'I'm sorry, Linus. I don't know what he meant by that,' Alison replied, as she and Linus left the room. James Faulkner stood up and looked over to where Michael was dancing with Heather.

After a few more minutes on the dance floor, Heather thanked Michael, then broke away from the dance. She went off to check her make-up in the ladies' room. Margaret came to stand next to her.

'You look upset. James seems to be annoying everyone tonight,' Margaret said.

'You don't have to tell me. I don't know how much more of this I can take,' Heather replied, wiping her eyes.

When she came back into the room of the party, she shuddered at what she saw. Michael and James were standing face to face, looking as if they were about to fight. Most of the other people at the party were watching with expressions of either amusement or horror.

'I told you to leave her alone,' James was saying.

'You're a drunken waste of space,' Michael said, preparing for a fight.

'James,' Heather called, coming between the two men. 'Shut up. You're making a scene.'

James and Michael grudgingly moved apart. Heather took James's arms and directed him out into the corridor. The audience to the scene dissolved away. Heather noticed Margaret looking at her quizzically.

Heather waited until she was alone with James before saying anything. 'This can't go on. Do you know how embarrassed I get when you're drunk and behave like this? It's over between us.' She took her engagement ring off and slid it into James's suit pocket. 'Take this back. I've decided it's all been a mistake. I never want to see you outside work again.'

Heather walked away, leaving James looking amazed.

'But why? I love you,' he shouted, but Heather had left.

James staggered to the bar and ordered another drink. He saw Sir Giles Palmer standing nearby, looking glumly around. Derek passed Sir Giles a tray of canapés, which he received without thanks. Sir Giles was notorious for making short visits to the firm's Christmas party, which were presumably designed to boost staff morale, but always had the opposite effect.

The sight of Sir Giles seemed to stir a memory within James's mind of something Heather had said to him the day before. Once Derek had moved away, James leant over Sir Giles menacingly.

'Why the hell do you pay Ringer so much?' James slurred.

Sir Giles looked back with distaste. 'I don't know what you're talking about.'

'Heather's been going through the accounts. She tells me you pay Ringer far more than he's worth.' James's words became more indistinct as alcohol overcame any inhibitions he may have felt when talking to the chairman of his company.

'You're drunk. I suggest you go home,' Sir Giles ordered. As James staggered away, Sir Giles changed his mind. 'Come back. What else did Heather say about the accounts?'

'She said there were lots of strange payments of money. I think that's what she said.'

This time Sir Giles allowed James to stagger back towards the bar. Sir Giles indicated for Derek to follow him as he left the party to return to his office.

Back in his office, away from the noise of the party, Sir Giles turned to Derek. 'Do you know what James has been saying?'

Derek shrugged his shoulders. 'James is drunk. He doesn't know what he's been saying himself.'

'Maybe not, but he's one of the people getting too curious about our business for my liking. Robin Lynch, that muckraker, for one – he was outside as we came in. He seemed to know James. That Heather woman he's been engaged to has also been asking questions about the accounts. She's cottoned on to some payments she says are strange.'

'Oh, my God.'

'That's right. I know Heather's type. Too bloody pure to be bought off. I want her silenced. I don't care how you do it. You know how badly our little trade would go down in court.'

Derek stood up. 'I'll see to it, Sir Giles. She'll be out of this company before you know it. She can't have seen much yet.'

Sir Giles dismissed him with a wave of his hand and returned to the party.

'I've been meaning to have a word with you.'

Sir Giles turned to see a drunken man he knew too well. He looked around to see if there was any way of escaping from Hugh Fretwell, one of his largest financial backers, who was advancing towards him.

As Fretwell never tired of telling people, he was the scion of an aristocratic family, whose ancestors were mentioned in the Domesday Book. For the last two generations, the Fretwell family had degenerated. Hugh Fretwell was its last representative and still had enough family money to invest in schemes that he hoped would make a profit. His latest venture was in film making, which, he had a vague idea, was full of glamorous women.

'Ah, Hugh, how good of you to come,' Sir Giles said, doing his best to hide his contempt for Fretwell.

'Never mind that,' Fretwell said, his voice becoming ever more slurred. 'Where are the profits from that latest film? It's doing great business, but I haven't seen any money yet.'

'Well, we have expenses to cover, of course. But let's not talk about business. It's Christmas. Let's see who I can interest you in.'

'Can't see much talent. I thought you'd have a few actresses for me to meet.'

'No, but I'm sure I can find someone interesting,' Sir Giles said, looking around. Suddenly, he saw Heather looking at James with obvious contempt. 'Let me introduce you to Heather Morgan – she's one of our executives. Heather – this is Hugh Fretwell, one of our backers.'

Fretwell took Heather's hand and held it too long for her comfort. 'Yes, we met the other day, didn't we, Heather? What's a pretty girl like you doing at Palmer Associates ...?'

Sir Giles walked away without hearing any more of Fretwell's well-rehearsed ancient chat-up lines.

Meanwhile, Fretwell guided Heather away from the centre of the party. 'Why don't I get you a drink while you tell me exactly what you do here?' he began.

'Oh, I'm an accountant,' Heather replied, taking the glass of wine that Fretwell had picked up from the free bar. 'I gather you're one of our backers. You must be interested in what happens to your money.'

Fretwell's demeanour suddenly changed. 'Yes, I certainly am. Why hasn't our latest film produced any money yet? It's been out for months, and everyone's talking about it, yet I can't see any money coming back to me.'

Just then, Heather saw James walking past. 'This is my friend, James Faulkner. You can talk to him about it.'

She saw James and Fretwell talking to each other as they left the room.

A few minutes later, Heather sipped more of her white wine. She had decided to order a taxi and go home alone. She finished off her glass. In the half-light, she failed to notice that the contents had turned suspiciously cloudy. That was the last memory Heather had until the following morning.

PART 2

INTERVIEWING THE SUSPECTS

Chapter 5

S ome time later, Heather Morgan opened her eyes and waited for them to clear. She was baffled; she remembered drinking a glass of wine at the office Christmas party, but little else. She must have travelled home from the party, but she knew she was not in her own flat. She could not work out where she was.

She looked around at mahogany-lined walls and realised she was in the Palmer Associates boardroom. She must have drunk too much and slept the night in the office. This would be embarrassing to explain to everyone, but no doubt she would eventually recover from the humiliation.

Then Heather noticed a shape that looked familiar on the floor in front of her. When her eyes had focussed, she realised that, yes – it was a body that was either dead or unconscious.

She stared, panic-stricken, looking for help from some imaginary quarter, at the skyline outside her City office. At least the City was still there, she told herself, but everything else seemed to be a bad dream. At first, she could not imagine why the streets were deserted, then she realised it was, of course, Sunday – the day after the party.

She closed her eyes, then opened them to look back at the floor in the hope that the body would somehow have disappeared. Then she realised that this was no dream. The body was still there in front of her.

Heather felt a wave of nausea coming over her, and she tried to breathe deeply. After a few breaths, she told herself to calm down. She knew panicking would do no good, and she forced herself to set out the position as calmly as possible. She tried to pull her thoughts together.

She looked down and realised immediately that the body belonged to her colleague and ex-fiancé, James Faulkner, but how he had come to be there she could not imagine. She reached out a hand and gingerly touched James's skin, hoping he was merely sleeping. Could they have had a drunken tryst together after the party in the boardroom? That would be embarrassing enough, but she knew such things happened at Christmas parties every year. But the body was cooling and she realised James had been dead for some time. He always seemed fit and healthy, so she could not imagine how he could have died from natural causes.

Her eyes drifted down to the bloodstained knife next to her, which looked as if it must be a murder weapon.

Some of the coldness from James's corpse seemed to enter Heather's body, as she shivered inside the expensive party dress she was wearing. She asked herself who could have murdered him, and looked around in case some unknown killer might be lying in wait to attack her. She screamed for help, but soon realised the office must be empty, as no one seemed to hear her.

Heather tried to think rationally and decide what she should do. She knew a good citizen would call an ambulance and get medical help for James, even though she was sure he was dead. As it looked like a crime scene, she thought the police would be the better people to call. Then, as she caught sight of her reflection in the mirror on the wall – she saw a dishevelled woman with a body in front of her – she realised that anyone, especially the police, would assume she had murdered James. She noted she had blood on her hands, and she could vaguely remember dropping the knife. She could not remember much else that had happened since she had arrived at the office Christmas party. Sir Giles Palmer, the firm's chairman, had made his annual appearance thanking them for all their hard work and then disappeared.

And then what happened at the party? Heather racked her memory. She had little recollection of anything since seeing James start to get drunk. She remembered how annoyed she had been when he had flirted with Alison at the party. He had also been saying far too much about Heather's suspicions over some

43

of the dubious payments she had spotted in the company's accounts.

Heather remembered she had decided in advance to break off their engagement and planned to go home alone. She felt for the engagement ring on her finger, but it was not there. Then she remembered giving it back to James. That meant she must have gone through with her plan to break off her engagement. Now everything was changed by James's murder.

Heather wondered for a moment if, in some way, she herself could be guilty of murdering James. She remembered being furious with James over his behaviour at the party, and fantasising about killing him. She recalled an old Victorian novel by Wilkie Collins where the hero found he had been hypnotised during the theft of a jewel and was unwittingly an accomplice to the crime. Could she have murdered James in some alcoholic rage and then forgotten about it? She knew she had been upset by James's flirting with Alison, but, no, she was sure she had not drunk that much. She could not imagine herself killing anyone, let alone James, no matter what state she was in.

But what should she do now?

She reminded herself she had a duty to call the police and tell them of the murder. If she was innocent, she told herself, she had nothing to fear, but she still dreaded the thought of being interrogated by some cynical detective.

The thought of the police reminded her of her ex-boyfriend. David Gould was a detective chief inspector in the City of London police, and she decided he would be a good person to call. He had still been friendly when they had met in the restaurant recently. He was a sensible man, and he would know what to do. She had kept his phone number, even though they had split up over a year ago; it was as if she wanted to keep some keepsake of their relationship.

After some rummaging around, she found her small notebook in the bottom of her handbag. As she remembered, his home and office numbers were still noted there. She picked up her mobile phone and, with shaking fingers, dialled the number she had for David Gould's office. Once the phone was answered, she shouted down the line, 'David, it's me, Heather. Something terrible has happened. You've got to help me.'

*

Detective Chief Inspector David Gould was looking through the papers on a possible fraud case, in his office at Snow Hill police station, when he picked up the phone. 'DCI Gould,' he announced. Suddenly, his voice changed from professional and formal to warm and personal. 'Heather, how are you? It was good bumping into you again ... Is this a social call? ... No, I see ... Take a deep breath ... Don't touch anything ... Don't panic ... Tell me the address ... I'll be right there.'

Gould walked out into the open-plan office. 'Philippa,' he called. 'We've got a call. It sounds serious.'

Detective Sergeant Philippa Cottrell stood up. 'Yes, gov. Are the uniforms there already?'

Gould stared at her, as she had reminded him of something he should have thought of. 'No, it's someone I know – a good friend. She phoned me directly, but you're right – the uniformed patrols should be there first.'

Cottrell followed Gould through to the station reception.

'We've got a call to an incident at 50 City Wall,' Gould told the duty sergeant. 'Send a car to follow us.'

'Yes, gov,' the sergeant replied, before barking orders into his intercom.

In the car park below the station, Gould held the door open for Cottrell. A couple of years before, the two had lived together for nearly a year, before Cottrell had walked out. They could have chosen to work in different divisions, but somehow, without anything being said, the two had instinctively agreed to return to work together and resume a formal relationship.

45

'Where are we going, David?' Cottrell asked as Gould drove them out of the station.

'I got a call from an old friend – there's been some sort of incident at Palmer Associates over on City Wall.'

'What sort of incident? What sort of friend?' Cottrell asked.

'It's serious. It sounded as if someone was dead.'

'Is this friend female, by any chance?'

'Yes, that's right,' Gould answered. His tone discouraged further questions, but Cottrell continued pressing him.

'And this friend . . .'

'Heather. Heather Morgan.'

'I remember her – you two used to be an item. You walked over to talk to her in the restaurant the other day. But I don't see why she should phone you now. Just because she knows you, she thinks the City of London police are at her beck and call, does she? Why didn't she phone 999, like everyone else? Does she expect a special service?'

'It's not like that,' Gould said. 'It sounds as if Heather's in serious trouble and she knows I'm in the police. It's natural for her to phone me.' After a few minutes' silence, he said, 'We're here now.'

As they got out of the car, Cottrell looked around. 'The patrol car's not here yet. We ought to wait for them. You know they should always be first on the scene.'

'Oh, come on, it's an emergency,' Gould said as he walked into the reception area of the office block. He showed his warrant card to the elderly security guard. 'I've had a call from someone on the twelfth floor. In the boardroom.'

The guard looked baffled. 'Twelfth floor? That's odd. There was a party last night, but I'm sure everyone's gone home. I'll take you up so you can see for yourself.'

The guard led Gould and Cottrell into the lift. The journey to the twelfth floor passed irritatingly slowly. Eventually the doors opened onto a plushly carpeted hallway.

'The boardroom's this way,' the guard said, leading the way to the right. After a few feet, he pulled out his pass key and opened a door. Gould and Cottrell followed him in, and they saw Heather standing there, dishevelled and with her cocktail dress smeared with blood.

'My God, Miss Morgan, what's happened to you?' the guard asked in shock.

Gould and Cottrell followed the guard into the room.

'David, thank God you've come.' Heather rushed forward. Gould held her, while Cottrell immediately donned a pair of transparent gloves and bagged the knife on the floor.

'Heather, take some breaths and calm down. What's happened?' Gould asked. 'Who is this man?'

'James – James Faulkner. I told you about him,' Heather answered between sobs. 'He's my fiancé – or was. I broke it off with him last night.'

Cottrell knelt down next to the body and felt for a pulse. 'He's dead,' she said. 'The body's starting to turn cold. There's a lot of blood, and it definitely looks a suspicious death. I'd say he's been stabbed. This knife might well be the murder weapon.'

'Call for the scene of crime staff, Philippa,' Gould said, then turned his attention to Heather. 'Now take deep breaths, Heather, don't touch anything, and tell me what happened.'

'I don't know, really,' Heather said, her voice unsteady. 'The office had a party here last night. There were a lot of people, of course. I came with James, but he got very drunk and started flirting with another girl. I'd had enough of it, and told him it was all off between us. I remember having a drink, then this morning I woke up here, with James dead beside me. I don't remember anything else. I'm sure I didn't kill him – I couldn't do anything like that – but I don't know how he died.' She looked around. 'The killers can't still be here, can they?'

'No, there was no one here when we arrived, and the boardroom was locked,' Gould said. 'Now, are you hurt?'

Heather was looking at her hands. 'No, I don't think so. This must be James's blood. How did it get on my hands?'

'That's what we'll have to find out. If you're not hurt, we'll have to take you to the station and test you for evidence.'

'Evidence? What evidence do you need? You don't suspect me, do you, David?' Heather gasped. 'You know I couldn't do anything like that.'

'I don't suspect anyone at this stage,' Gould said, 'but testing you is for your good as much as anyone's. If you're innocent, it'll clear you. I'd do the same if it was my mother. Philippa, take Miss Morgan in for testing. I'll wait here for backup.'

Just then, two uniformed constables rushed in. 'We got the call, gov, but what are you doing here?' one of them asked.

'Heather – Miss Morgan – phoned me directly, so DS Cottrell and I drove here first.'

'It seems unorthodox, sir, but how do you want to play this?'

'Follow the usual steps for a suspicious death. Phone for the doctor first, before you move the body, but I'm sure he's dead. Then phone all the scene of crime officers; we'll stay out and leave the scene for you as much as we can.'

Cottrell took Heather firmly by the arms. 'Come with me, Miss Morgan. We need to get you tested. Then the doctor will give you the once-over.'

After the journey in the police car, which passed in silence, Cottrell led Heather to a cell in the basement of Snow Hill police station. Cottrell went to a cupboard and took out a white boiler suit. 'Remove your outer clothes and put this on,' she ordered.

Heather looked at the boiler suit and shuddered. 'That's hideous. I can't wear that.'

'We can send out for some of your own clothes in due course, but that's the best we can do for the moment. Put it on, please. This isn't a fashion show.' Cottrell put on some plastic gloves from the cupboard and took out an evidence bag. 'Give me your outer clothes and I'll put them in this bag for forensics.'

48

'Can't I be on my own while I change?'

'No.'

'Can I see David?'

'DCI Gould will be along later. Your clothes, please.'

Heather silently removed her party dress and tights. Then she stood embarrassed in her bra and pants.

Cottrell checked over Heather's underwear. 'There's no blood on those. You can put the boiler suit on now.'

'How long will they keep me here?'

'As long as necessary. The police doctor will be along to examine you soon.'

'Is that really necessary? I'm perfectly well.'

'Yes, it certainly is necessary,' Cottrell said, and left the room, locking it behind her.

Heather sat disconsolately for twenty minutes before Cottrell returned with a middle-aged man, who was carrying a medical bag. Cottrell waited outside the room as the doctor entered.

'I'm Doctor Coombs,' the man said. 'How are you feeling?'

'Terrible. I don't like being treated like a criminal.'

'I can't help you there, I'm afraid. I'm just here to check you're fit to be interviewed,' Dr Coombs replied in a breezy manner. 'Were you injured in the incident at all?' He pointed at the blood on Heather's hands.

'No, I don't think so,' Heather replied vaguely.

'You don't think so?' Coombs echoed. 'Don't you know?'

'I can't remember what happened,' Heather replied, starting to cry.

'I'll have to take a blood sample. Do I have your permission? It's to test for the presence of drugs or alcohol.'

'Yes, if you must, but I don't do drugs, and I didn't drink much alcohol – just a couple of glasses of wine.'

The doctor took a blood sample and a small clipping of hair and sealed them in small polythene bags, then he looked at her hands. 'I can't see any injury. If you're not hurt, the sergeant will

49

want to take that blood off your hand. I'll call her.' He went to the door to let Cottrell in and left.

Cottrell took out a box of tissues and another evidence bag. 'Wipe your hands on these, please,' she ordered Heather. Afterwards, Cottrell placed the tissues in the evidence bag and started to leave.

'Is that all?' Heather called out.

'Yes, thank you. You'll have to wait for DCI Gould to come back before we decide what to do.'

'I want to go home and get some fresh clothes.'

'That won't be possible.'

'Have I been arrested?'

'No, you are voluntarily helping us with our inquiries. But you must understand, if you try to leave, I will be obliged to arrest you.'

'Then I want to see my solicitor,' Heather said.

Chapter 6

At that moment, Gould was still at the murder scene, with the two uniformed police officers. He stood just outside the door into the company boardroom. The dead man, identified by Heather as James Faulkner, was stretched out on the floor, and Gould looked around for clues, making sure he did not contaminate the crime scene.

The blood-soaked knife was in an evidence bag. It was the obvious weapon, and Gould wanted to inspect it thoroughly, but he knew he would have to wait for his forensics colleagues to test it before he could study it closely.

He knew he had to examine the evidence impartially. He ran through his feelings for Heather. They had been very close until she had broken the relationship off. He still shuddered at the memory of her tearful recriminations on that day. She had accused him of being obsessed with his work. He knew it was true, but the accusation still hurt.

As a police officer, Gould realised it was his duty to find the murderer in this case, even if it proved to be Heather. He told himself the fact that he knew her and did not believe she was capable of killing anyone was not necessarily a handicap to the inquiry. It would force him to look around for other suspects. Gould wanted to make sure that even the sharpest defence barrister would not be able to accuse him of being too ready to arrest Heather. He knew most of his colleagues would have arrested her on the spot, but Gould could not reconcile the woman he used to know with murder.

He asked himself if he was letting his personal feelings get in the way of his judgement as he looked around for some way of clearing Heather. He persuaded himself any competent senior investigating officer would do the same, though he knew quite a few who would jump to the easy conclusion that Heather had killed James in some lovers' spat.

However, as Gould looked around, at first sight, there was no evidence that even the best barrister could have used in Heather's defence. When Gould and Cottrell had arrived, Heather had been on her own in the boardroom, holding what looked like the murder weapon. The key to the boardroom was on the floor beside her, so she had presumably locked herself in, which looked very suspicious, and it was difficult to see who else could have killed James. Gould sadly shook his head as he closed the door behind him, to preserve the scene of the crime.

Gould knew that there was a whole subcategory of crime stories called locked-room mysteries. He remembered, with derision, some of the solutions to such mysteries in fiction. There were icicles shot through the keyhole that killed the victim, then melted away. One involved the murderer killing the victim with a frozen leg of lamb, then cooking and eating the murder weapon. Did a Sherlock Holmes story involve a trained mongoose climbing down the chimney, or had he imagined that? But proving Heather innocent when she had been found alone in a locked room with the body of a murder victim, whom she admitted to arguing with that evening, seemed just as implausible as any of those.

Gould looked out of the window at the neighbouring skyscrapers, vaguely hoping to see a long-range sharpshooter who could have killed James, or any bullet holes in the windows. Then he shook his head, as he reminded himself that the victim had been stabbed and the apparent murder weapon was right next to him.

It would be a challenge for any investigator to find any suspect with a greater motive, means and opportunity than Heather Morgan. Most people would find it obvious that Heather had killed her fiancé, and they could be right. Perhaps the best hope for Heather would be to submit some sort of self-defence plea, if she could argue that James had been attacking or even raping her.

Just then Gould recognised the police surgeon coming along the corridor.

'Hello, David, what have we got here?'

'A stabbing,' Gould said. 'Please let me know when we can move the body.'

The police surgeon entered the boardroom, bent over the body, touched the neck, then took the corpse's temperature. 'Yes, he's dead all right. Rigor mortis has set in. He must have been dead for at least eight hours. You can take it to the morgue for a post-mortem.'

'Eight hours?' Gould echoed. 'That's strange.'

'Why?'

'Our suspect was locked in here when we arrived. Why would she stay with the body all that time?'

'That's out of my area,' Coombs said. 'But in this normal room temperature, eight to twelve hours would be a reasonable estimate.'

'Thank you, doctor,' Gould replied. 'Has your colleague seen our suspect?'

'Is that the attractive young woman – Heather Morgan, I think her name was? I saw her in the distance, but didn't get too close. I didn't want any cross-contamination.'

'Thank you, doctor,' Gould replied in a sad tone. 'I can guarantee I'll be careful.'

Just then, as the surgeon left, three forensic examiners arrived at the door of the boardroom. After a nod from Gould, the photographer was the first to enter the room and took a large number of shots of the body and the scene as a whole. Then he left and the fingerprint expert entered and begun to dust all the visible surfaces. He picked up the exhibit bag with the knife and placed it carefully in his case. Then the third technician took samples of the many bloodstains surrounding the body.

'This was reported by a woman called Heather Morgan,' Gould said. 'She was by that knife when I came in.'

'There are spatterings of blood over the table and carpets. They're probably the victim's, but we'll have to check, of course. Somebody certainly stabbed him – it looks as if this is the murder weapon – and if her fingerprints are on the knife, she's looking a dead cert for the perpetrator.' Just then the technician saw Gould's pained expression. 'Why the long face? It should be a nice and easy case for you.'

'You're probably right, but I know her, and I don't think she could do it.'

Just then, a pair of hospital orderlies arrived with a stretcher. 'Yes, you can take the body away now,' Gould told them.

Once the body had gone, Gould saw more bloodstains on the carpet where it had lain. 'There's more blood for you to sample,' he told the scene of crime officers. He turned to the uniformed constables. 'I'll leave you here while I get back to the station.'

Chapter 7

When Gould returned to Snow Hill police station, he called DS Cottrell into his room. 'How has Heather been? Does she have a solicitor yet?' he asked.

'We've allowed her to make her single phone call. She's in one of our boiler suits, which she's unhappy about. I'm expecting her solicitor shortly.'

'The evidence doesn't look good for her, does it, Philippa?'

'At first sight, it looks as if she's a murderer, if that's what you mean,' Cottrell replied. 'Perhaps you should stand down. You mustn't let any friendship stand in the way of the investigation.'

'I won't give her any special treatment, but we have to offer her every chance to prove her innocence, as we would with any suspect,' Gould said. 'Don't forget I know her, and I can't believe she would do anything like this.' Cottrell did not reply but maintained a sceptical silence. 'I see you don't agree. I'll let you ask the difficult questions.'

Half an hour later, Gould and Cottrell entered the interview room. Heather was sitting next to a short, balding man, whom Gould recognised as a duty solicitor.

'Hello, Heather,' Gould said. 'Good morning, Mr Bradshaw.'

'I am representing Miss Morgan, DCI Gould. I have interviewed my client, and she is prepared to answer questions,' Bradshaw announced.

'Very good,' Gould pressed the switch on the tape recorder. 'This interview started at 11.30am on December 17th in the presence of Detective Chief Inspector David Gould.'

'Detective Sergeant Philippa Cottrell.'

'Anthony Bradshaw, solicitor.'

'Heather Morgan.' The four participants called out their names for the benefit of the recording.

'Miss Morgan – Heather,' Cottrell began. 'We are investigating the recent suspicious death of James Faulkner at the offices of Palmer Associates. I must stress that you're a person of interest. Mr Bradshaw will have explained to you what that means. To start with, I'd like to go back in time. Tell us about your relationship with James Faulkner – when did it start?'

'That's difficult to say exactly,' Heather began, after a moment's thought. 'It somehow just started about six months ago. We work together – I'm his boss – and we were both single. He asked me out, and suddenly we were a couple. Then a few months later we became engaged – but we hadn't fixed a date for the wedding yet.'

'And was your relationship going well?'

'No, I'm afraid it wasn't, to be honest. Not at all.' Heather looked at Bradshaw, who signalled for her to continue. 'In fact, I'd decided to break it off. I'd just told James it was all over during the party. I'd given his ring back to him.'

'And why was that?'

'Everything, really. I'd decided we just weren't compatible at all. He didn't seem fully committed to marrying me – or anyone. His flirting with other women at the party was the last straw.'

'How did he react to your breaking it off?'

'He said he was surprised, but I don't think he can have been. He told me he loved me, but I didn't believe him. Not after the way he behaved at the party.'

'By "the way he behaved", you mean flirting with other women, do you?'

'Yes, also getting generally drunk and obnoxious. He was even rude to Sir Giles Palmer – the chairman.'

'Then, at the party where you ditched him, he was murdered, with you alone in the room with his body. From our point of view, you have to admit it looks suspicious.'

Heather started to cry. 'Do you think I don't know that? But I couldn't kill anyone.'

'We'll see about that,' Cottrell said. 'You told me you were engaged to the dead man, but had broken it off with him. Please tell me what else you remember about the party.'

'Well, everything is very hazy.'

'Hazy? What do you mean, hazy? Are you saying you can't remember events from last night?'

'I remember James and I arrived together. I drove his car, as I was worried he had been drinking. I gave him back the key. It was a red MG. It should still be in the company car park.'

'We'll check that. And did you stay together for the whole party?'

'No. Before long, he was chatting up some girl – Alison, her name is. She's a secretary in the firm – very vulgar, and pretty enough to hate on sight. I knew they'd been an item sometime in the past.'

'How did you feel about that?'

'Pissed off, of course,' Heather said. 'But I'd decided to break off the engagement by then, so I suppose that I had no right to object.'

'Who else did you speak to?'

'All the usual crowd. Derek Ringer – he's my boss, Margaret Prestwood – she's my best friend at work, Michael Dawson – he's another executive – he was being quite sweet to me – even Sir Giles Palmer deigned to speak to me.'

'Please tell us what you know about the death of James Faulkner,' Gould said. 'Speak slowly and steadily, and describe everything even if it doesn't seem relevant.'

Heather took a deep breath. 'James and I arrived at the office party at around nine o'clock. I wasn't looking forward to it, but felt I ought to make an effort. There were some journalists hanging about outside as we walked in. God knows how they had heard about the party. There's been a lot of bad publicity for the company recently. Someone James used to know – Robin Lynch, the editor of *Dirty Money* – was there, and shouted out questions.

'I remember coming into the party. It was held in the large office room. There were hideous Christmas decorations all round. I remember seeing a lot of my colleagues – quite a few of them I try to avoid all year – in this one big room, and grabbed a drink.

'I can't really remember everyone who was there. I know I met Sir Giles Palmer – the boss man. He was hosting the party, so it was polite to speak to him, but he didn't say much. As I said, I was annoyed because James was flirting with a pretty blonde girl called Alison – she's one of the secretaries in the office. I seem to remember she slapped James, as he was pestering her. They were both very drunk, to be fair.'

'You admit you were annoyed?' Cottrell echoed. 'How annoyed were you by the end of the party?'

'Well, I was furious with James. He was making me look a fool,' Heather replied, before she realised the implication of what she had said. 'Oh, let's say I was sad, not really angry. I'd decided I'd had enough of the engagement even before I saw him flirting with Alison. It was like a load off my mind, knowing that I didn't have to bother with him any more, except at work. Assuming we carried on working together, of course.'

'Just carry on with what happened at the party, please, Heather,' Gould interrupted, with a reproachful glance at Cottrell.

'There were the usual people from the office. Derek Ringer, of course, was there.'

'Derek Ringer? Is he a senior person in the company?' Cottrell asked, preparing to make notes on her pad.

'He's my direct boss. He's between me and Sir Giles Palmer. I expect you'll want to speak to him.'

'I'm sure we will. We'll want to interview everyone we can trace who was at this party with you. Please continue,' Cottrell said in a firm tone.

Heather closed her eyes to concentrate. 'Well, there were quite a lot of people. I mentioned a journalist called Robin Lynch, shouting questions as we came in. He's written about the company – basically he hates us, for some reason. James said he went to school with him, which seems a strange coincidence. I hope James wasn't leaking stuff to Lynch, but I can't be sure. James said he saw Lynch talking to a man in a brand-new Land Rover – James seemed upset about it, but I don't know why.

'At some point, James and Linus Murray – he's from our LA office – were arguing over Alison, which made me look even more stupid. Michael Dawson was being nice to me. He could see I was upset. Then James and Michael had an argument.'

'What about?'

'About me, I suppose you could say. But I don't think James knew what he was doing by then. Margaret came up to me and sympathised, which made me feel worse, and I decided to go home by taxi. I remember I spoke to a man called Fretwell – he's an investor in the company. I think he might have brought me a drink. After that, it all goes blank, and I can't remember anything until I woke up in the boardroom.'

'You woke up with James Faulkner's body in front of you,' Cottrell said. 'Did anyone enter the boardroom during the party – anyone apart from you and the dead man, that is?'

'Not as far as I know. I remember looking at it through the small window and thinking how spotless it looked. I expect it was kept locked to keep it tidy in there during the party.'

'You had a key by you when the guard came to let us in. Do you know how it got there?'

'No. I've never needed to have a key for the boardroom.'

'You had no key and no idea how you got into the locked boardroom,' Cottrell echoed, making notes. 'Yet that is where we found you and your dead fiancé at ten o'clock this morning. To be honest, Miss Morgan, you are looking the prime suspect for the murder of Mr Faulkner. I expect your solicitor will want to explain to you the serious position you are in. Some of your answers aren't at all convincing. I suggest you take the next set of interviews more seriously than this one. You might like to review your story.'

'I don't know what you mean. Believe me, I am taking this all very seriously. And it's not a story; it is the truth,' Heather said, as the tape recording was switched off.

Bradshaw leant across the table. 'I must ask you to allow Miss Morgan to leave now, detective chief inspector. She's had a terrible shock and would like to go home.'

'Not as big a shock as Mr Faulkner had when he was knifed,' Cottrell said.

'My client and I have every sympathy with the dead man's family, but, unless you wish to arrest my client, I must ask you to release her. She's extremely stressed. She's answered all your questions, and will be happy to help again in the future.'

'Yes, we have all the forensic information we need from Miss Morgan, but it is still to be tested. If you can collect a change of clothes from her home, she can be released,' Gould told Bradshaw, ignoring Cottrell's reproachful glare.

Chapter 8

The next day, Gould and Cottrell looked down at James Faulkner's naked body, at Saint Bartholomew's hospital, close to Snow Hill police station. Cottrell shuddered as the pathologist made the first incision. She had never overcome her revulsion at seeing a human corpse cut open as if it were an animal on a butcher's block, and hoped she never would become desensitised to the sight. The two officers watched and listened as the pathologist dictated into a small tape recorder.

'We have a well-nourished male aged about thirty,' the pathologist was saying. 'There are no marks on the body apart from the incisions in the upper torso.' He ran his hands over James's legs, pelvis and midriff. 'The deceased seems to have been healthy – when he was alive, of course.' He chuckled to himself, while Gould and Cottrell tried to hide their impatience. Gould knew it was standard practice to examine the rest of the body before studying the obvious cause of death, but it did not make it any less irritating. 'I see our guests are getting impatient. Let's look at the upper torso. There have been, I would say, three incisions with a sharp implement, any one of which could have caused death.'

Cottrell showed him a photograph of the knife found near Heather when the body was located. 'Could this have done it, doctor? This was found close to the body.'

The pathologist studied it closely. 'Yes, that would have done the job very nicely, if *nicely* is the *mot juste*.' Gould and Cottrell exchanged glances as the pathologist chuckled again. 'If the blood matched the deceased's, then I would say it's almost certainly the murder weapon. Well, that's it, officers. I'll let you have a written report in the morning.'

'Would it take any particular strength to inflict these injuries, doctor?' Gould asked.

'No, not if the knife was sharp. I wouldn't rule out a woman doing it, if that is what you're implying. Fifty or more years ago, pathologists would rule out a woman stabbing someone, but nowadays we're not so chivalrous, you might say. I would think the murderer was right-handed and facing the victim, but that's all I can say.'

'Any clues on the killer's height?' Cottrell asked.

'Again, my predecessors used to be very specific about this, but I don't know how. No, I can't say, other than not very short and not very tall.'

'Can you tell us when he died, doctor?' Gould asked. 'The police surgeon said he had been dead about eight hours when he was found.'

The pathologist checked his notes. 'Yes, I see. From the temperature of the corpse that my colleague measured, I'd probably agree with his estimate.'

'Thank you, doctor, that's very useful,' Gould said. 'If you can stitch him up again by this afternoon, I have arranged for his parents to identify him.'

*

Later the same day, Gould directed an elderly couple into the interview room, and waited while they took their seats. 'I'm sorry for your loss, Mr and Mrs Faulkner.'

Gould had previously accompanied James's parents to the autopsy room, where the post-mortem had been held. The body had been made as presentable as possible to spare the relatives' feelings. The attendant had pulled down the covering sheet, and Mr Faulkner had nodded confirmation of their son's identity, while Mrs Faulkner sobbed.

'There is no way I can console you, and I know you want time to grieve quietly,' Gould said now, as a constable brought them cups of tea. 'But if you can answer my questions now, it should help us bring your son's killer to justice.'

'Thank you, inspector,' Mr Faulkner replied, as his wife sobbed next to him, 'but James was lost to us for many years before he died.'

'What do you mean, sir?' Gould asked.

'We live up in the Scottish Highlands – we've always been dairy farmers. But it wasn't exciting enough for James. He moved down to London when he was eighteen. He never returned.'

'Lots of young men move to London to make a career, Mr Faulkner. Leaving home is quite normal nowadays, but you sound bitter. Was there some unpleasantness behind him moving away? Had you lost touch with him?'

'My son and I hadn't spoken for two years, Mr Gould. We didn't approve of his way of living.'

'And why was that, sir?'

'Oh, we knew he was only interested in making money and chasing women. We're Presbyterians, Mr Gould. We don't approve of those sorts of things.'

'And you're saying you haven't tried to contact James for the last two years?'

'No. We love him, but he chose a different path, which we know now ended up with him dead.'

'I see. Does the name Heather Morgan mean anything to you?'

Mr and Mrs Faulkner looked at each other and shook their heads. 'No. Who is she?' Mr Faulkner asked.

'She was engaged to your son. I'm surprised he didn't tell you about her.'

'Engaged? How could he be?' Mrs Faulkner spoke for the first time. 'James was engaged to a local girl.'

Gould was too stunned to speak.

'I see you don't know,' she said. 'James seems to have forgotten as well.'

Gould recovered his poise. 'No, that's very useful information. Do you have any details of his first fiancée?'

'Her name's Sandra. I'll write down the last address I have for her.'

'That will be very useful, Mrs Faulkner,' Gould said. 'Can you tell me what sort of childhood James had?'

'He was always very happy. Very good at rugby and all sorts of sports, James was. Not like Stuart, who was more bookish.'

'Stuart? Who is he?'

'James's brother, of course,' Mrs Faulkner said, obviously impatient at being interrupted. 'He's a doctor down here. He's done very well for himself. He's a credit to the family. We stayed with him over the weekend.'

Gould sat up in his chair. 'Are you saying you were in London last weekend? Please tell me where the two of you were between 7 pm and 2am on Saturday night.'

'We were staying with Stuart,' Mr Faulkner said. 'We don't go out much at our age. I'll write down Stuart's address, but, as I say, we haven't seen James for a long time – neither has Stuart, I'm sure.'

'Do you know of any friends James had?'

'No, not really,' Mr Faulkner replied after some thought. 'He lost touch with all his local friends when he moved away. The only one I can think of who he might still be in touch with is his best friend at school – he was called Robin Lynch. I believe he's some sort of journalist in the City.'

Gould looked up from writing his notes. 'Is that the Robin Lynch who is editor of *Dirty Money* magazine? His name has come up in this investigation.'

'Yes, that could be him. He always wanted to be a journalist, but I don't know what job he ended up doing. Is he famous?'

'Yes, I think everyone in the City has heard of Robin Lynch. He's behind quite a few revelations of scandals. People either love him or hate him. Thank you, Mr and Mrs Faulkner. I will have a word with Mr Lynch. The constable will escort you out. We can give you a lift to your son's house, if you need it. I'm afraid we won't be able to release the body yet.'

*

Gould and Cottrell's next visit was to the Central London Pathology Laboratory located in University College Hospital.

'I've brought you here because I've found something very interesting,' the laboratory scientist began, checking her records. 'All the blood found near the body and on the knife you brought me belonged to the deceased. So, no surprise there. We obviously took a sample from the chief suspect. I believe her name is Heather Morgan. None of the blood on the knife or on the body is hers, but when I tested her, we found traces of a drug.'

'Drug? What drug?' Gould asked, startling the scientist with the force of his question.

'Ketamine – it's a strong sedative. It's often called the main date rape drug. It dissipates quite quickly, so we were lucky to find it. The amounts are small, but definitely there.'

'The suspect said she woke up close to the body, feeling woozy, after several hours.'

'That would be consistent with the known effects of ketamine.'

'And ketamine, of course, is used for anaesthetic purposes in hospitals – or by inadequate men for purposes of rape, as you mentioned. Or it could be used to silence someone and frame them for a murder they didn't commit,' Gould said, his voice rising in excitement.

'Any of those purposes are possible,' the scientist said, 'but I'll have to leave it to you to decide which is correct in this case.'

65

Chapter 9

Early the following morning, Gould called a meeting of the detectives involved in the case. Cottrell and DS Fox, a newly promoted detective sergeant recently transferred from the Surrey force, were assisting him.

'We'll have to interview everyone at the party,' Gould said.

'I have a list from the security people of everyone officially invited,' Fox said, handing it over.

'Could anyone have entered the premises without an invitation?'

'The security guards say not, and there's no sign of forced entry, but it's only ordinary office security – so I suppose an intruder could have bluffed their way in.'

'Very well. It's most likely the murderer is on this list, but we'll keep an open mind, and ask if anyone saw an intruder. Have you sent out the invitations for interview yet?'

'Yes,' Cottrell said. 'The first ones have been arranged, and Foxy and I have drawn up this list of questions.'

Gould took the list from Cottrell and skimmed through it. 'Yes, these seem reasonable. Who's the first one?'

'An executive called Linus Murray is waiting for us. He's an American.'

'Yes, Heather mentioned him. Lead on. I'll be interested in what he has to say.'

Cottrell led Gould down to the interview room of the police station. Linus Murray sat opposite at the table. Even seated, his formidable bulk dominated the room.

'Thank you for coming in, Mr Murray,' Gould began. 'We are investigating the death of James Faulkner at the offices of Palmer Associates on Saturday night.'

'I understand. I was there.'

'So I understand. First, can you tell us about yourself? I'm told you are on loan from your company's Los Angeles office.'

'Yes, sir, I am over here for a year,' Linus said, his strong American accent seeming out of place in the British police station.

'And what is your role in Palmer Associates?'

'I'm what's called an accounts executive. I was transferred over here to help some of our American customers. They like to have a familiar accent when they phone in.'

'I understand you have a relationship with a young woman called Alison Coates.'

'You seem very well informed, chief inspector. Yes, I have nothing to hide. Alison and I have what you might call an understanding, sir,' Linus said.

'Please tell us what you saw at the party, Mr Murray,' Gould continued.

'Alison and I arrived together about eight. I was surprised to see so much drinking. It's not like that in LA. Everyone over there is on a health kick.'

'And did you notice James Faulkner at the party?'

'I should say I did, inspector. James was trying to pick up my girl. They were dancing really close together. After a while, I stepped in and took Alison home; it was getting embarrassing. She was getting upset.'

'We've heard she was getting drunk and slapped James Faulkner.'

'That's kinda true. At least it saved me from hitting him. Let's say I thought taking her home would be better all round.'

'Did you speak to Faulkner at all during the incident?'

'Yes, I told him to back off or I would punch him into the middle of next week. He looked kinda scared. It's useful being an athlete sometimes. It frightens some folks. They think I'm some sort of boxer.' Linus chuckled to himself. 'Mind you, I work out a lot and am pretty strong, so maybe James was right to be scared.'

67

'The incident could be said to give you a motive for killing James Faulkner, Mr Murray,' Cottrell said.

'I can't see that I had a motive. I kept my girl, after all. It was James Faulkner who lost out in our little encounter.'

'Do you know anyone else who would want Faulkner killed?' Gould asked.

'Well, Heather Morgan was looking daggers at him all night, so she must be a suspect. And everyone knows Mike Dawson is sweet on Heather. Now James is out of the way, he has less competition. Yes, I would say Dawson had a motive.'

'Did you see anyone going into the boardroom while you were at the party?'

Linus thought. 'No. I don't believe I did. I think it was locked.'

'You described having a violent argument with James Faulkner at the party, Mr Murray. How well did you know him before then?' Cottrell asked.

'I knew he had a fling with Alison in the past,' Linus said. 'James and I had exchanged words in the past few months, it's true, but, in general, I guess we kept out of each other's way until the night of the party.'

'When it all kicked off, apparently,' Gould said.

Linus said nothing.

'Can anyone vouch for your movements after ten o'clock that night, Mr Murray?' Cottrell asked.

'Well, I went home with Alison around ten, and we went to bed together. Neither of us went out again.'

'So you can give each other alibis, but no one else can corroborate. That might not carry too much weight with a jury, Mr Murray.'

'Especially as I'm a foreigner. I know the picture,' Linus said with a sigh. 'I can't help that. I can only tell you the truth.'

'I've been looking at your personnel file, Mr Murray,' Gould said. 'You seem to have some very impressive qualifications. All sorts of degrees, including one from Harvard. Somehow you don't seem to come from an Ivy League background.'

'Yeah, well, I studied under the GI bill after a spell in the army, so it didn't cost much.'

'I think we'll follow up with some of these universities and see if they remember you. Can you give me the names of any of the lecturers who might remember you? Unless you have something to tell us first ...'

'No, I have nothing to hide, but I can't remember any of the lecturers. Now, if that's all ...' Linus walked slowly out of the interview room, ducking his head to avoid hitting it on the doorframe.

Gould turned to Cottrell. 'If that man's got a degree from Harvard, I'll eat my hat. I wonder what he's really doing over here. I'm suspicious of Mr Murray. He may not have killed James Faulkner, but he certainly has something to hide.'

Chapter 10

In the afternoon, Gould and Cottrell looked at the CCTV image of Margaret Prestwood waiting in the Snow Hill station interview room.

'How does she look to you, Philippa?'

'She doesn't look like the typical City executive. I've never seen anyone quite so hippyish working in the City before.'

'I see what you mean. Does she look nervous to you? Most people are when they are about to be interviewed by the police, even if they're innocent.'

'No, she seems quite dispassionate, really.'

'That's what I think. I'm not sure if that makes her less or more suspicious. Still, let's go in and talk to her. We've let her stew for long enough.' Gould led Cottrell into the interview room.

'Thank you for waiting for us, Miss Prestwood,' Gould began. 'We met at the restaurant last week, didn't we? As you know, I'm DCI David Gould. I'm senior investigating officer in charge of this case, and DS Cottrell will take notes. Are you ready for the interview?'

'Yes, thank you, Chief Inspector,' Margaret began. Her voice struck Gould as being vaguely Australian.

'I'm primarily investigating the murder of James Faulkner two nights ago. But I would like to go back in time to make sure I know the background of people at the party. When did you start working for Palmer Associates?'

Margaret looked at the sky through the window high above the desk, as she considered her answer. 'I started working there two years ago. I'm an accounts executive.'

'Where did you work before then?'

'I was brought up in Australia – near Sydney – then backpacked to Europe after university, like lots of Aussies do. I just never went back. I've worked for various City firms. I like the money here. It makes up for the awful climate,' Margaret added with a slight smile.

'Tell me about your responsibilities.'

'Well, I handle some of our principal clients. If they have any problems with work we are doing for them, they come to me.'

'I know Palmer Associates is called an international finance company, but that doesn't mean much to me. Please tell me more about what the company does.'

'Well, companies that have a project they need money for come to see me. If it seems likely to be profitable, we arrange finance.'

'What sorts of goods do your clients make?'

'Oh, no, inspector, they don't make things you can touch. Our client companies work in the service industries – film production and other things.'

'That sounds glamorous.'

'Not our side of it. It's just a question of introducing people with money to the film producers who need it.'

'Which people with money?' Gould asked.

'Well, one of them was at the party – Hugh Fretwell.'

'Tell me about him.'

'Oh, he was born into money. He's the tail end of a noble family. From the look of him, by the time he was born, the character of his ancestors had gone, but some of the money was left. Hugh Fretwell likes to back films. He thinks it brings him closer to glamorous starlets, but I don't know if he's ever actually met any. He seemed keen on Heather, though.'

Gould leant forward. 'You're saying this man Fretwell was paying too much attention to Heather Morgan at the party.'

Margaret nodded. 'Yes. He thinks money makes him irresistible to women, but he's still a fat loser. A rich fat loser, to be fair.'

Gould nodded to make sure Cottrell had made a note of

Fretwell's name. 'We'll follow that up, Miss Prestwood. Now, I believe you are good friends with Heather Morgan. How did that come about?'

'I'm not sure, really,' Margaret said, her gaze shifting to the far corner of the interview room. 'We were two of the few women in this part of the office, and we started chatting. Then, after a while, we began having lunch together. It's good to talk with another woman sometimes. We chatted about the usual girly things – what men we were going out with, why we weren't paid as much as men, what clothes we were going to wear, that sort of thing. Heather was single when we met, and she didn't seem to be looking for a man in her life. I was surprised she got engaged to James Faulkner. I wasn't sure he was right for her, but I suppose it was her decision.'

'Let's talk about the evening of the party. Please tell me what you saw.'

Margaret sipped a glass of water. 'It started off like a normal party. I arrived soon after eight o'clock. There was Sir Giles Palmer – the head man. He puts in an appearance every Christmas, just to show willing. There was Derek Ringer, who's a simpering sycophant who follows Sir Giles around like a bad smell. He's managing director. I told you about Fretwell. I suppose you're interested in James Faulkner, as it was him who was killed. He was getting drunk. I could tell Heather was getting annoyed with him. He was chatting up any attractive women in the place. I'm not sure how long their engagement would have lasted if James had lived.'

'Go on.'

'James was behaving badly, as I said. He was dancing closely with Alison; she's Sir Giles's secretary. I know she and James had a fling before Heather came on the scene. Heather was upset with them, and I don't blame her. Alison's current boyfriend – he's called Linus Murray – had a few angry words with James. James backed off after that. You wouldn't want to cross Linus if you could help it. He's a big strong guy.'

'We've already interviewed Mr Murray,' Gould said. 'Please tell us what happened at the end of the party.'

'It got less tense after old Palmer had left. Ringer went with him, of course. We knew we had to be out by midnight, so things slowed down about then.'

'Are you sure Sir Giles and Mr Ringer both left early?'

'Well, no, they looked as if they were preparing to go, but I didn't see them leave as such.'

'Did you see Heather leave?'

'No. I looked out for her around eleven, but I assumed she left. From what I now know she was stuck in the boardroom all night.'

'Yes, she was,' Cottrell said. 'I'm surprised you didn't check to see she got home safely – after all, you were friends.'

'I knew she had James with her. I thought she was his responsibility.'

'When did you leave the party, Miss Prestwood?'

'Oh, just after eleven.'

'Did anyone see you leave?'

'I'm not sure. I left quietly.'

'Did you see anyone enter the boardroom at all?'

'No. I noticed it was locked, but after then I didn't take much notice of it.'

'How well did you know the dead man?' Gould asked, taking over the questioning.

'Well, he was Heather's fiancé, as you know, so his name came up when we talked. As I said, to be honest, I never thought they were well matched. Heather was too good for him.'

'It sounds as if you didn't like James Faulkner.'

'I didn't really, but I had no reason to kill him.'

'No one said you were a suspect, Miss Prestwood,' Gould said, as Margaret shrugged. 'Apart from Heather Morgan, can you think of anyone else with a reason to kill James Faulkner?'

'I suppose I can't,' Margaret said, gazing into the corner of the room. 'I should mention Michael Dawson. He's another accounts executive. He was being very attentive to Heather at the party. I think he secretly fancies her. He could be said to have a motive to get rid of James. Michael was in the army, so he would know how to silence someone. He might have thought killing James would leave him clear to make a move for Heather. I don't know what else to say. Except that I am sure Heather could never kill anyone.'

Chapter 11

On their way to their next interview, Cottrell, who was driving the official car, turned to Gould. 'Why are we going to see the next suspect at home, David?'

'I thought it would be interesting to see what sort of property this man Ringer has. They say he's got a day off, and I fancy surprising him at home. It's good to get out of the City and see how these people live. According to Heather, Ringer lives high on the hog. Let's see if she's right.'

Gould carried on idly watching the Surrey countryside through the car window until he noticed Cottrell had been unusually silent for the whole of the journey. 'Is anything wrong, Philippa?'

'No, nothing.'

'Yes, there is. You think we should arrest Heather, don't you?' Gould asked.

'You're the boss,' Cottrell said shortly. 'You make the decisions.'

'Yes, I'm the boss, and I'm asking for your opinion.'

'I just don't see what else you want before you arrest Morgan. She was in the room alone with the body and her fingerprints are all over the knife. Faulkner's blood is all over her hands. She had the motive – lots of people saw her arguing with Faulkner. She admits she'd just broken off their engagement. Either she killed him in anger, because of the way he was treating her, or it could be in self-defence if he tried to attack her in a jealous rage, which seems more likely. Either way, she's the one who killed him. Can't you persuade her to come clean and claim provocation? She'd get a light sentence. Especially if you put in a good word for her – that should be easy, since you know each other so well.' Cottrell could not conceal the bitterness in her voice.

75

'That would make life easy for us – except I believe Heather's innocent,' Gould said. 'Let's wait until we've interviewed everyone who was at the party, shall we? We need to have all the facts before we arrest anyone. I know Heather, and I can't believe she's capable of murder, no matter the provocation.'

Cottrell shrugged her shoulders and remained silent.

'You're not jealous of her, are you, Philippa?'

Cottrell put the brakes on so suddenly she and Gould jolted forward.

'Don't flatter yourself, sir,' Cottrell spat out, before she calmly resumed driving.

*

After they had parked, Gould and Cottrell stood outside their destination: a large detached house in a leafy suburb of Guildford. Gould was still aware of friction between them, but told himself to restrict himself to his official duties. As they walked up the drive of the house, he mentally computed the cost of the house on the open market. It seemed way beyond the reach of most middle-ranking executives, which was what Derek Ringer claimed to be.

Cottrell rang the doorbell. A tired-looking middle-aged woman came to the door.

'Mrs Ringer? I'm Detective Sergeant Cottrell of the City police. This is DCI Gould. Could we speak to your husband, please?'

Mrs Ringer looked worried. 'There's nothing wrong, is there? Is it about that Morgan woman? I don't know why you haven't arrested her yet.'

'Could we speak to your husband, please, Mrs Ringer?' Cottrell repeated in a firmer tone.

Mrs Ringer stood aside to let the two police officers in.

As they waited in the sitting room, Derek Ringer came in. He was dressed in smart casual clothes, as if he had just finished a round of golf. He closed the door of the room, leaving his wife in the hall. 'What's this, inspector? I've got a day off. Can't you see me at the office?'

'I'm interviewing the witnesses at home, Mr Ringer,' Gould said, looking around. 'This is a very pleasant home, I must say.'

'I'm sure you haven't come to talk about my property,' Derek replied impatiently. 'Since you're here, let's get on with it.'

'Very well,' Gould said. The two detectives sat down, and Cottrell prepared to take notes. 'For the record, can you tell us your exact role in Palmer Associates?'

'Oh, for heaven's sake, I'm managing director, while Sir Giles is chairman and founder. It's set out quite clearly on our website – if you know how to look at that.'

'I find it useful for witnesses to describe their roles in their own words, Mr Ringer. Now, what time did you arrive at the party at Palmer Associates on Saturday?'

'About half past eight, I suppose.'

'Please tell me everything you remember about the party.'

'We have a Christmas party every year. Sir Giles feels it is good for staff morale. He always puts in an appearance, which is very good of him. He arrived at the party soon after me.' Derek's voice grew warmer as he extolled the virtues of his boss. 'I must say I was ashamed of what Sir Giles saw when he came to the party this year.'

'Ashamed of what, sir?' Gould asked.

'The scene between James Faulkner and Heather Morgan, for one.' Derek's mouth pursed with distaste. 'Palmer Associates has always been a respectable company. People shouldn't have rows like that in public. It lowers the tone.'

'Please say precisely what you saw, sir,' Cottrell said, with her pen poised above her notebook.

'Well,' Derek continued in an offended tone, 'as I remember, James was very drunk and made insulting remarks to Sir Giles. Fortunately, Sir Giles was very gracious and ignored what he said. Most bosses would have sacked him, but he didn't. Later

I saw James having a row with Michael Dawson. I think they both fancied Heather Morgan. Then Heather shouted at James that their engagement was ended. As I say, it was very distressing.'

'What exactly were the insulting remarks the deceased made to Sir Giles?' Gould asked.

'Oh, James wondered what Sir Giles did in California. Then James raved about some suspicious payments in the company accounts. As I say, he was very drunk and not making much sense.'

'And what does Sir Giles do on his trips to California, sir?'

'Company business. We're an importing and exporting company, so obviously Sir Giles has to travel.'

'What sort of thing do you deal in?'

'Mostly copyrighted material. Not the sort of thing that you can touch or see.' Derek's voice conveyed the impression that the trade of the company was too complex for the police officers to understand.

'I see. How about the other matter – something unusual in your accounts?'

'I tell you, James was drunk. He wasn't making sense.'

'Then you won't have any objection to police auditors looking at your books?' Gould asked.

'I'm not sure about that. You'll have to consult Sir Giles.'

'I will do that. A few more questions, if I may. Do you know anyone with a motive to kill James Faulkner?'

'I don't know much about James's private life, but he seemed to think he was God's gift to women. Some jealous husband or boyfriend could have wanted him killed – or Heather Morgan could have killed him, of course. She was glaring at him whenever I noticed her.'

'And did you see anyone enter the boardroom?'

'No. Sir Giles left orders that it was to be kept locked. We like to keep it clean for our more important clients.'

'So, when did you last see James Faulkner at the party, Mr Ringer?'

'I had no reason to notice him especially, chief inspector. He was just another junior member of staff. I remember him speaking to Mr Fretwell – he's one of our investors – at about ten, but I don't remember seeing him after that.'

'Now I'd like you to tell us what else you remember about the party where the murder took place.'

'I didn't see very much of a fight, if there was one,' Derek said. 'As I say, I saw Heather drag James away to a corner of the room, then she was talking angrily to him. Telling him off for being drunk, I suppose. After that they separated. He went back to the bar and I remember Heather talking to Margaret Prestwood. Heather and James disappeared after that and I naturally supposed they'd gone home. I left at about eleven o'clock, I'd say – and that's all I know.'

'Thank you, Mr Ringer,' Gould said, as he and Cottrell rose. 'That will be all for the time being.'

Chapter 12

After the two officers had returned to Snow Hill police station, they sat at Gould's desk and prepared for the next interview.

'This will be a tricky interview, Philippa,' Gould said. 'It will be a good opportunity for you to take the lead.'

'Thanks for the opportunity. Sir Giles Palmer has told us he's bringing his solicitor with him.'

'That's usually a suspicious move for a preliminary witness interview. Why spend money on a solicitor unless he has something to hide? But, in his case, it might just mean he has money to throw away.'

'Well, let's go and find out,' Cottrell said, looking out of the window. 'That looks like his Daimler outside.'

Gould and Cottrell entered the interview room to meet Sir Giles Palmer, who was looking at the tatty furnishings with evident distaste. His solicitor pointed to the chair for him to take. Sir Giles looked around as if for help, but none was forthcoming. Eventually, he pulled out the chair and perched on the edge of it. He seemed to be making sure that the peeling cover on the chair touched as little of his pinstripe suit as possible.

'Sir Giles is prepared to answer your questions, chief inspector,' the solicitor began, as Sir Giles nodded wordlessly.

'Thank you, but DS Cottrell will conduct the interview,' Gould said, indicating for Cottrell to take the lead.

Sir Giles raised his eyebrows, looked to his solicitor for help, then finally looked towards Cottrell, whom he had obviously previously regarded as some sort of clerk. 'Very well, can I help you ... sergeant?' He seemed to imbue the word *sergeant* with as much contempt as he could muster.

'Sir Giles,' Cottrell began, 'we're investigating the suspected murder of a man named James Faulkner at the offices of your company on the 16th or 17th of December. For the record, please describe your role in Palmer Associates.'

'I would have thought it obvious, but, as you ask, I started the company from scratch and brought it to where it is now – a major company. I am chairman. Derek Ringer runs affairs on a day-to-day basis, but the company obviously bears my name.'

'And can you tell me how many times you had spoken to Mr Faulkner before the party?'

'I'm not sure that I had ever spoken to him. I had seen him and knew he worked in accounts, but that is all. The Christmas party is a regular event I hold to boost morale, but I don't know many of the staff there personally.'

'When did you arrive at the party?'

'I arrived at about half past eight. I think the staff appreciate me turning up. I came with Derek Ringer.'

'Can you describe when you spoke to Mr Faulkner at the party and what you talked about?'

'James was becoming drunk and embarrassing. He had his hands all over various women who kept moving away from him.'

'Any woman in particular?'

'My secretary, for one. I think there might have been some affair between them in the past. Alison Coates is her name.'

'We'll be sure to interview Miss Coates, Sir Giles. And I gather the deceased man spoke to you as well?'

'Yes, he did. He wanted to know about my recent trips to Los Angeles. Damn cheek. It was none of his business. He also wanted to know confidential information about our accounts. Then he asked about Ringer's salary. I'd probably have sacked James if he hadn't been killed.'

'It sounds as if the killer did you a good turn. When did you last see Mr Faulkner at the party?'

'About ten, I would say. I had no reason to speak to him after the way he spoke to me.'

'Were there any other conversations at the party that we should know about?'

'I didn't stay long. Hugh Fretwell was there – he's one of our backers. He wanted to know about the profits for a recent film we had invested in, but I told him that, after all the expenses, there wasn't much money left to go around. He wasn't happy about that. There's not much else I can tell you.'

'Did you see anyone enter the boardroom during the evening?'

'No. I gave instructions for it to be kept locked. I didn't want people spilling drinks or fooling around during the party.'

'And do you know anyone with a motive to kill Mr Faulkner?'

'There's only one person I know of, and that's Heather Morgan. I'd like to know why you haven't arrested her yet.' Sir Giles turned to look at Gould. 'She obviously did it. I could tell she was getting annoyed with James getting drunk, so she had a motive.'

'Did you see the clash between Morgan and Faulkner yourself?' Cottrell asked.

'No, it's just what I heard.'

'We are only interested in first-hand evidence, Sir Giles. Perhaps you could encourage your staff to come to us with any first-hand evidence they may have. Not many of them have come forward with useful evidence yet.'

'Very well. Is that it? Is that what I have been dragged here for?'

'It would help us considerably if you allowed us to look at the company personnel files of the people who were at the party.'

Sir Giles looked startled. 'That information is strictly confidential.'

'As you wish, Sir Giles, but we could always go to the courts and gain access. That would take time and might imply your company is unwilling to help the police. That would not be good for your company's good name.'

'Oh, very well, I'll tell Alison to give you access.'

'Thank you, Sir Giles, that will be very useful. Now, unless you have anything you want to add ...'

Sir Giles shook his head.

'Very well. Please let DCI Gould or me know if anything more occurs to you.'

'I certainly will,' Sir Giles said. 'If that is all, I must press on with more important business. I have a banquet at the Guildhall to attend. I expect your commissioner will be there. I play golf with him. I might ask him to check on the progress of your investigation, if indeed you are making any. Goodbye, sergeant – and you, chief inspector.' Sir Giles left the room. He looked back at the interview room and the two detectives with undisguised contempt.

'That was one annoyed baronet,' Gould said to Cottrell, once the solicitor had left after his client. 'He didn't like being interviewed by a lowly sergeant, especially a woman.'

'I don't see my aim in life is to irritate people like Sir Giles Palmer,' Cottrell said, keeping her voice level to conceal her annoyance. 'I'm a police officer, who happens to be a woman. Why did you insist on me asking the questions? Was it just to annoy Palmer?'

'No. I thought it would be useful experience for you. Annoying Palmer is a perk, though. I wonder how he'll react. We've got this Hugh Fretwell man to interview next. That'll be outside the station – I've arranged to see him at his club. Then we've got Alison Coates to interview. The police computer has thrown up something very interesting about her.'

'Does she have a criminal record, then?'

'No, she doesn't, but her surname rang a bell with me. It turns out her grandfather is Alf Coates, a criminal gang leader. He's been in and out of prison all his life. It will be interesting to see if he is involved in the company.'

'Do you think this killing could be tied to old man Coates?'

'I'm not sure, but I wouldn't put anything past him. I've arranged to see him in one of the pubs he owns. He's been out of prison for too long. The Met hasn't been able to pin anything on him. It would be great to put him behind bars, where he belongs.'

Chapter 13

Before the start of their next interview, Gould and Cottrell looked around the foyer of a gentlemen's club in Pall Mall. It was a comfortable oasis in the centre of London, which the members presumably appreciated. They no doubt had to pay handsomely for the privilege, though most of them could easily afford the fees. Once the police officers had given their names to the uniformed receptionist, they were asked to sit in the comfortable leather seats.

Gould looked through the notes he had brought with him. 'This is Hugh Fretwell's home patch, Philippa. I thought it would be interesting to tackle him here. We can learn more about how he lives.' He kept his voice down to avoid disturbing the elderly visitors scattered around the room.

'He lives very comfortably, by the looks of it. I wonder if he has ever had to work in his life.'

'I doubt it. He probably has a pile of inherited money that he wants to invest in films as a hobby. As Margaret Prestwood said, he probably also thinks it is a way of meeting beautiful women.'

'He won't meet many women here, beautiful or otherwise. I don't suppose they're allowed in. I wonder if that's why we are being kept out in the foyer,' Cottrell said.

Just then, the police officers heard an aristocratic voice.

'DCI Gould and DS Cottrell, isn't it?' Fretwell said, as he came forward, arm outstretched. 'Won't you come into the study, where we receive visitors? It's quiet and comfortable in there.'

Fretwell led Gould and Cottrell into a room lined with antique books and invited them to take a seat. 'I heard about the murder at the party at Palmer Associates. It sounded dreadful, just dreadful. But how can I help?'

'Thank you for your cooperation, Mr Fretwell,' Gould began.

'We understand you attended the party at Palmer Associates on the 16th of December. First, how did you come to be invited? I understood it was just for staff.'

'Well, I enjoy investing in films. Giles Palmer sometimes approaches me with a project that he thinks might interest me. It's just an extra little hobby of mine.'

'And how many films have you invested in with Sir Giles?'

'At least six. The last one was very successful. I was hoping to see some return on it, but nothing has appeared yet. I wanted to talk to Palmer about it, but he kept fobbing me off. He said there weren't any returns on the films. In the end, I insisted on attending this party, as a major investor, so I could talk to Palmer face to face.'

'Did you think there was anything suspicious about the fact that you had not received any money on your investment?'

'God knows what's been going on with the profits I was hoping to earn. Palmer waffled about needing to cover expenses, but I was suspicious. I didn't really learn anything more at the party, so I am still worried.'

'I'd like to concentrate on the evening of the murder, Mr Fretwell,' Cottrell said. 'What time did you arrive at the party?'

'It must have been around nine o'clock.'

'You say you spoke to Sir Giles and he fobbed you off. Who else did you speak to?'

'I had a nice chat with a charming young lady called Heather. I'd met her a few days before, when I visited the offices to speak to Palmer.'

'Heather Morgan. Yes, we know about her. What did you talk to her about at the party?'

'Oh, just the things you talk to attractive women about,' Fretwell said, smiling at Cottrell, who glared at him. 'I think I brought her a drink from the free bar. She took it, then walked away. She seemed to have other things on her mind.'

'What sort of drink did you get Heather Morgan?'

'Oh, white wine, I think it was. There were a few glasses left by the bar and I gave one to her. Is that important?'

'It could be. Now, the victim was a man called James Faulkner. Did you speak to him?'

'I may have done. Do you have a photo of him?'

'Yes, this is James Faulkner,' Gould said, passing over a photo of the victim.

'Oh, yes, I saw him getting drunk, but I can't tell you any more, I'm afraid.'

'We have two witnesses who say they saw you talking to him.'

Fretwell paused. 'Yes, I remember now. I had a conversation with him about finance, but he didn't tell me very much. I can't tell you anything about his murder.'

'You seem to be one of the last people to have spoken to Mr Faulkner before he died, Mr Fretwell.'

'Well, I can't help that, but he was definitely alive when I left the party – at about half past ten.'

'Did you see anyone enter the boardroom during the evening?'

'I wouldn't know where the boardroom was.'

'And can anyone prove you left at the time you say, Mr Fretwell?'

'No, I suppose not. I took a taxi and went home. I live alone, so I can't produce any witnesses after that. But I only met James Faulkner once. I know nothing about the man or his private life. Why would I want to murder him? I guess his killing was some sort of domestic dispute. The *Evening Standard* said some woman was found with the body. Perhaps she killed him.'

'Thank you, Mr Fretwell. We will be in touch,' Gould said, as he led Cottrell out.

Chapter 14

By the following day, the boardroom of Palmer Associates had been cleared as a murder scene. Gould had decided to interview the remaining witnesses in the boardroom. He told Cottrell he would be interested in seeing their reaction to being close to the location where James's body had been found.

The next interview was arranged to be held with Alison Coates. Gould and Cottrell sat on one side of the large conference table, while Alison sat opposite them. She seemed scared, and was looking down at the table, avoiding eye contact with the two officers. She had a pile of files in front of her.

'Sir Giles asked me to give you these files,' Alison said in a sulky voice.

'Yes, your company personnel files will be very useful.' Gould picked up the first file. 'Michael Dawson. I see he used to be in the forces. I'll put out some feelers. The army always keep good records, and they owe me a favour. Let's look at yours next, shall we?' He looked through the files and pulled out one with Alison's name on it. 'Alison Coates. Home address in Elephant and Castle, then you moved to Dulwich.' He picked up the next file on the pile. 'Then there's your boyfriend Linus Murray, who lives at the same address. A degree from Harvard. That's impressive. I wonder how much he had to pay for that.'

'What do you mean?' Alison asked. Her voice had moved from antagonistic to genuinely baffled.

'Miss Coates,' Cottrell began. 'There's nothing to be worried about, but we need to ask you some questions about the murder of James Faulkner on the 16th or 17th of December. Are you willing to ask questions now, or do you want a solicitor?'

Alison jumped. 'A solicitor? Why should I need one of them?'

'No reason at all,' Cottrell said, 'if you have nothing to hide.'

'No, I haven't done anything.'

'Very well, then. For the record, please tell us your role at Palmer Associates.'

'I'm secretary to Sir Giles and sometimes to Mr Ringer.'

'And what time did you arrive at the party?'

'About eight o'clock. I came with Linus – he's my boyfriend and works here too.' Alison glared at Gould. 'But you seem to know that already.'

'Let's talk about James Faulkner, the deceased man. Various witnesses saw you talking to him at the party. How well did you know Mr Faulkner?'

Alison shifted uncomfortably in her chair. 'Not very well. I just saw him around the office.'

'That's not what we've heard. I'd advise you to tell the truth, Alison. Let me ask again. Had you ever met James Faulkner outside the office?'

'No, not really,' Alison said.

Cottrell gave a theatrical sigh and crossed her arms. 'Would you like to continue this discussion at the police station, Alison? Do you know how long the prison sentence is for perjury?'

Alison looked in turn from Cottrell to Gould. After a long pause, she replied. 'I might as well tell you. I have done nothing to be ashamed of. Yes, James and I were a couple for a short time, but it never really worked out.'

'How long ago was this?'

'It ended about two months ago.'

'He became engaged to Heather Morgan three months ago.'

'If you say so.'

'So you were going out with him while he was engaged to Heather Morgan?'

'I suppose so,' Alison said, thoughtfully. 'He said he was seeing someone else. That's why there was nothing between us any longer. There was for a while, but it didn't last long. I didn't want to play understudy to some other girl.'

'Did he mention Heather Morgan at all? Only you must agree it seems strange to go out with you when he was engaged to Heather.'

'It was odd. She was his boss, so he mentioned her from time to time, but only when we talked about work. I always felt James wasn't all that keen on Heather – not in that way. I was surprised when I heard about their engagement. I'm sure James would have broken things off with her before too long, if he'd lived. I think he realised he'd made a mistake.'

'Do you think he would have gone out with you instead?' Cottrell asked, with a slight ironic smile.

Alison shrugged her shoulders. 'I don't know. Oh, I'm not flattering myself I was really his type – he probably saw me as a bit of rough, who he could drop when he wanted to. We had a sort of jokey, flirty relationship by the end. I just don't think Heather was his type either. They never really seemed a couple to me.'

'Please tell us what else you saw at the party.'

'I spent most of the time with Linus – Linus Murray. As you know, he's my boyfriend.'

'Did you speak to James Faulkner at the party?'

'Well, yes, we had one dance together, just for old times' sake. I didn't think it would do any harm. But Linus came over and told him off, and took me home.'

'How did James react to that?'

'Not too well. I think he might have wanted to hit Linus, but realised he would come off worse. Linus is pretty fit.'

'We understand you slapped James Faulkner at the party, is that right?'

'Yes, he said something about having me first and leaving the rest of me for Linus. He seemed to think I was some sort of tart to be passed around.'

'It sounds as if you were pretty angry, Miss Coates,' Gould said.

'Yes, I suppose I was. I had a bit too much to drink as well, to be honest. But Linus took me home before the end of the party – at about half past ten. James was still fighting fit when we left. In fact, he looked as if he might fight with Michael Dawson.'

'Did you speak to Heather Morgan during the party?' Cottrell asked.

'No, I don't think she likes me. The executive women look down on us secretaries – they think they're better than us. But we know more of what goes on in the company than they do. Also, Heather must have learnt that James and I had been out together in the past, and she may have hated me for that.'

'You told us you see a lot of what goes on in the office.'

'Yes, I do. The bosses tend to forget about us secretaries – but we know more than they think.'

'What sorts of things?'

Alison crossed her arms, suddenly looking like a sulky child, and looked defiantly at Cottrell. 'Just things.'

'Did you see anyone enter this boardroom during the party?'

'No,' Alison said, looking around the room. 'Sir Giles told me to lock it before the party started. He wanted to keep it tidy.'

'Do you keep a key to this boardroom, Alison?'

'Yes, of course. I need to put out the papers for Sir Giles's meetings.'

'Please show me the key.'

Alison took a key from her handbag and passed it to Cottrell.

'I'll keep this for the time being,' Cottrell said, carefully depositing the key into an evidence bag and sealing it. 'And do you know anyone with a motive to kill James Faulkner?'

'That cow Heather, of course – Heather Morgan. She broke up with James on the night of the party. You could tell she was furious with him.'

'How about you and Linus Murray? You both argued with him at the party.'

'I told you James was alive when Linus took me home, and we didn't go out again.'

Cottrell nodded to Gould, in case he wanted to continue the questioning.

'Where were you brought up, Miss Coates?' Gould asked, in an unfriendly tone.

'Near the Elephant and Castle, like it says in the file. We're an old-fashioned Cockney family – not like most of the ones that work here.'

'Coates is a famous name in that area, isn't it, Alison?'

'I don't know what you mean.'

'I looked your surname – Coates – up on the police computer. It nearly blew the system. Do you know why?'

Alison stared sullenly ahead.

'Your family is one of the longest-running crime families around, isn't it? You're Alf Coates's granddaughter, aren't you? The Met have been trying to put him and the rest of your family away for years, but they've never managed it.'

'Yeah, what about it?' Alison's cockney accent suddenly became stronger. 'Yes, Granddad used to be a crook. He said he knew Reggie Kray in his heyday. Everyone around here used to look up to my granddad. At least he kept the streets safe. You should hear the tales he tells about the police and what he'd like to do with them – with you, that is.'

'Is he why you don't want to help the police, Alison?' Gould asked. 'Crime families never really go straight, do they? They just find new ways of making money – still crooked, of course, just different. They used to sell stolen goods at market stalls; now they sell dodgy investments to people with too much money. Why are you really working here just as a secretary, Alison? Have your family sent you here to keep an eye on their investments? Do your family invest in Palmer Associates? Why would they do that, unless it was for some crooked reason? Or are your family trying to move into Palmer Associates?'

'So I'm to blame for some crimes my granddad did, am I?' Alison's accent was becoming more cockney as anger rubbed off the sheen of whatever expensive education she may have had. 'I haven't done anything. Granddad was right. You're always trying to pin crimes you can't solve on our family. Well, unless you're going to arrest me, I'm leaving.'

'Yes, you can leave. Give my regards to your granddad, though. He might remember me from when I was in the Met. He was one of our best customers. Tell him I'll be in touch,' Gould called after Alison as she stormed out.

'She was pretty angry when she left, wasn't she?' Cottrell said, after a pause. 'I suppose she could be an innocent secretary, as she claims. We can't blame her for what her grandfather does.'

'You don't know these gangs as I do, Philippa,' Gould said. 'The young ones aren't allowed to leave their past behind. If they do try to leave, their families follow them. If Alison started out innocent, her grandfather wouldn't have let her stay that way for long. An interview with Alf Coates is called for.'

Chapter 15

Later that day, Michael Dawson drummed his fingers on the table in the boardroom of Palmer Associates. 'Is this going to take much longer?' he asked DS Fox. 'I have an important meeting to go to.'

'It will take as long as necessary, Mr Dawson. DCI Gould will be with us as soon as he can.' Fox knew that Gould was waiting outside, delaying the start of the interview to test Michael's reaction. 'I hope you agree solving a murder case is more important than your meeting – about some investment, is it?'

'Something like that. But I'm more worried about Heather. I know you brought her in here when she reported James's death. It's monstrous that you are treating her as a suspect. I know she couldn't do anything like murder.'

'You seem very concerned about Miss Morgan's welfare, Mr Dawson. Do you have some sort of relationship with her?'

'I'm just a friend, but I know she wouldn't hurt anyone.'

'Well, the more thoroughly you answer our questions, the faster we can proceed and find the murderer. If Heather Morgan's not a killer, she doesn't have anything to worry about.'

Michael nodded impatiently. 'Yes, I know the official line. Now, what questions do you have for me?'

Gould entered the room and nodded at Fox to continue.

'For the tape,' Fox said, 'DCI David Gould has just entered the room. For the record, Mr Dawson, please tell us your role in Palmer Associates.'

'I'm an accounts executive, if you know what that means.'

'Yes, I believe I do. It is the same job title as Heather Morgan.'

'Yes, we worked quite closely together. I have the greatest respect for her.'

'You were seen talking to Miss Morgan at the party for some

time. Everyone we've spoken to tells us they believe you were trying to make a play for her. Would that be true?'

'Yes, your spies are well informed. I would be happy to see more of Heather. But, for some reason, she had shackled herself to James Faulkner.' Michael looked at the police officers with obvious puzzlement. 'God knows why; she was always far too good for him. But perhaps I don't understand women.'

'It sounds as if you didn't have a high opinion of the dead man.'

'High opinion?' Michael replied with a sneer. 'No. James is – or was – a complete waste of space.' He paused, then, when neither Gould nor Fox responded, continued. 'But that doesn't mean I killed him. Why would I?'

'You might think it would free the way for you to make progress with Miss Morgan,' Fox said. 'That could be one strong motive to kill James Faulkner.'

'I suppose it's a motive, but it doesn't prove anything. What evidence do you have that makes you think I killed James?'

'We are just investigating the events at the moment, Mr Dawson. We are not accusing anyone yet. Please describe the events at the party as you remember them.'

'Well, I got there about eight. It was a normal sort of Christmas party to start with.'

'Did you go on your own?'

'Yes, I'm single and went on my own. I admit I was pleased when I saw Heather arrive, even though she was with James,' Michael said. 'After a while, I walked over and had a pleasant conversation with her. We had a talk about work, and we danced together. James was drunk and it became unpleasant. He threatened me, but when I pointed out I was trained in unarmed combat, he backed down and drifted away. It was embarrassing for everyone, but I felt most sorry for Heather. I could tell she was furious with James. The three of us started with the company at about the same time and Heather and I became quite friendly. I told her I would be there for her if she wanted to break up with James. She didn't say anything, but you could tell the engagement wasn't going to last.

'By about eleven, the party seemed to be dying out. People had to catch last trains and so on. I lost track of Heather. I assumed she had gone home.'

'Heather Morgan never left the party.'

'I know that now. I'm sorry I couldn't protect her, but it wasn't my place. Perhaps if I'd stayed at the party longer, none of this would have happened. But Heather came with James, so I assumed they would leave together.'

'Do you remember precisely what Mr Faulkner said to you?'

'Yes, he told me to leave Heather alone. James was drunk and angry at that stage. I was tempted to punch him into the middle of next week, which I could easily have done. I learnt some ways to disarm an enemy in the army. But I moved away to avoid a scene. I didn't want to embarrass Heather ... or the company.'

'When did you last see James Faulkner?'

'About an hour before I left.'

'What time did you leave the party, Mr Dawson?'

'It would be about half past eleven,' Michael said, after a moment's thought. 'I had a last train to catch then.'

'And did you see anybody entering this boardroom, Mr Dawson?'

'No, I believe it was kept locked. I assumed it was to keep some of these people out. A good idea, if you ask me.'

'Can you tell us anything else to cast light on how James Faulkner came to be killed?'

'No. Many people at the party probably wanted to kill him, the way he was behaving, but I can't help you more than that.'

'When you say most people had a motive, do you mean Heather Morgan – and yourself?'

Michael shrugged his shoulders. 'Yes, I suppose I do. But Linus Murray had as good a motive as me. He was jealous because

James was flirting with Alison. Why don't you interrogate him? Perhaps Alison killed James – they were having a lovers' tiff in the middle of the party.'

Gould indicated to Fox that he would take over the questioning. 'We will interview everyone at the party in due course. Let's start with you first. How long have you worked at Palmer Associates, Mr Dawson?'

'About a year. I started around the same time as Heather.'

'And before then, where did you work? Somewhere else in the City, I imagine?' Gould asked, picking up a pile of papers and riffling through them. He hoped Michael would believe they were his staff records. 'Are you happy to tell us?'

'I've nothing to keep secret. I think you know my background already. I'm proud to say I was a captain in Her Majesty's Forces.'

'Which regiment?'

'The Special Air Service.'

'Very honourable, I'm sure. You must be tough to be in the SAS, so I've been told. I imagine you were trained in unarmed combat – including how to kill people with a knife.'

'Don't be melodramatic. I did my duty, but I'd only kill for queen and country. I don't wander around London killing people. I wouldn't murder some jumped-up office boy like James Faulkner.'

'So, as an officer, you must have had an honourable discharge.'

'I consider myself honourable—'

'But the army didn't,' Gould continued. 'When I say you were tough, you were too tough even for the SAS, weren't you, Captain Dawson?'

Michael shifted uncomfortably in his chair. 'You mean that business over the hostages, don't you?'

Gould nodded.

'That was for queen and country,' Michael said. 'Those men were our enemies. I acted in self-defence. Those men were terrorists and they would have killed me without even thinking about it. I know the brass in the Ministry of Defence said I'd gone too far. But most of the men on the board were paper pushers – they'd never fought in a combat zone. They wouldn't know what it was like out there. So I was given a dishonourable discharge, after all I'd done for my country.' He stared ahead, his forceful personality making the police officers flinch. 'But I was honourable then, and I am honourable now. I don't tolerate enemies to my country then, or to my company now, but I didn't kill James. Was there anything else, detective chief inspector?'

'No, Mr Dawson,' Gould said, 'but I expect we will be in touch. If you remember anything else, it would be in your own interest to let me know.'

Chapter 16

Alf Coates looked around at the entrance hall of the Pall Mall gentlemen's club. He could not fail to be impressed by the surroundings. He thought back to the terraced house in Mile End where his mother had raised him and his brothers, and wondered how many of those houses would fit into this club. No doubt, if his late mother – always a snob – could see him now, she would be impressed by how far he had come. Alf knew, however, that he could have bought the whole establishment by the time he was twenty-one.

He realised the membership of the club looked down on him and his class, but he did not care. He was happy to go along with the fiction that they and their class still owned the country. If he showed them his bank account, he knew the staff would fawn over him, but he was happy to keep the real level of his income to himself. When the commissionaire, dressed in a uniform suitable for a Swiss admiral, called Alf's name, his voice conveying utter contempt, Alf merely smiled to himself.

'That's me, mate,' Alf said, knowing how annoyed the man would feel to be addressed in such a way.

'Mr Fretwell will see you now, sir,' the commissionaire said, as he led Alf through the carpeted rooms. Eventually, they stopped by an armchair in which Fretwell was sipping a whisky.

'This is Mr Coates to see you, sir,' the commissionaire said, before he walked off.

'Ah, Mr Coates, how do you do? Why don't you take a seat?' Fretwell said. 'Your message said you wanted to see me, but not what about.'

'Yes, thank you for seeing me, Mr Fretwell. I must say this is a smart establishment. I run a pub in the East End, but that is quite a bit different.'

'I imagine it is. Now, I was surprised to receive your phone call. What can I do for you?'

'It's more a question of what we can do for each other. I happen to know you are a major investor in Palmer Associates. I've heard there was a murder at a party there last weekend.'

'You seem very well informed, Mr Coates. May I ask how?'

'Let's just say I have good contacts, and I know how Palmer Associates operates. Now, I'm guessing that your investment in the company has not been as profitable as you might have hoped.'

Fretwell stared at the other man. He decided that, while Alf might be rough and uneducated, he was not a fool. 'I don't propose to discuss my finances with you. What do you want, Mr Coates?'

'I'd like to take your investment over from you, Mr Fretwell. From what I've heard, you've lost most of your family's fortune. I don't think you have much choice.'

Fretwell gulped. He thought about having Alf thrown out, but something about the way the man presented himself told him that would not be sensible. He decided to test the water. 'How much are you offering, Mr Coates?' His eyes widened as Alf quoted a figure. 'That's half of what it was worth a month ago.'

Alf smiled. 'Yes, but twice as much as it is on the open market, now there's been all that bad publicity. *Dirty Money* has been slagging the company off good and proper. Firms with bad press and where murders are committed tend not be considered good investments by the people who run pension funds, do they?'

'What do you know about the bad publicity?' Fretwell asked.

'I'm not saying. That's a take it or leave it offer, Mr Fretwell. I have my cheque book here. I know what I would do in your position.'

Fretwell stared as Alf wrote out a cheque. He wondered whether to hold out for more money, but a glance at Alf told him the price was not negotiable. He silently shook Alf's hand. Within five minutes, Fretwell had the cheque in his pocket, as Alf left the gentlemen's club and returned to his East End pub.

Chapter 17

David Gould, looking through the transcripts of the interviews so far, felt that a large part of the mystery of James's murder seemed to lie in Los Angeles. He picked up his list of international contacts. The City of London police were often the lead for the United Kingdom in international liaison issues, and Gould had contacts in many overseas police forces.

He soon found the details of Lieutenant Jeff Zug of the international branch of the Los Angeles police department. They had collaborated on a fraud case two years previously, and Gould had taken his details as a useful potential contact. He mentally checked the eight-hour time difference between Britain and California, and, calculating Zug would be at his desk, phoned him.

'Zug, LAPD,' came the familiar tones of Gould's acquaintance.

'Hello, Jeff. David Gould here – from the City of London police.'

'David? Oh, hi, it's good to hear your voice. It's been a while – two years, isn't it? How are things over there?'

'Fine. I'm dealing with a murder here in the City at the moment, and you may be able to help,' Gould said. 'The victim works for a character called Sir Giles Palmer. Palmer does some film finance work. He seems to visit LA a lot, and I wondered if his name had come up on your radar at all.'

'Giles Palmer, you say,' Zug replied. There was a pause. 'I'll make a note of it, and check our records. But offhand, it doesn't ring any bells.'

'Yes, that would be very helpful,' Gould said. 'The other thing is there is a character called Linus Murray, an American citizen from LA. He claims to be well qualified, with a degree from Harvard among other things, but I don't believe him.'

'Linus Murray, you say,' Zug replied, after another pause. 'Again, no bells are ringing, but fax me over any details, and I'll be happy to look into him.'

'Thanks, Jeff. I'll send the papers over straight away.' Gould put down the phone. He had the satisfied feeling of a successful call, but something gnawed at his mind. Was it his imagination, or had Zug hesitated before denying any knowledge of Giles Palmer or Linus Murray? Gould's policeman's instinct told him he was being lied to.

He half-smiled, as he told himself it would be ridiculous not to trust a fellow police officer. He knew he had a good professional relationship with Zug and should be able to trust him to provide any helpful information. He decided he must have imagined Zug's hesitation.

*

Lieutenant Zug put down his phone and looked thoughtfully through the window at the sidewalk outside LAPD headquarters. He hated lying to a fellow police officer and friend such as David Gould.

Zug was preparing a strong case against Giles Palmer for organising snuff videos. He looked forward to eventually ensuring Sir Giles served time in one of southern California's tougher prisons for several counts of murder. Zug had a sense that Sir Giles would not last long against the black and Hispanic gangs that controlled the jails in Los Angeles. The thought of Sir Giles's likely fate in a Californian prison gave him a definite sense of anticipated pleasure.

However, Zug knew that every time he seemed to be making progress in the case against Sir Giles, there seemed to be some sort of leak in his organisation, which sent everything back to square one. It was as if Sir Giles had some police officers, either in Los Angeles or in London, in his thrall. Extending the investigation to London was only multiplying the possibility of further leaks. He was sure that Gould was honest, but he knew he had to keep his inquiry secret.

Zug shook his head and hoped Gould would someday forgive his white lie. He locked his papers in a file and made sure he wasn't being overlooked. He was all too aware that the corrupt police officer could be in his own force as easily as they could be in London.

*

Heather Morgan stood outside the offices of the company where, as far as she knew, she was still employed. She pushed open the door as confidently as she could. She showed her pass and ignored the receptionist, who spoke frantically into her intercom.

As Heather walked through the dealing room, the normal hubbub of conversation stopped. As she had expected, everyone in the office seemed to know about her recent history. No doubt they had been discussing her possible guilt as they had drunk their coffees that day.

Keeping her eyes fixed straight ahead, Heather walked towards her desk. She felt sure that if she could just reach it, everything would be back to normal. She counted the steps to herself – one, two, three. She told herself that once she reached her chair, she could hide behind her computer screen and become less visible.

With a sense of relief, Heather moved her swivel chair. She was about to sit on it, but then uttered a scream. Sir Giles Palmer was sitting in her chair.

Sir Giles smiled without mirth. 'You weren't expecting to see me, were you, Miss Morgan?'

'No, Sir Giles,' Heather stammered.

'The feeling's mutual. I couldn't believe it when they told me you were back in the office.'

'Yes, well, I was feeling better, so I felt I could come in.'

'You were feeling better, were you?' Sir Giles asked, standing up to tower over her. 'Tell me, how long does it take to feel better after murdering someone?'

'But I didn't murder James,' Heather stammered. 'I'd never do anything like that. The police haven't charged me at all.'

'Maybe not yet, but I'll see about that. Everyone says you used to be DCI Gould's girlfriend. Is that true?'

'Yes, Sir Giles, but that's nothing to do with it. David is an impartial police officer.'

'Well, I'm not impartial, and I'm telling you to leave,' Sir Giles said as he started to walk away. 'You're fired, young lady. You can pick up your P45 from personnel on the way out.'

Heather mouthed as if she wanted to reply, but no sound emerged from her mouth. She picked up her bag and left the office, conscious of the curious and hostile stares from other people around her.

Chapter 18

The next day, Gould led Cottrell into an unprepossessing office close to Fenchurch Street station. He knocked on the door labelled *Dirty Money* and waited for a reply. After a while, a man in a dingy suit came and opened the door.

'Yes?' the man demanded. 'Who are you?'

'Mr Lynch,' Gould said, flashing his warrant card. 'I'm DCI Gould of the City police. This is DS Philippa Cottrell. Could we have a word with you?'

Lynch looked at them with suspicion. 'Do I have to let you in? Do you have a search warrant?'

'No, I'm just asking to talk to you about a murder. I'm sure you'll want to help the police.'

'What happens if I don't?'

'We could get a search warrant without much trouble. It would cover everything in this office.' Gould looked around. 'It would keep us busy for at least a week. It might stop you putting out your next issue. There should be some interesting stuff in those files.'

Lynch stared at Gould dubiously. 'Well, I suppose you can come in. I should warn you I never release anything about my investigations to the police.'

'We understand.'

Lynch reluctantly stepped to one side and allowed Gould and Cottrell in.

When they had sat down, Gould pulled out a photograph from his briefcase. 'Mr Lynch, I believe you know this man.'

Lynch picked up the photo and stared at it. 'It looks like James Faulkner. I was at school with him. How can I help?'

'Mr Faulkner was found dead at the office of Palmer Associates on the morning of the 17th of December.'

'My God, I didn't know. That's terrible,' Lynch replied with a convincing shudder. 'We go back a long way.'

'You've written a highly critical article about Mr Faulkner's company, Mr Lynch. And you were seen outside the company's offices on the night he died. We are trying to talk to everyone who knew James Faulkner. Can you tell us how you came to meet him and what you know about his background?' Gould asked.

'We were good friends at school together until about eighteen,' Lynch said. 'Then we went to different universities. I remember we met again the year we both graduated. We met up at a party in London. It was strange to see someone from my old hometown. It's four hundred miles away on the Scottish border – and feels four hundred years in the past. James argued with his father once, and he hasn't gone back for a long time. But I lost touch with James after that.'

'Yes, we've spoken to Mr Faulkner senior. He agrees you and James were best friends at school. It appears he didn't approve of James's career. He seems to live by a different set of values from his son.'

'Well, old man Faulkner belongs to a different world from us in the City. Whether he's right or wrong, I'm not sure. Anyway, I hadn't seen James for three years or so, but he suddenly phoned up last week, and we met for a drink after work. It must have been just before he was killed.'

'What did you talk about?'

'I suppose it can't do any harm to tell you. He said he had suspicions about his company's accounts. But there was nothing concrete I could use. I warned him that if it became known to potential employers that he leaked information to me, he would never work in the City again.'

'What did he say to that?'

'Oddly enough, he didn't seem worried. He seemed to think I could give him a job, but I can't afford to feed my family, let alone pay new staff, as you can see.' Lynch indicated his untidy office.

'And did James mention anything else? His fiancée, for instance. He was engaged to a young woman called Heather Morgan. She worked for the same company.'

'Yes, he did mention a fiancée in his firm. I was surprised he would risk both their careers by talking to me. That is, unless he was planning some major change that didn't involve his fiancée. I got the impression the engagement wasn't going well.'

'And did you tell anyone about this conversation, Mr Lynch?' Gould asked.

'No, of course not. I always respect my informants' privacy. I wouldn't be able to keep this magazine going if people didn't trust me to keep their secrets.'

'Heather Morgan says you called out Faulkner's name when he was entering the party. That seems quite tactless. I am sure Faulkner did not want his employers finding out he knew you. They might think he was the person who had been leaking information to you.'

'James wasn't my main source.'

'And who was?'

'I won't reveal that information to the police, Mr Gould.'

'And did you enter the company's offices at any time that night, Mr Lynch?'

'No, of course not. I wouldn't have been allowed in, anyway.'

'Yes, but it is only an ordinary office, not Fort Knox,' Gould said. 'I am sure you could have entered it illicitly, if you tried hard enough. And it does seem curious that James Faulkner was killed quite soon after speaking to you in public. We have a witness who saw you talking to an elderly man in an expensive-looking Land Rover on the night of the party. Were you reporting back to someone on the success of your campaign against Palmer Associates? A suspicious mind would think you betrayed your friend Mr Faulkner to someone who then had him killed before he could talk any more. And I'm paid to be suspicious.'

'What do you think I am?' Lynch demanded, his Scottish

accent becoming more pronounced as his anger grew. 'I'm not some sort of establishment spy. Everyone knows I'm a thorn in the side of the big City firms. They all hate me. Why would I betray James to organisations like that?'

'I think everyone in the City knows that money has a way of making people forget their scruples,' Cottrell interjected. 'Perhaps a bribe from someone interested in Palmer Associates would be a good enough reason to betray an old school friend that you hadn't seen for several years.'

Lynch stood up. 'I don't think this conversation is going anywhere. I must ask you to leave now, DCI Gould and DS Cottrell.'

Gould gave Lynch a piercing look. 'Very well. I expect we will be in touch again quite soon, don't you, Philippa?'

'I can guarantee it, gov. Bye for now, Mr Lynch,' Cottrell said, as she and Gould prepared to leave.

As they returned to their car, Gould turned to Cottrell. 'I'd like to learn more about that man. How did he know so much about Palmer Associates? He could be blackmailing companies by threatening to reveal even more about their activities. If he did enter that Christmas office party, which he could have done, he and Faulkner could have had some sort of argument that ended in Faulkner having a knife in his chest.'

'I'm not so sure, gov,' Cottrell said. 'How would he know where to find the key for the boardroom? I'm still betting the killer's an employee of Palmer Associates. Heather Morgan still ticks all the boxes for me.'

*

After the two police officers had left, Lynch dialled the number of one of his contacts. 'I've just had the police around. They want to know who my contact in Palmer Associates was.'

A rough male cockney voice came on the phone. 'And what did you tell them?'

'Nothing, of course. I'm not a squealer.'

'That was a very wise move. I don't like people who squeal to the police. The last person who did that is no longer with us.'

'Are you threatening me? How did you get all that information you sent? You don't sound like the sort that Palmer would employ.'

'Let's just keep things as they are now. It's better all round – for you as well as me.'

'Well, I don't like dealing with people like you. I won't be publishing any of your stuff any more, unless we can deal face to face.' Lynch slammed the phone down. He noticed that his hand was shaking afterwards.

Lynch had a feeling that his contact was genuinely dangerous. He preferred the more genteel world of financial journalism, and regretted encountering Palmer Associates. He lit a cigarette and pondered his plans.

Chapter 19

Two days later, Heather waited in a wine bar close to Liverpool Street station. She was nursing a glass of sparkling water in her hand. She could tell that the waitresses were anxious for her to leave, and for her place to be taken by a customer with more money to spend. She ignored their glares, then waved when the person she was waiting to see arrived.

'Heather, how good to see you,' Margaret said, greeting her friend with a peck on her cheek. 'How long has it been since we've had a chat?'

'Too long,' Heather replied, with a sigh. 'You know I was sacked a few days ago. I've been stuck at home since then. No one in the City will give me a job now, so there's nowhere else to go. I've already had my fill of daytime television and TV dinners. Believe me, time passes slowly when you don't have a job and you know your money will soon be running out.'

'Well, let's make this my treat, then,' said Margaret. 'After all, I still have my salary.'

'Thanks, Margaret. You're a true friend.'

Heather pointed out a starter and main dish on the menu. She reflected it would be good to have a square meal for once.

When the waitress had left, Heather turned to Margaret. 'Tell me what's been happening at Palmer Associates, since I ... left.' She was trying to put on a bold front by not using the word *sacked* again.

'Well, Michael Dawson has taken over your old job. That's the main change. He seems to have jumped into the fray to build his little empire. I don't know why you like him so much. I'm suspicious of Mr Dawson. I'm going to see what I can dig up on him.'

'But the police must already be looking into all this,' Heather said, reaching out for Margaret's hand. 'You don't want to cut across them. It could be dangerous. You saw what happened to James. You don't want that to happen to you.'

'How do you mean? Why should what happened to James happen to me? You're scaring me.'

'I don't know anything specific. But we both know the real murderer is still somewhere out there. He's killed before, so he has nothing to lose by killing again.' She hesitated. 'And are Linus and Alison still a couple?'

'Yes, they're still together,' Margaret replied. 'Why do you ask?'

'There's something strange about those two. I think one of them could have killed James. What do you think?'

'I don't know, but I wouldn't want to cross Linus Murray,' Margaret said, with a shudder. 'He always looks as if he could kill anyone without a second thought.'

'I didn't see them around at the end of the party, but they could have been there. And I've never been sure about Alison's family,' Heather said. 'I've seen some of them, and, believe me, they are rough.'

The two women had their meal together, still talking in the comfortable manner of old friends.

Chapter 20

Gould and Cottrell walked up to James Faulkner's brother's house in Wimbledon. It struck them as the type of expensive house that a doctor might be expected to own. After a while, a bearded man, bearing the faintest facial similarity to James Faulkner, came to the door.

'Good afternoon, Dr Faulkner,' Gould began. 'I'm DCI Gould and this is DS Philippa Cottrell. We phoned and you agreed to see us.'

'Ah, yes, I remember. Do come in,' Stuart Faulkner said, leading them into the sitting room of the house.

After they had taken their seats, Gould began the interview. 'Thank you for agreeing to see us, Dr Faulkner. First of all, may I say how sorry I am about your brother's death.'

Stuart Faulkner gazed at Gould coldly. 'Thank you, chief inspector, but I see death every day as part of my job. My brother and I were not close, so I don't need your sympathies.' He spoke with a definite Highland accent.

'I understand, sir, but I must ask you some questions to help us investigate your brother's suspicious death. Could you tell me the last time you saw him?'

'It must have been three years ago or so. It was at our home near Inverness.'

'So you're saying you had no contact with him at all when you were both working in London, Dr Faulkner. That seems strange.'

'Yes, but we travelled very different paths in the last few years, chief inspector. We were both brought up in the same God-fearing household. I was grateful for it, while James was not. He went into the money-making parts of the City as soon as he could. I am proud to still be a member of the church where my father is an elder.'

'Yes, we've interviewed your father. I believe he and your mother were visiting you when your brother was killed on Saturday evening.'

'That's correct. We had a quiet dinner together at home then.'

'Can anyone else vouch for that?'

'No, it was just the three of us. I wasn't aware we would need a witness.'

'Do you know very much about James's life in London, Dr Faulkner? Were you aware he had a fiancée?'

'No. James and I had a severe argument when he left home. I advised him not to follow the path of greed and dissipation, but he obviously did not take my advice.'

'And have you ever been to the offices of Palmer Associates in the City of London, Dr Faulkner?' Cottrell asked.

'Is that where James worked? No, I have never heard of the organisation and would have no need to visit it. If that is all, chief inspector, I don't believe I can help you any more. Now, I have a surgery to attend ...'

'Yes, that will be all,' Gould said, standing up. 'This is my card. Please phone me if anything occurs to you about your brother's death.'

'I will, but I doubt it, somehow,' Dr Faulkner said, guiding the two police officers to the front door.

'James Faulkner certainly had a cold family,' Gould said to Cottrell, as they walked back to their car. 'No wonder he moved away to London and wasn't in contact with them. I suppose either his father or his brother could have killed him, as they were so ashamed of him.'

'We mustn't forget the killer would have needed an office pass to get into the building,' Cottrell said. 'I can't see either of them knowing how to get hold of the key to a boardroom in a building they'd never visited.'

'You could be right, but I want them included in our list of suspects until we are certain we have found the guilty man.'

'Or guilty woman. I can't get the feeling that Heather Morgan is responsible out of my head.'

*

The following day, Margaret Prestwood walked up to Heather's old desk in Palmer Associates. Michael Dawson was looking through some paper files, but put them down when he saw Margaret approaching.

'Hello, Michael,' Margaret said. 'It didn't take you long to take over Heather's job, did it?'

Michael shrugged. 'I was offered the job, so I took it. I don't have to apologise to you or anyone else. I'm sure Heather is happy it's me rather than anyone else. She knows I'm on her side. If she ever comes back, I'll make way for her.'

'Vey altruistic, I'm sure,' Margaret sneered. 'It's nothing to do with the extra money, of course, is it?'

'The money helps, but I want to keep an eye on what's going on here. Do you have any ideas on who killed James?'

'I have my suspicions.'

'Who?'

'You,' Margaret said. 'You had the motive. You want to get into Heather's bed, and killing James puts you ahead. As well as hoping for sex, it's the extra money and power.'

'I didn't kill James,' Michael said, his voice rising in anger. 'He wasn't worth bothering with. Why don't you tell the police your theories if you're so confident? They'll laugh in your face.'

'We'll see,' Margaret said, as she walked away.

In the next corridor, she passed Alison and Linus, sharing a coffee together.

'Hello, you two,' Margaret said. 'I'm trying to arrange a get-together at the pub on Friday lunchtime. Are you up for it?'

Alison and Linus exchanged glances. Alison shrugged her shoulders.

'I guess that'll be fine. We'll be there,' Linus said.

Chapter 21

On Friday, Heather looked around the crowded pub, thronged with lunchtime customers. She shuddered as she turned to her friend. 'I'm not sure this is a good idea, Margaret.'

Margaret snorted. 'Yes, it is. It'll be great. It's the only way to clear your name. I've invited everyone we know to discuss who we think killed James.' Just then she saw Alison and Linus come towards the table. 'Hello, you two. What would you like to drink?'

Alison and Linus ordered drinks and then noticed Heather seated at the table. Alison edged away. 'Come away, Linus. I didn't know that woman would be here.'

Heather stood up. 'No, come and have a drink. I know about you and James. I don't blame you. He didn't care about either of us. Now he's dead, we should forget about him. We're both victims in our ways.'

Alison sniffed. 'The difference is I didn't kill him. I couldn't do that,' she said, grasping Linus's hand.

'I know, honey. Neither of us would,' Linus said. 'But let's listen to what Heather has to say.'

Just then, Michael Dawson arrived, holding a pint of bitter. 'Hello, Heather,' he said, reaching across to kiss her cheek.

'Hello, Michael,' Heather said, turning her head away. 'How do you like having my job?'

'It's fine,' Michael said. 'I'm keeping an eye open for suspicious payments, as you said.'

Margaret returned with Linus and Alison's drinks. 'Well, we're all here. I wanted to talk about who we think killed James. I think we all know it wasn't Heather.' Michael and Linus nodded, while Alison looked down at her drink. 'I'm guessing it was ordered by someone in our management team.'

'What makes you say that?' Linus asked.

'I heard James asking awkward questions about the accounts and salary levels at the party. Ringer was looking very annoyed about it. What could be easier for Ringer than to kill him to keep James quiet and put the blame on Heather?'

'So what do you want us to do about it?' Michael asked.

'I say we ought to keep an eye on what's going on in the company now,' Margaret said. 'Together, we can find out things that the police can't.'

'This is all nonsense,' Alison said, standing up. 'Let's go, Linus. I don't want to drink with the woman who murdered James. He wasn't a bad man, even if he ditched me. I'm happy now I have you. I've got to get back to work. Some of us still have loyalty to the company.'

'OK, honey,' Linus said, finishing his drink. 'We're leaving.' He followed Alison out of the pub.

'I told you it wouldn't work,' Heather said, close to tears. 'They all hate me in the company.'

'I'm sorry that Alison was so hostile to you,' Margaret said. 'I didn't think that she would still be so jealous. She can't really think you killed James.' She finished her drink and stood up. 'Come along, Heather. I think some retail therapy is in order. You know I always need your fashion advice.'

'I suppose that might cheer me up, but it would just be window shopping for me,' Heather said, rising to her feet. 'Goodbye, Michael. Thank you for coming.'

'Bye, Heather. I think I'll stay. I'll keep an eye on your job for you,' Michael said, as Heather and Margaret left.

Once on his own, Michael stared after the two women. He was not sure why Margaret was asking these questions. It seemed as if she were conducting a one-woman investigation of the Faulkner murder. He doubted that the police would welcome one of Heather's friends duplicating what they should be doing.

Michael wondered what to do about it. He could phone David Gould and tell him about Margaret's amateur detective work. He smiled when he thought of how Gould would haul Margaret back into the police station and berate her for bypassing the police.

Then again, Michael wondered if Margaret could possibly uncover valuable information about the murder on her own. She obviously had no police powers, but she knew the office system inside out. She would know where to look and who to interview to find out the truth about the unusual payments that Heather had talked to him about. All in all, it would be good to stay aware of whatever Margaret was investigating.

*

Sir Giles Palmer looked up in annoyance at the hesitant knock on his office door. As he expected, Derek Ringer appeared nervously around the door.

'Yes, what is it, Derek?' Sir Giles asked, not trying to hide his impatience.

'I'm sorry to bother you, Sir Giles, but I think you should see this letter I've received. It's from a firm of solicitors in South London,' Derek said.

'Can't you deal with it? What do they want?'

'They say they represent a sizeable shareholding in the company, and they are demanding an extraordinary general meeting.'

'Which shareholding? I own nearly half of the shares, and I haven't sold any lately. That old fool Fretwell is the second biggest and he won't want to rock the boat.'

'I can only think Fretwell's sold his shares to someone else. He seemed pretty unhappy when I last saw him – at the party.'

'I might have known Fretwell would betray us. Who's he sold them to?'

'I don't know, but, looking at the address, it may be one of the main customers for our ... specialist materials. He calls himself Alf Jones and he runs a pub in Elephant and Castle.'

'Damn! Can't we turn him down? He still can't have a majority of shares.'

'I don't think that would be seen to be ethical, Sir Giles. I'm the registrar of the company, and I have to follow the rules. If a major shareholder wants a general meeting, he's entitled to have one. Besides, it may be a good opportunity to find out what he's planning.'

'Very well, arrange a meeting if you have to. But that's one too many nuisances for me to deal with. DCI Gould is getting on my nerves, with his fawning over that Morgan woman instead of arresting her. I'll get rid of him, so I can tackle Mr Jones – or whatever his real name is.'

'Yes, Sir Giles,' Derek said, turning away, before stopping on his way out of Sir Giles's office. 'Excuse me, Sir Giles, but you don't run the police. How can you get rid of a detective?'

Sir Giles smiled with satisfaction. 'You don't know how the City works, do you? Just watch me, Derek. Watch my next steps.'

Chapter 22

The next day, Gould looked around at the meeting room in Snow Hill police station. A small squad of detectives had been assigned to this case, and they were waiting in subdued fashion for Gould to address them. DS George Fox had worked on previous cases with Gould; however, most of the others were new to him. Photos of the main persons of interest were displayed on screens around the room.

Gould generally adopted a collegiate style in such meetings. He liked to hear the views from junior colleagues, both to gain new insights and as a way to gauge the calibre of the detectives who had been assigned to him.

'Welcome to the team, ladies and gentlemen,' Gould began, looking around the room. 'As you know, you have been assigned to this investigation of the murder of James Faulkner, an executive at Palmer Associates here in the City. I've called this meeting to run over the facts and see who the suspects are. With any luck, we should find some fruitful lines of inquiry. We've conducted all the initial interviews and it's time to see what we have learnt from them.

'Let's start with the basics. James Faulkner, a thirty-year-old executive at Palmer Associates, an international trading company, was murdered late on Saturday 16th December after a Christmas party. His body was found in the boardroom of the company. His fiancée, Heather Morgan, was found near the body, so she's an obvious suspect. Morgan had broken off her engagement to Faulkner earlier that evening. Her fingerprints were the only ones on the knife that killed Faulkner and his blood was on her hands, but she reported the crime to us – to me, in fact, as she knew me – and you would think if she was guilty she would have made a better job of covering her tracks.

'So, let's run over the forensic evidence. DS Cottrell and I attended after a call from Miss Morgan at 9am on Sunday 17th December. The security guard let us into the boardroom, using his pass key.'

'So it was locked from the inside,' DS Fox interrupted.

'That's right – at least at first sight. The key was on the floor, inside the door. There were no fingerprints on it. That looks bad for Morgan, but the guard says there were several other copies of the key in the building, so an unnamed culprit could have left one beside the body to incriminate Morgan, then locked the door on their way out. There was a large amount of the victim's blood on the knife, on Morgan's clothes and hands, and on the carpet. So, either she is the murderer, or someone was trying to frame her.

'The most interesting recent discovery is that we also found a trace of the date rape drug ketamine in Miss Morgan's bloodstream. We are keeping that information to ourselves. No one outside this room must know that. Not even Heather Morgan knows about it. It looks to me like someone else murdered Faulkner and framed Morgan. The victim had been dead for hours by the time we entered the room, and any killer would have made their escape before then.'

'Or the obvious suspect – Heather Morgan – could be guilty,' Cottrell interrupted. 'And the ketamine was self-administered or irrelevant – perhaps a trick to fool us. Who knows why she stayed so long with the body before calling us? But it doesn't mean she's innocent.'

'Thank you, Philippa; it is possible that Morgan is guilty, of course,' Gould said, giving Cottrell a reproving glance. 'But we'll give this suspect the benefit of the doubt for the time being. She's at home and not going anywhere at the moment, so we can arrest her at any time, but only if we build up a strong enough case against her. I insist we look at all the other possibilities before we tie ourselves down to one. I don't want any miscarriages of justice in this case. Let's talk about the motives of possible suspects.

'We've found that Faulkner had been annoying a lot of people during the party. He upset his superiors – that's Sir Giles Palmer and Derek Ringer – by querying some dodgy accounts at the company. Palmer could have given the orders and Ringer carried them out. From what I can see, Ringer would do anything Palmer told him to do. Ringer seems to be paid a huge salary for his job, so he's obviously a loyal servant, but would he kill someone on Palmer's orders? Palmer and Ringer must both be suspects; either or both of them could have killed Faulkner or had him killed. The next person of interest is Margaret Prestwood.' Gould indicated her photo on the screen. 'She's another long-term employee who was at the party, but she seems to be a good friend of Morgan's, with no obvious motive.

'Another line of inquiry is that, rather than being connected to the victim's work in the company, it could be a domestic crime. Faulkner fancied himself as quite a ladies' man. He had been flirting with a secretary called Alison Coates at the party. They had gone out together in the past, including after he was engaged to Heather Morgan. Perhaps Coates and Faulkner were still involved with each other, in some way. Perhaps Coates didn't take kindly to being dumped in favour of Morgan; with her family background – which I'll come to – Coates is used to fighting for what she wants. Witnesses say she slapped Faulkner hard at the party. So, could it be a lovers' tiff between James Faulkner and Coates that ended in murder? There has been some ill feeling between Coates and Morgan, so Coates might have taken pleasure in incriminating Morgan for the murder.

'Coates has a current boyfriend, Linus Murray, a visiting American executive – a super fit guy – and they were living together. Murray could have murdered Faulkner out of jealousy, or to cover up some other criminal activity. I'm suspicious of Murray. He doesn't seem to be the classic American executive. We need to find out more about him. What's he doing in London, anyway? I've asked Jeff Zug in the

Los Angeles police department for any information, but he hasn't come up with anything yet.

'Murray says he and Coates went home before the end of the party, while the victim was still alive, but we only have their word for that, and they could have returned in time for the murder. They've given each other alibis, so, if one of them did it, they would both have to have been involved. I wouldn't put the murder past either of them.

'Alison Coates also has an interesting family background. Her family are all members of the Coates criminal gang.' Gould waited until the murmurs of recognition from the detectives present died down. 'Her grandfather is Alf Coates – we've all heard of him. His gang used to terrorise the East End with threats in the old days; now they may be interested in moving into the City. It's probably easier money for them. Is Alison some sort of spy for the Coates gang? She says we can't blame her for the sins of her family, which I suppose is true. She may be as innocent as she says, but I doubt it. We know Alison and Faulkner had an affair a few months ago, but now he was engaged to Morgan. Knowing her background, I can imagine Alison persuading her grandfather or one of her grandfather's thugs to kill Faulkner out of jealousy. Or could she and Murray have returned to the party and killed Faulkner themselves? We need to look at both those possibilities.'

Gould stopped to take a sip of his tea, but his staff knew better than to interrupt his talk.

'Morgan also has an admirer called Michael Dawson,' Gould continued. 'He was jealous of Faulkner for being engaged to Morgan. Dawson and Faulkner exchanged angry words during the evening. Could some fight have got out of hand? We've found out that Dawson was in the SAS – a trained killer, in fact. He was even thrown out of the forces for bending the rules too much in treating suspects, so we know he has a quick temper. Dawson had a strong motive for killing James Faulkner, and he would know how to do it. Could Dawson have drugged Morgan for some sexual reason? Perhaps Faulkner interrupted them, and Dawson killed him to keep him quiet.

'Let's talk about Faulkner's family background, which seems strange. His parents are Bible-bashers from the Highlands of Scotland. James rebelled against them, and they say he had no contact with them. At the time of the murder, his parents were staying with James's brother, Stuart, a doctor living in Wimbledon, who seems as cold as their father. I can't see how he was involved, but let's keep an open mind. Did Stuart Faulkner come to the City and end up killing his brother for some reason? He says he hadn't seen his brother for over a year, but he could be lying. It seems most likely that the killer is one of the people with security clearance who attended the party, but it might have been possible for some intruder to gain access. We have to follow that up.

'Then there's Robin Lynch. He's well known in the City as an investigative journalist. Some people regard him as a spokesman for the common man, and others would call him an unscrupulous muckraker. A week before the murder, he published an article making allegations about Palmer Associates' accounting practices. Ringer asked Morgan to investigate this. Who leaked all that information on Palmer Associates to Lynch? Apparently, Lynch is an old school friend of Faulkner's, which seems a strange coincidence, if he wasn't involved. After the article was published, Lynch says he received a call out of the blue from Faulkner saying he had his own suspicions about the accounts of Palmer Associates. Lynch says he hadn't seen him for some three years before then. What was Faulkner suspicious about? Why would he risk his job by leaking confidential information to Lynch? Who leaked the earlier information if it wasn't Faulkner?

'I think we must have doubts that Lynch is really the moral crusader he claims to be. Perhaps Lynch betrayed Faulkner by phoning Sir Giles Palmer, who then had Faulkner killed. We know Lynch was in the lobby of Palmer Associates on the evening of the Christmas party, and so was close to the scene of the murder. He says he didn't come into the building, but he could be lying. Heather Morgan spotted Lynch talking to an elderly man in an expensive-looking Land Rover that night. Could he have been reporting back to someone with money on the success of his campaign against Palmer Associates?

'Let's suppose Lynch broke in, or someone – Faulkner or someone else – let him in. If he didn't let Lynch in, perhaps Faulkner encountered him, there was an argument, and Faulkner ended up dead. It all hangs together, but there's no hard evidence to suggest that happened in fact.

'Other people at the party included Hugh Fretwell, a rich investor – the original public-school twit type. He was unhappy about some missing money and admits talking to Faulkner at the party. Could he have blamed Faulkner for some reason? He seems to have been the one who gave Morgan the drink that may have contained ketamine, but he says he just passed the nearest one to her. Someone else could have dropped the drug in the drink.

'I mentioned that Morgan's best female friend at the company was Margaret Prestwood. She was at the party at the relevant time. Could she have had some motive for killing Faulkner we don't know about?

'I think that covers the main suspects. I want us to divide up and find out whatever we can on all of them. What was Faulkner suspicious of? Was he right and is something rotten in the company, or was he being paranoid? Let's find out the backstories on Faulkner and all the suspects. What was Palmer up to on his trips to California? I'd welcome any other suggestions on our next steps.'

After a moment, Cottrell stood up. 'I suggest Foxy and I,' she said, indicating DS Fox, 'draw up a timeline and see how many of these suspects have alibis for the time of the murder. There's a danger we're confusing ourselves talking about motive. We'll end up like the Kennedy assassination, with scores of candidates wanting the victim killed. You talked about motives. I'd like to talk to this group about opportunity.'

'OK, Philippa, the floor is yours,' Gould said.

Cottrell came to the front to address the assembled detectives. 'The crucial points in time are when James Faulkner was last seen alive and when DCI Gould and I found him dead the next day. Faulkner was seen, drunk and argumentative, at around 11pm on Saturday 16th December, and we responded to a call from Heather Morgan at around 9am on the next day. He was found in the boardroom, which was locked when we entered it. Heather Morgan was there with a knife close by. Her fingerprints and DNA were on the knife, which had Faulkner's blood on it. Faulkner's blood was also on her hands. There doesn't seem any doubt that it was the knife that killed James Faulkner. So Heather Morgan is the obvious suspect.'

'Yes, we know you're suspicious of Heather, but let's look at some other suspects,' Gould interrupted. 'As I say, we'll assume, for the time being, Heather is innocent.'

'Very well,' Cottrell said. 'Let's start with the assumption that Heather Morgan is innocent and see where that takes us. We know the murderer killed Faulkner in the company boardroom, which was kept locked. There was no blood outside the boardroom, so we can assume the murder took place where the body was found. The perpetrator or perpetrators drugged Miss Morgan with ketamine and led her into the boardroom, then placed the knife in her hand to incriminate her. They must have locked the door from the outside, taking care to leave a spare key next to the body. They seem to have made a key for the purpose as the known keys are all accounted for.

'The temperature of the corpse indicates that Faulkner was killed between 11pm and 1am. It is strange that Miss Morgan was in the boardroom all this time, if she was innocent, but she would say she was drugged, which is confirmed by the drug found in her bloodstream. That doesn't let her off the hook, though. She could have taken the drug herself to confuse us, or for some recreational purpose.

'So, who could have done it, if it wasn't Heather Morgan? Do you have the table I started, Foxy?'

'Yes, here it is,' DS Fox said, posting a lined sheet of A1 paper on the board.

'The murder, as I said, took place in the boardroom between 11pm and 1am,' Cottrell said. 'Under our assumption, Heather Morgan was drugged and placed there either before or after the murder. Let's see who was around then.

'There are a few tangential people who are suspects but were not seen in the buildings. There's Faulkner's family, to start with. His parents look too old to go around killing people and drugging young women, but his brother could be a suspect. He's a doctor, so he has easy access to ketamine. He says he hadn't heard of Heather Morgan, but he could be lying; if he was, he would have known how to frame her. Let's show Stuart Faulkner's photo around to people at the party.

'There's Robin Lynch. He was seen outside the office earlier in the evening. He wasn't invited to the party, but, as DCI Gould said, he could have been allowed in, or entered illicitly. He could have killed Faulkner and framed Morgan. Perhaps Lynch has some criminal motive, and he's not as squeaky clean as he pretends. He could have some financial incentive to drive down the share price of Palmer Associates.

'Then there are the suspects known to have been at the party. Michael Dawson admits disliking Faulkner, and seems obsessed with Heather Morgan. He says he left the party earlier, but he could be lying. He was trained to use a knife when he was in the forces. So I could see Dawson killing Faulkner if he lost his temper. He says he regarded Faulkner as what he calls a *waste of space*. So perhaps they had some argument we don't know about.

'Alison Coates and Linus Murray say they both left early and went home to bed. Their only alibis are each other. They could be guilty as a team, but probably not individually. Margaret Prestwood seems to have been Morgan's best female friend at work. Prestwood has no obvious motive, but no alibi. Then there are the two senior people in the company: Sir Giles Palmer and Derek Ringer. They were at the party, and may have reasons to want Faulkner silenced permanently. Are there any other suspects we can think of?'

'There's Alison Coates's family,' Gould said. 'If she didn't kill Faulkner herself, a quick phone call would bring one of that bunch of crooks out of the woodwork. Alf Coates would kill someone with no trouble, either by himself or employing one of his gang to do it.'

'Yes, we'll include him on our list,' Cottrell said. 'And there's Hugh Fretwell, a major backer in the company. He was disgruntled about the lack of return on his investment. He was seen talking to Faulkner before he was killed. Fretwell may well have given Morgan the drugged drink at the party, perhaps innocently. Fretwell looks harmless, and I can't think of a motive for him to kill Faulkner, but we must include him as a suspect. But we mustn't forget the suspect we haven't included on the list yet.'

'Who's that?' Gould asked, though he knew the answer.

'Heather Morgan – the most obvious suspect of all,' Cottrell said. 'She admits arguing with Faulkner and breaking off their engagement on the night of the party. She was found with the body the next day. Motive, means, opportunity – Heather Morgan had the lot.'

'You're right, of course,' Gould said, 'but I want to eliminate everyone else before we arrest her. I don't want to go for the obvious suspect just to close the case. Is that clear to everyone?'

The assembled detectives looked at each other, before they gave reluctant nods.

'So, what are the next steps, gov?' DS Fox asked Gould.

126

'We'll draw up a timeline of what we know happened at the party. Philippa's right. We know we have lots of people with a motive – we need to narrow it down to people with opportunity. The perpetrator unlocked the boardroom late in the evening at the party, and persuaded James Faulkner, a large healthy man, into it. It would have taken two strong men to force Faulkner against his will into that boardroom. Faulkner would have resisted, and no one heard any struggle. It seems the victim entered the boardroom voluntarily. So how could someone – the murderer, presumably – have persuaded him to go in there?'

'By promise of sex,' Fox suggested, to jeers from his colleagues.

'No, Foxy,' Gould said, 'that's an excellent suggestion. It ties in with what we know of Faulkner's character. That points to a woman – Alison Coates, for example; we know he fancied her in the past. At a stretch, Margaret Prestwood could have done it. I don't imagine she's his type, but, after a few drinks, from what we know of him, he would follow anything in a skirt.'

'Or it could be a man who promised Faulkner information if he was trying to find some dodgy transactions in the company,' Fox said.

'Yes, that would point to Ringer or Palmer or both,' Gould said.

'Or Heather Morgan could have invited him for a quick chat about the break-up, and she lost her temper and stabbed him,' Cottrell said.

'But we have witnesses who say that Morgan had thrown Faulkner's ring back at him. What else was there to talk to him about?'

'As a woman myself, I can tell you any woman would have lots of things to clear up – like making sure he gave his key back to her and took all his stuff out of her flat. Morgan did none of those things before he died, as far as we know.'

'How about getting a warrant to search Morgan's flat?' Fox asked. 'We've already searched Faulkner's, using his father's permission.'

'That's a good idea. If Morgan's defence is correct, there must be an extra key to the boardroom out there, and we'll also search the whole of the office,' Cottrell said. 'Palmer can give us permission for that.'

Gould looked around at the assembled detectives. 'So nearly everyone is a suspect,' he said. 'That doesn't get us very far with a murderer or murderers wandering around free. What can we do to narrow the field some more?'

'With all due respect, gov, the only one we can make a convincing case against is Heather Morgan,' Cottrell said. 'I respect what you say, but we must look at her. She had motive, means and opportunity. The forensic case against her is strong. We could probably get a conviction against her with the evidence we have now.'

'Yes, that's exactly what the real killer wants. Do we think she took that date rape drug herself?' Gould asked.

'Do we know who else could have put the ketamine in her drink?' Fox asked.

'The doctors say the drug can take up to half an hour to take effect,' Gould said. 'So it would have to be someone still at the party at around 11 pm. Who do we know was there then?'

'Fretwell admits passing Morgan a drink,' Cottrell replied, 'but, unless he's a brilliant actor, he didn't know it was doctored. Prestwood was there. She was Morgan's friend, and she had no known motive. Murray and/or Coates could have returned to the party. We know Coates disliked Morgan and was angry with Faulkner. She could have asked Murray, or one of her granddad's hired thugs, to put the drug in Morgan's drink. There was no record of an uninvited person entering, but no doubt a professional criminal could have broken in. Palmer and Ringer were there, as was Dawson, so there are still too many suspects for comfort. You won't like the other two options.'

'Try me,' Gould said.

'One possibility is that Faulkner put it in her drink. Let's say he was hoping to have sex with her either at home or in the boardroom. Perhaps he was trying for some sort of sexual revenge by humiliating her in the office for ditching him. If that's the case, it still indicates Morgan killed him, but arguably as an act of self-defence, assuming he tried to rape her in the boardroom. You could phone her brief and offer to go easy if that's her defence.'

'But Heather denies killing Faulkner at all,' Gould said, 'and I don't want to reveal the ketamine angle. I aim to keep that up our sleeves, and not tell anyone.'

'The final option is that Morgan took it herself after killing Faulkner out of anger or jealousy, just to put us off the scent.'

'Please tell me you're not going to say, "Hell hath no fury like a woman scorned."'

'No, but clichés often turn out to be true,' Cottrell said in a defensive tone.

'Well, Heather hasn't admitted anything so far, and I don't think she will. We'll try to eliminate the other suspects before making any offers. I don't want to be responsible for a miscarriage of justice.'

DS Fox spoke. 'It seems there are two broad options. Either this murder is a crime of passion, which points to Alison Coates, Linus Murray or possibly Michael Dawson – or Heather Morgan, of course. Or it's a financial crime, which points to anyone in the company, Lynch or perhaps Fretwell – if he had some motive we haven't found yet.'

'Let's start with the passion motive,' Gould said. 'Alison Coates or Linus Murray could have come back to the party and killed Faulkner. They're providing alibis for each other, so if either of them did it, it was a joint enterprise. Or Alison could have phoned her granddad to have Faulkner eliminated out of jealousy.'

'Do we really think old man Coates would have done that?' Fox asked. 'From what we know of his reputation, he'd kill as part of a crime deal, but I imagine if Alison was just jealous, he'd tell her to go back to bed and forget about it. Alf Coates wouldn't want police going all over his activities because of some silly girl's lovers' spat.'

'Then let's assume it was a financial crime,' Gould said. 'We'll get an expert to go over that article in *Dirty Money*. It's too much of a coincidence it came out just before Faulkner's murder.'

Fox was making notes on the A1 sheet on the board. 'So, there's the financial crime network – Lynch, or anyone in the company. And the jealousy motive – Alison Coates, Murray, Dawson or Morgan. If you draw two circles around these people, what strikes you?'

'Alison, Murray, Dawson and Morgan are in both circles,' Gould said. 'I'd like to follow Alison, Murray and Dawson – and Alf Coates. Someone among the people we have just talked about is laughing at us.' He stood up to conclude the meeting. 'We cannot have that. It is time to take some action to flush them out.'

'What do you mean, gov?' Fox asked.

'I aim to go after the corporate side of the dead man's life. We are going to put the cat among the pigeons with this lot. I'm going to start with Linus Murray, then that pompous oaf Giles Palmer. Murray's got something to hide. I'm going to tell him the US police have him on their files.'

'But you said Jeff Zug hadn't heard of him,' Cottrell said.

'I know that, and you know that, but he doesn't. If he has a record and learns he's under suspicion, I'm betting he's going to make a run for it. I'll interview him and tell him we're on to him, then, Foxy, you tail him. He hasn't seen you, has he?'

'No, gov,' Fox said.

'And what about Palmer?' Cottrell asked.

'We'll interview him formally. He's getting too comfortable for my liking.'

'But he has influential friends, sir,' one of the detectives said. 'We don't want to annoy Sir Giles unnecessarily.'

Gould glared at the detective. 'You're new here, aren't you? I'm going to forget you said that. We have to go where the evidence leads, no matter who it upsets. I'm going to visit Alf Coates to give him a scare as well. I'm ending this meeting now. You have enough work to be getting on with.' He left the room without further comment.

After Gould left, there was an embarrassed silence. Once the rest of the team had left the conference room, Fox turned to Cottrell. 'I hope the boss knows what he is doing.'

Cottrell sighed. 'So do I, Foxy. Heather Morgan ticks all the boxes, and I'm guessing she's as guilty as sin, but he doesn't see it. I'm happy to look at every other suspect to keep the boss happy, but I'm going to make sure we keep Heather Morgan in our sights.'

*

The next day, Gould and Fox arrived at the offices of a firm of chartered accountants in Moorgate. Peter Thomas, who was a paid advisor to the City of London police, was seated at his desk with the *Dirty Money* article in front of him. He was well known as a long-time City expert, who had the world-weary air of someone who has seen all the various financial fashions come and go.

'Thanks for seeing us, Peter,' Gould said, sitting opposite him. He handed Thomas a file of all the press cuttings from *Dirty Money* that covered Palmer Associates. 'We need your help in analysing this article by a Robin Lynch. A man called James Faulkner who worked for this company was killed at their Christmas party, and we suspect this article played a part.'

Thomas peered at Gould over his half-moon glasses. 'Murder's not my area of expertise, David, but I'll do my best.' His expression conveyed a background numbers man's distaste for anything as basic as the subject of murder. He skimmed through the article. 'Yes, I read this when it first came out. What did you want to know?'

'First of all,' Gould said, 'what is Lynch accusing the company of, and is it illegal? We've interviewed him, but he wasn't helpful.'

Thomas removed his glasses and drew a deep breath, before addressing Gould in the manner of a doctor delivering news of a fatal disease to a patient. 'He's saying Palmer Associates, which I've always considered a most respectable company, is investing in ways of which its investors wouldn't approve.'

Gould sat up. 'What sort of ways?'

Thomas sighed. 'The article is not very specific. Lynch says they invest in films that are not the sort your mother would want to see. But that could mean anything or nothing. As for investments in pharmaceuticals, he says they are not the sort sold at Boots: again meaningless on its own.'

'Would you say he is implying they invest in pornography and illicit drugs?' Gould asked, keen to tie Thomas down.

'Implying without saying it, to avoid libel, I would say,' Thomas said.

'And would you say Palmer Associates are breaking any accountancy laws?'

'You would have to check the terms of any capital issues, but if Palmer Associates invested in a company in good faith, and that company did any of these things, then Palmer could plead ignorance.'

'But if he did not act in good faith?'

'Then Sir Giles Palmer could be charged with conspiracy,' Thomas said, sadly. 'If that were the case ...' His voice tailed away.

'Yes?'

'That would damage the City's good name. Already Palmer's share price has plummeted because of this article. If you could prove bad faith by Palmer himself, he would probably be forced out.' Thomas gazed at Gould. 'Another thing is that if as respectable a company as Palmer Associates were involved in pornography or drugs, that would call the whole future of the City of London into doubt.'

'I realise that would be bad for the economy,' Gould said.

'Disastrous, I would say. And, knowing how the establishment in this country protects itself, it would be unfortunate for whoever first raised it. Someone might decide to get rid of the messenger. The loss of a detective chief inspector might be seen as a price worth paying to keep it quiet. Do you take my meaning, DCI Gould?' Thomas asked, with a smile devoid of humour.

'You're the second person to try to scare me, Peter. I hope no one tries to threaten me,' Gould said, standing up. 'Thank you for your time. I expect I will want to interview Sir Giles again.'

PART 3

CAT AMONG THE PIGEONS

Chapter 23

The following day, Gould and Cottrell waited in their police car outside the offices of Palmer Associates. Gould turned to Cottrell and indicated the twelfth floor. 'Somewhere in those offices, Faulkner's murderer is laughing at us. It is up to us to make sure whoever it is faces justice.'

Cottrell looked at Gould. 'These are going to be two difficult interviews, David. Are you prepared for them?'

'We all know you can't always be popular as a police officer. Sometimes, one must do the right thing, even if it upsets those in charge,' Gould said. 'Are you ready?'

'Yes, gov,' Cottrell said, as she followed Gould out of the car.

The two officers did not talk as they entered the offices of Palmer Associates and took the lift to the top floor. Alison was waiting for them when they walked out of the lift.

'Hello, Miss Coates,' Gould said, in a cold voice. 'We have an appointment with Sir Giles.'

'Yes, Sir Giles is expecting you,' Alison said, her practised smile fading as she saw Gould's severe expression. 'Please come through.'

Sir Giles stood up as Alison led Gould and Cottrell into his room. 'Ah, good morning, officers. I trust you have come to tell me you have arrested that Morgan woman for the murder of her fiancé. I'm surprised it's taken this long, but as long as you arrest the right man – or woman, as in this case – I suppose not too much harm has been done.'

Gould shook his head. 'All I can say is that investigations are proceeding into the murder of James Faulkner, Sir Giles. I'm afraid DS Cottrell and I have a few more questions to ask you.'

Sir Giles urbanely gestured for the officers to take seats behind the large table, as he took the more imposing swivel chair. 'I'm surprised you have further questions, Mr Gould, but I am happy to help if I can.'

'You will have read the article written by Mr Robin Lynch that appeared in *Dirty Money* recently. It made serious allegations against your company. For the record, do you have any comments to make on it, Sir Giles?'

'Yes, I read it, and largely ignored it. It seemed to take care not to make specific allegations, as far as I could see. If it had, we would of course have sued for libel,' Sir Giles replied, with the air of a respectable householder disposing of rubbish.

'It seems to be implying the company deals in pornographic films, and drugs, without exactly saying so.'

Sir Giles shrugged. 'Yes, that seems to be the insinuation, but there was no truth in the allegations, of course, so I took the decision to ignore the article.'

'Yet I understand Miss Heather Morgan was given the task of seeing who in the company had been leaking information to the press. Why was that necessary if there was no truth in it?'

'I assumed the allegations came from somewhere in the company. Obviously, we do not tolerate disloyalty of that kind. Yes, Miss Morgan was given that task, but I do not think she found anything useful. She's been sacked now, of course.'

'We have been told that the dead man, James Faulkner, knew Robin Lynch and spoke to him on his way into the party.'

'I am disappointed if James was the guilty man, but, as he is dead, he cannot do any more damage now, can he?'

'What were the questions Faulkner asked you at the party, Sir Giles?'

'He seemed to think I was paying Derek Ringer too much money. It was none of his business, so I ignored him.'

'Why do you think he was asking about that?'

'I've honestly no idea, but Derek Ringer is my trusted managing director, and is paid accordingly.'

'Mr Faulkner may have wondered if he was paid so much

because some of his activities were illicit and you wanted to buy his silence.'

'I'll forget you suggested that, DCI Gould. Now, is there anything else?'

'No, Sir Giles, I will call that a day now. Thank you for meeting us.'

Gould and Cottrell noticed the look of undiluted hate Sir Giles directed at them as they left his office.

Gould stopped at Alison's desk. 'I wish – in fact I insist – to use your boardroom as part of the investigation into James Faulkner's death.'

Alison looked up from her typing. 'I don't think Sir Giles will be happy about that.' She noticed Gould's demeanour. 'But if I don't tell him, he won't know, will he?'

'Thank you, my sentiments exactly. Then please tell Mr Linus Murray we want to have a word with him.'

'Linus? What for?'

'I'd like to tell him directly, Miss Coates. We don't have to give members of the Coates family advance warning of police operations.'

Alison pressed an intercom. 'Linus, honey, Inspector Gould wants to see you.'

'Sure thing. I'll be right there.' Gould and Cottrell recognised Linus Murray's voice, and within a minute he had joined them.

'We would like a word with you in the boardroom, Mr Murray,' Gould said, indicating the room behind them. He led Linus in, then Gould and Cottrell sat down opposite him. 'This was the site of the murder of James Faulkner, Mr Murray. Is there anything else you can tell us of that matter now you have had a chance to think about it?'

'No, inspector. As I told you, Alison and I had left the party before it happened.'

'So you say,' Gould said, pulling open a file. 'I've been looking into your history, Mr Murray. I phoned Jeff Zug of the Los

Angeles police department to see if he knew you. Shall I tell you what he said?'

'Yes, what did Lieutenant Zug say?'

'They have a long record on you. He's about to fax it over to me. I'd like you to visit Snow Hill police station tomorrow so I can discuss it with you.'

'There must be some mistake; I have never been in trouble with the police, but sure thing, I'll be there. I have nothing to hide.'

'I'll see you tomorrow at 2pm then,' Gould said, keeping his gaze fixed on Linus's face.

After Linus left, Gould turned to Cottrell. 'That man's a criminal, even if he has enough confidence for two people.'

'How do you know he's a criminal? He didn't react aggressively.'

'Exactly; he didn't seem surprised he had a police record. And how did he know Jeff Zug is a lieutenant? I never told him that. Foxy should be following him home. With any luck, he'll make a break for it. Somehow, I don't expect him to report for questioning tomorrow.'

*

DS Fox looked at the images from the various security cameras located close to the offices of Palmer Associates. Unfortunately, there were none that showed the entrance to the offices. Fox reflected that that would have been ideal in confirming the various witness statements regarding when the partygoers had left the party.

More promisingly, there were two traffic cameras trained on the street outside the offices. The more interesting one showed a large top-of-the-range Land Rover waiting on a yellow line around eight o'clock, when the party was starting. There appeared to be a large elderly man at the steering wheel, but his face was obscured. The number plate was very clear, however, and it showed a number registered to Alfred Coates, whose name had already come up in the investigation.

Soon after eight o'clock on the video, a youngish man came over to the man who Fox assumed to be Coates. The pedestrian spoke to the driver for a few minutes, then walked away. Although the image was grainy, Fox felt sure the pedestrian was Robin Lynch. The fact that there appeared to be collusion between Lynch and Coates threw a fresh light on the investigation, and Fox picked up the phone to report to DCI Gould.

'Gov,' Fox said, 'I've just confirmed a car registered to Alf Coates was outside the party on the night of the murder.'

'Great work, Foxy. I think it is time to pay Mr Coates a visit.' Gould's voice came down the phone. 'And I want you to follow him to see what he does afterwards.'

*

Later the same day, Gould led Cottrell into a pub situated near the Oval cricket ground. While many of the local pubs had been updated to cater for the increasingly upmarket clientele in the area, it was obvious that the Cornwall Arms had not been altered since the days when the Kray twins controlled many of the local businesses. Gould smiled to himself as he noted that the public and saloon bars still had separate entrances. He walked over to the far corner of the saloon bar area, where a seventy-year-old man sat counting bank notes.

'Hello, Alf,' Gould said. 'I thought I might find you here.'

'Why, Mr Gould,' the old man said, after putting the bank notes away carefully. 'What are the City police doing down here? I thought you never left the Square Mile. And who is this lovely young lady?'

'I'd travel a long way to see you, Alf,' Gould said, taking a seat. 'And this is DS Philippa Cottrell.'

'Charmed to meet you, my dear,' Alf said, with a lascivious sneer.

140

Cottrell glared at Alf. 'Lay off the old-world charm, Mr Coates. I am a police officer and you are a professional criminal. I am not your dear.'

Alf smiled wryly. 'Well, now the pleasantries have been sorted out, let's get down to business. To what do I owe the delight of this visit?'

'We are investigating the murder of a Mr James Faulkner at the offices of Palmer Associates in the City of London, after a party on the evening of the 16th of December. Can you tell us where you were on that evening?'

Alf thought for a long time, with the obvious aim of annoying the two police officers. 'Well, I'm truly sorry to hear of any man's death. James – Faulkner, was it? The name doesn't mean anything to me, but then I never go into the City of London. It's like a foreign country up there. I'm sure on the 16th of December I was around this pub. It takes up most of my time. Why do you think I might be involved in this alleged crime?'

'It is not an alleged crime. We are investigating a murder. We have photos of an elderly man in an expensive Land Rover outside the offices of Palmer Associates on the night of the murder. Does that sound familiar? I've checked and you own a new Land Rover. The number plate on the DVLA computer matches the one shown in the photo.'

Alf smiled. 'Yes, well, I reported that motor nicked a couple of weeks ago, but the police haven't been able to find it. They always say there's a shortage of manpower.'

Gould proceeded, ignoring Alf's reply. 'The other connection is that I believe you have a granddaughter called Alison. She was there at the party. She has an American boyfriend called Linus Murray, of whom we have strong suspicions. When did you last see Miss Alison Coates?'

'I can't quite remember, but I don't think I can be held responsible for what my granddaughter does or who she meets, Mr Gould. Nor do I have to explain the whereabouts of my car at all hours of the day and night. Now, if there is nothing else, it has been a pleasure to see you again and meet your charming assistant.' Alf pointed to the door.

'I am only charming when I want be, Mr Coates,' Cottrell said.

Gould stood up. 'Well, thank you for seeing us, Mr Coates. Please be sure to give us a ring if you have any sudden flashes of memory about any visits to the City. DS Cottrell, we will leave Mr Coates to get on with running his ... pub, and other things, for the time being.'

'It's been a pleasure, officers,' Alf said, as Gould and Cottrell left.

'Did we get anything out of that interview, David?' Cottrell asked, as they returned to their car.

'Not really, but it's good for the police to pay these characters a visit from time to time. Trouble is, he's right. He has no contact with the City as far as we know, and I don't know why he would want to murder Faulkner. But I can't believe Alison Coates is as innocent as she claims to be, and there's something definitely suspicious about that Linus character she goes around with. Old man Coates may be a tough nut to crack, but I aim to find out what Alison and Linus Murray are up to.'

Once the two detectives had left the scene, they did not observe Alf Coates looking thoughtfully after them. He then called to the man behind the bar. 'I'm off for the rest of the day; I'm going to see my granddaughter. I have something to discuss with her.'

Alf took the keys for his Land Rover, which now had a different registration number from the night of James Faulkner's murder, and drove away. He did not notice DS Fox following at a discreet distance.

Chapter 24

Later that evening, Alison opened the door of the small flat in Dulwich that she shared with Linus Murray. She put down her shopping bag and sighed. She told herself she had had a tough day. Walking into the kitchen, she opened the door of their American-style fridge and pulled out an alcopop. She smiled as she recalled how, when they had moved in, Linus had insisted on a large fridge, and how he made fun of small British ones. Just then, she heard a noise from the main bedroom.

'Linus, honey, is that you? I didn't realise you were home,' she called, turning to greet her boyfriend with a welcoming smile.

She froze when she saw who entered the room.

'Granddad,' she gasped. 'How did you get in?'

Alf Coates smiled. 'You don't think some feeble Yale locks could keep an expert like your old granddad out, did you?'

'No, that was a silly thing to say. I meant why are you here and how did you find me?'

'Let's skip the how bit. The same thing applies to that. The why question is more interesting. I've heard there have been unusual things happening at that poncey firm you work at.'

'Too right, there's been a murder. I've had that DCI Gould haul me over the coals because you're my granddad.'

'Gould? Yes, I know him. He's been to see me. I know most of the top brass in the Met. Gould's different from the others, though. He moved over to the City, because he was too honest for the Met. He's what you might call a worthy opponent.'

'Very gentlemanly, I'm sure, but this isn't a game of cricket. If you're involved in any dodgy business in the City, I don't want to be a part of it. I want to make my own way in the world.'

'I don't think I can allow that, Alison, love. Do you know how many people were after your job as Palmer's secretary? How do you think you got it?'

Alison winced. 'Oh, my God. You threatened to break a few kneecaps, did you, persuading them to take me on? I might have known.'

Alf smiled. 'No, but I did persuade some other girls who were strong candidates not to apply. Now, there's no reason to thank me ...'

'Thank you? I'd like to throttle you. I want to make my own way in my own career without any help from you.'

'As I say, there's no reason to thank me. But I was grateful for all the things you told me about Palmer's activities.'

'I didn't feel good about that,' Alison said, embarrassed. 'It wasn't good looking through James's papers when he was out of the room. I felt like a tart – sleeping with him for secrets. He looked down at me anyway, because I'm lower-class. I don't know what he'd call me if he knew I was spying on him for you. And how did all that stuff end up in that magazine? Did you have a hand in that?'

'I'm not saying. It was good of you to help me, though. That's what families are for,' Alf said, making himself comfortable on one of the kitchen chairs.

'You needn't be so pleased with yourself,' Alison said, her voice rising in anger. 'That DCI Gould is on to you. He's no fool. I would watch my back if I were you.'

Just then, a soft American voice came from the hall. 'Is this gentleman bothering you, honey?'

Linus came in. Alf Coates stared at him as if he were from another planet.

'Who the hell are you?' Alf asked.

'I might ask you the same question. I live here.'

Alison intervened. 'Linus, this is my granddad. Granddad, this is Linus, my boyfriend.'

Linus smiled and offered his hand. 'I've heard about you, sir. Your name goes before you.'

Alf looked at him suspiciously. 'What do you mean?'

'You're one of the top crime bosses here in London, aren't you?'

Alf nodded. 'You could say that.'

'Well, my family controls most of the crime in LA. We should have lots of interests in common, wouldn't you say?'

Alf turned to Alison, who was staring open-mouthed. 'Did you know anything about this?'

Alison seemed to come out of her state of shock. 'No, I damn well didn't. I don't think I know anything anymore. Who the hell are you really, Linus?'

Alf and Alison both turned to Linus.

'I'm sorry about this, honey,' Linus said. 'I've been in a criminal gang since I was fifteen. I joined your company in LA to find out more about profits in the film finance industry, then transferred to London. My loyalties are to my gang. My real boss is very interested in expanding into this area. I came over here to see what opportunities there might be. You're just a lovely bonus.'

'So I'm just a means to an end, am I?' Alison shouted. She stormed over to Linus and slapped his face as hard as she could.

Linus winced and then smiled. 'I guess I deserved that. Now, shall we get down to business?' he said, pulling a gun from his pocket.

Alf and Alison instinctively backed away.

'There's no need for a shooter, son,' Alf said. 'Why don't you put that gun away and we can talk?'

Linus smiled. 'I like your style, sir. OK, I don't want any trouble. Let's talk, as long as we all know I'm tooled up.'

The three of them sat down at the kitchen table, as Linus returned the gun to his pocket.

'So, why have you been fooling around with my granddaughter?' Alf asked.

'I'm sorry about that. You might call it mixing business with pleasure.'

Alison snorted. 'Is that supposed to make me feel better?'

'Have you really been honest with me, honey?' Linus asked. 'I don't remember you mentioning anything about your grandfather really being a godfather. Now, let's put our cards on the table and say what each of us knows about Palmer Associates.'

Alf and Alison exchanged glances.

'All right, I'll talk. But I don't want any competition on my home turf,' Alf said.

'I'm sure we can work something out based on mutual respect,' Linus said. 'Why don't you tell me what your plan is?'

'Why don't you go first, son?'

'OK. My boss keeps an eye out for companies with larger-than-normal profits. Palmer Associates always seems to pay out a lot of money, even when the films make losses. That seems pretty clever to us. We think Palmer's real films may be on the criminal side, which also appeals. That's about it. Now you.'

'It's very similar. I know the types of films that Palmer finances,' Alf said. 'Believe me, *The Sound of Music* they ain't. Palmer doesn't know that I've just taken a large number of shares in his company. It should be a useful sideline for me.'

'It seems as if we have a good deal in common. I'm sure we can work something out. We don't mind you having the English market, while we have the American side stitched up. Why don't we have a drink to seal the deal? Alison, honey,' Linus ordered, 'get out those bottles of champagne we bought the other day.'

Alison, perhaps in a state of shock from seeing two of the most important men in her life conspiring together, silently obeyed Linus's abrupt order. She obediently laid out glasses for the two men to toast their newly forged criminal conspiracy.

*

Outside Alison and Linus's building, DS Fox checked his watch and updated the events recorded in his logbook. DCI Gould had ordered him to follow Alf Coates as a major suspect for James

Faulkner's murder. Fox had still been convinced that Heather had murdered James in some sort of jealous rage, and inwardly he had seethed at what he regarded as a waste of time in following Coates.

Fox had checked the Range Rover's number plate with the DVLA computer in Swansea, and Alf Coates's name had come up as a person of interest. Fox had seen Linus Murray arrive later and would dearly have loved to know what the three suspects were discussing. Perhaps Gould was right after all. He decided to make a call and tell Gould about this meeting straight away.

'Gov,' Fox said, 'there's been an interesting development. Linus Murray, Alison and old man Coates are all together at Murray's house. I'm outside now. How do you want to play it?'

Gould snorted. 'That old crook Coates said he'd never heard of Linus Murray and didn't know much about his granddaughter. Coates doesn't do family get-togethers – they must be discussing some sort of crime. I bet Faulkner's murder is part of it. I'll be there as soon as I can. If Coates leaves first, follow him rather than Linus.'

'Yes, gov.'

After five minutes, and before Gould could arrive, Alf Coates left the house and climb into his Range Rover. Fox followed Alf's vehicle through the crowded streets to his pub close to the Oval. Fox stayed outside until Gould phoned to send him home at the end of his shift.

*

Philippa Cottrell waited impatiently outside the office of Palmer Associates. She was keeping an eye out for Michael Dawson's departure from work. She had drawn what she felt was the short straw of following Michael. Fox had sat in on Michael's police interview, so Gould had decided that, to avoid recognition, Cottrell would be better assigned to Michael.

Around a quarter to six, Cottrell saw Michael leave through the front door of Palmer Associates. She prepared to follow him, but then noticed he stopped suddenly. Heather Morgan had just left a nearby department store and set off along the busy street, and Michael walked in the same direction.

It became clear that Michael was following Heather for some unknown reason. Cottrell followed Michael, who was tailing Heather into Saint Paul's underground station. The three of them went onto the westbound platform and waited until the tube train arrived. Cottrell was worried Heather might recognise her, but Heather seemed oblivious to the two people following her.

The journey proceeded uneventfully as Heather left the tube and walked along the road in Swiss Cottage where Cottrell knew she lived. Heather let herself in with a latch key. Michael waited on the street behind a tree until the light went on in the first floor of the building, obviously Heather's flat. He then turned and walked without expression towards the nearby Swiss Cottage tube station. Cottrell decided to stop him.

'What are you doing here, Mr Dawson?' she asked.

Michael Dawson turned around, startled. 'Who are you?'

'I am Detective Sergeant Cottrell, investigating the murder of James Faulkner,' Cottrell said, showing her warrant card. 'I repeat: what are you doing here, Mr Dawson?'

'Just walking home. I'm not breaking any law, am I?'

'I will ask the questions, Mr Dawson. You will answer them. Do you want to talk to me here or at the local station?'

'I was just going home,' Michael answered, his eyes conveying panic.

'I don't think so. You live in a different part of London altogether. Why were you outside Heather Morgan's flat?'

'If you must know, I happened to see Heather on the street, and wanted to make sure she arrived home safely.'

'You were following her. Stalking her, one might say.'

Michael looked appalled. 'No, you've got me wrong, officer. Someone framed Heather for that murder. They're still out there, and she's in danger. I am merely making sure she comes to no harm.'

'Did she ask you for protection?'

'No, of course not.'

'If Miss Morgan wanted protection, she would ask the police. I'm sure she doesn't want some strange man following her home.'

'I'm not a stranger. We're friends.'

'Maybe so, but I don't want to see you following women home again. Do you understand?'

Michael nodded.

'If someone did frame her, we will deal with it,' Cottrell said. 'You are a suspect at the moment. You were at that party and were seen talking to James Faulkner. You could have killed him.'

'You can't think I killed James. Why should I?'

'I could think of several reasons why you could be regarded as a suspect. You could move yourself up to the top of the list of suspects if you don't leave Miss Morgan alone.'

Michael seemed about to reply, but simply mumbled an apology and turned away.

As Cottrell watched him walking down the dark street to the tube station, she could not decide whether he was a criminal or an innocent man infatuated with Heather Morgan, misguidedly trying to protect her. She could make a case for Michael as the murderer of James Faulkner, but somehow she did not think he was.

She shook her head and reminded herself that her duty was to follow the evidence, which, in her view, still pointed to Heather Morgan as the murderer, even though her detective training made her regard Michael's behaviour as suspicious.

*

The following morning, Gould called another progress meeting to discuss the latest developments in the investigation into James Faulkner's murder.

'Let's run over what we have from yesterday,' Gould said. 'Foxy, tell us about Coates.'

Fox checked his notebook. 'Alfred Coates was at his pub for most of the day. Various criminals known to us visited the pub during that time. Whether it was to see Coates or just to have a drink is not known.'

'Chatting to his mates is probably the only reason he keeps that pub open,' Gould said. 'It's a great place to meet all his criminal cronies. Carry on.'

'Yes, gov. You and Philippa visited at around 1715 and left shortly after. At 1730 Coates left in his Range Rover and travelled to Dulwich. There he apparently broke into his granddaughter's flat. He was seen tampering with the lock on one of the windows. Alison Coates entered at 1750 and then Linus Murray entered at 1800.'

'You're saying he broke into his granddaughter's flat? That's a damned strange thing to do,' Gould said.

'Yes, gov,' Fox said. 'Then Coates left Alison's flat at 1820 and returned to his pub. He was there until I ended my shift at 2145.'

'So Linus, Alison and old man Coates had a meeting for around twenty minutes,' Gould said. 'Knowing Coates, it was probably some kind of criminal conspiracy. That's worth following up. Thanks, Foxy. How about you, Philippa?'

'As agreed,' Cottrell began, 'I followed Dawson after work. What was interesting was that he saw Heather Morgan leave a shop, apparently by chance, and followed her home. Once she was there, he travelled to his own address. I was worried by his behaviour and stopped him.'

'You did what?' Gould asked. 'You were only supposed to be observing.'

'I used my initiative, as he was acting so suspiciously. He claimed he was only following Morgan home as he was worried about her safety. I warned him to desist and said we would protect her if she was in danger. I followed him home, and he travelled there without incident. To be honest, I could not decide if I believed him or not.'

'There's no law against a man following a woman he fancies home,' Gould said, 'but, I agree, it definitely seems suspicious.' He stood up and started to pace the room. 'Dawson seems to have a very protective view of Heather. He could have killed Faulkner if he thought he was treating her badly for any reason. Dawson probably sees himself as a knight in shining armour.'

Fox spoke up. 'According to his army files, Dawson came from an all-male background – a boys' boarding school, then straight into the army. Sometimes, men like that don't know how to deal with women in the workplace. He may be overprotective of Morgan, but it doesn't mean he killed Faulkner.'

'I wouldn't like some creepy man following me home from work,' Cottrell said, her voice rising with indignation. 'But I agree with Foxy that he didn't seem to want to harm Morgan. It was as if he was making sure she arrived home safely, just as he said.'

Gould brought the meeting to a close. 'Don't forget we are trying to investigate the murder of a man – James Faulkner – and all of our suspects are still in the frame. We seem to have put the cat among the pigeons quite nicely. I'm going to apply for a search warrant for Palmer Associates tomorrow. We'll meet again after that.'

*

The next day, Sir Giles Palmer's Rolls-Royce purred up to the clubhouse at Hindhead golf course and parked in his regular reserved spot. Sir Giles climbed out of the back seat and looked around at the splendid view of the South Downs. He smelled the fresh air with satisfaction. His natural home was in the crowded office blocks of the City of London, but he enjoyed his weekend golf games.

Not even the sight of Derek Ringer walking towards him could dampen his spirits. Sir Giles would rather avoid Derek at weekends if he could, but knew that at least Derek would be sure not to defeat his boss at golf, and playing Derek was the only way Sir Giles could avoid a humiliating defeat.

'Ah, Sir Giles,' Derek said. 'How good of you to let me have a round with you.'

'Yes, Derek,' Sir Giles replied. 'Has our playing partner arrived?'

'Playing partner, Sir Giles?' Derek echoed, nonplussed for a moment.

'Yes. I see him there now.' Sir Giles stretched out his arm to greet his guest. Bob Watson, commissioner of the City of London police, shook Sir Giles's hand.

'Thanks for the invitation, Giles,' the Commissioner said. 'It's been a long time since we had a round.'

'Yes, I wanted to have a chat, and there's no substitute for golf to get to know one another, is there? Have you met Derek Ringer, my managing director?' Sir Giles asked, as Watson and Derek shook hands. 'We'll have a chat later, shall we, Derek?'

Derek immediately sidled away, realising that Sir Giles was hoping for a chat with Watson on his own. 'Of course, Sir Giles,' he said, obviously disappointed.

Sir Giles and Watson walked to the first tee and started playing. At the fourth tee, once Watson had hit a particularly good shot, Sir Giles raised the issue that was uppermost in his thoughts. 'Bob, you may have heard that there was an unsavoury murder at our offices just before Christmas. That was a great shot, by the way.'

'They'll be reducing my handicap soon,' Watson said. 'Yes, I'd heard about that. David Gould's on the case. He's a good man.'

'Is he? I'm not sure about that,' Sir Giles said, striding ahead along the fairway.

'Why? Is there some problem?'

'Yes. Tell me, Bob, is it ethical for a detective to investigate a crime where an ex-girlfriend is a suspect?'

Watson caught up with Sir Giles. 'No, it's not. Are you saying that's what Gould is doing?'

Sir Giles prepared to take his second shot, which landed close to the green. He gave a satisfied smile. 'Yes, so I understand.'

Watson started to walk towards his ball, which was resting fifty yards further on. 'Tell you what, Giles. Come along to my office next week, and we'll discuss this further.' He hit a shot that landed on the edge of the green.

'Nice shot, Bob,' Sir Giles said. 'I'll do that. Would Wednesday morning be convenient?'

'Yes, that will be fine,' Watson said, as he aimed up his putt. 'Now, with any luck, I'll make a par here . . .'

Chapter 25

Heather Morgan sat in the coffee bar near her home, staring at her half-drunk cappuccino. She had read through the job vacancies in the *Evening Standard* but had not seen anything for which she could apply. She told herself that something would turn up soon, even though she did not know when. She looked at the office workers hurrying by to their next appointments, wishing she could once again be one of them.

Just then, a youngish man she remembered seeing on the night of the party approached her. 'Heather Morgan? My name's Robin Lynch. I was an old school friend of James's. I wanted to say how sorry I am that he was killed. You must be devastated.'

Heather smiled uncertainly. 'I remember you from the night of the party. James said he knew you. I don't think you should have shouted his name like that. It put him in an awkward position. But thank you for your sympathy. No one else will talk to me. Most people in the City think I'm some sort of murdering hussy and I should be in prison.'

'Well, I'm sorry about that, but that's mainly why I wanted to speak to you. I'm a journalist and I am planning to write a piece about James's murder. I'm happy to put your case to the public. I can guarantee I will quote everything you say accurately.'

Heather looked at Lynch with suspicion. 'Why don't you think I killed James? Everyone else does.'

'I know a lot about your company, and I don't think you're the murderer. You've probably seen the piece I wrote on Palmer Associates two weeks ago.'

'I should say I did. Giles Palmer wanted me to find out who leaked that information to you. I'd still like to know that, and I'm sure the police would also be interested.'

'Well, I had another source originally, but, before he was killed,

James phoned me up and said he was suspicious of the accounts of Palmer Associates. I'm sure that caused someone to murder him. It's too much of a coincidence otherwise.'

'Have you told the police about this?'

'I don't think they trust me. I've had your friend DCI Gould give me a grilling. I don't know if he suspected me of killing James, but I had no motive and could not have got into that office, even if I'd wanted to.'

'How do you know David's my friend?'

'I'm a journalist. I make it my business to know things like that. It's true, though, isn't it?'

'We used to know each other. But I don't know whether I should talk to the press,' Heather said cautiously. 'I don't think David would want me to.'

'Screw the police. They don't care about you. I'm sure they're plotting to put you away as soon as they can.'

'Well, supposing I were to talk to the press, why should I talk to you? Something like the *Daily Mail* would give me more coverage. Your paper's not exactly world-famous. What's your circulation?'

'Never mind about that. People in the trade know about me. If you gave me a statement, the big papers would be sure to pick it up. At least you can trust me, as James and I knew each other for ages.'

Heather hesitated. 'James did mention you once or twice, it's true. Perhaps give me your phone number and I can think about whether I trust you, and if I want to talk to you about this.'

Lynch passed over his business card. 'I look forward to hearing from you. It would be in your interest to talk to me.'

'Goodbye, Mr Lynch,' Heather replied, holding his business card. She ordered another coffee as Lynch disappeared into the City crowds.

155

Chapter 26

The commissioner of the City of London police put down his gold Parker pen with a theatrical flourish. Checking through his desk calendar, Bob Watson remembered that, after their golf game, Sir Giles Palmer had asked to see him. Watson had no idea what Sir Giles wanted, but, as in all official interviews, his aim was to try to intimidate his visitor by stressing the importance of his own police rank. From their talk on the golf course, Watson knew that Sir Giles was unhappy with Gould's investigation. He checked in his mirror that his impressive uniform was in place as he rose to greet his guest.

'It's good to see you again, Giles. At the golf course the other day, you said you wanted to see me,' Watson said, as his visitor entered and took a seat. 'Perhaps you could start right at the beginning.'

'Thanks for agreeing to see me, Bob. As I said, it's about your force's handling of the murder in my offices on December 17th,' Sir Giles began. 'As far as I can see from reading the press, there's a cast-iron case against an ex-employee of mine, a young woman called Heather Morgan. When the police arrived, she was discovered with the body of her fiancé in a locked room. Everyone I've spoken to says you have a solid case against her. I can't see what other evidence you need, but she's allowed to wander around London free. She even had the nerve to come to my office, wanting her job back.'

'Well, you'll understand, Giles, that we have to go where the evidence leads. I've got one of my best men on the case. I'm sure DCI Gould is doing everything possible to uncover the killer.'

'I'm not at all convinced of that. I've been making enquiries about this DCI Gould. I've found that the main suspect was once a girlfriend of his. I feel that there are very good reasons to think he's covering up for her.'

'Yes, you said something along those lines before,' Watson said. 'Are you sure? That's a serious charge to make.'

'I assure you these are facts. And I can also say that unless Gould is taken off the case, I will have to inform the press about what I have discovered. I'm sure we can both imagine the sort of headline they will come up with. I'm always happy to support the police, but only when they are conducting things properly. Someone's been leaking against my company to that rag *Dirty Money*, and it might be time to do some leaking of my own.' Sir Giles's voice rose in anger as he spoke.

'I wouldn't go to the press making unfounded allegations if I were you, Giles. We don't look kindly on people interfering with our inquiries.'

'Well, I leave it in your hands, Bob,' Sir Giles said, standing up. 'I hope you're able to do something about this man Gould.'

'I'll certainly investigate what you have told me.'

'Good, then I expect I'll see you again at the golf course at the weekend. Are you in the Stableford competition?'

'Yes, but my handicap keeps edging up. Not like yours, eh?'

'Well, if I can just keep that slice out of my game ...'

The two men continued to talk about golf as the Commissioner escorted Sir Giles to the lift.

*

Later that day, Gould returned to his office after lunch. He walked through the open area where his team of detectives were located, then stopped in surprise when he saw the Commissioner talking to Cottrell. Gould went over to them, and noticed that they stopped talking when they saw him.

'Can I help you, sir?' Gould asked.

'Yes, come with me, David,' Bob Watson said, leading Gould to the Commissioner's large office.

'Did you want to brief on our murder inquiry, sir?' Gould asked.

'Yes, that's what I want to talk about,' the Commissioner said. 'Take a seat. I've had a visit from Sir Giles Palmer. I believe you know him.'

'Yes, he's the head of the company where the Faulkner murder took place.'

'Well, he's come to see me, and he's made serious allegations against you. He's convinced this Heather Morgan woman murdered her fiancé in his boardroom, and he wants her to face justice. He claims you won't arrest her because she used to be your girlfriend.'

'No, that's not true,' Gould said. 'That is, it's true that I used to know Heather. She's only one of a long list of suspects. We must look at them all carefully. The inquiry needs to be thorough.'

'Why didn't you hand the investigation over to someone else, bearing in mind your association with one of the main suspects? And, according to DS Cottrell, Heather Morgan originally called you instead of 999.'

'Yes, but that was just because she knew me. I would treat her the same as any other suspect.'

'You should have forwarded the call straight through to the emergency desk. According to Cottrell, she had to remind you to call the uniforms to come with you.'

'Well, yes . . .'

'I'm sorry to say this, David, but you're suspended until further notice. You're a fine officer, but I'll arrange for someone not so closely involved with the main suspect to head the inquiry. Hand over your warrant card to me now. Then you must leave the station. I should have you escorted out, but I'll spare you that indignity.'

Gould glared at the Commissioner. 'But Palmer's a major suspect. You can't just do what he says. I'm planning to make arrangements to search his home, as well as Ringer's. I've already applied for a warrant to go through his office.'

'I don't think so, David. I'm unhappy with the way this

investigation is going. I'm worried your friendship with this Morgan woman is clouding your judgement. I'm appointing another senior investigating officer – a new man from the Met.'

'But I feel I'm just about to make progress, sir.'

'Does this progress involve arresting Heather Morgan?'

'I'm looking at all other suspects first, sir. Obviously, I'll follow the evidence and arrest Heather if necessary.'

'I see. David, you have a large team of detectives on this case. How many of them agree with your approach?'

'I don't know, sir.'

'Well, I do. I've spoken to Fox and Cottrell, and they're both worried your judgement's been clouded.'

Gould started to protest further, but then spotted the Commissioner's furious expression, and silently handed over his warrant card.

Gould walked out of his meeting with the Commissioner with his thoughts in a whirl. In the adjoining office, he saw a detective chief inspector from the Metropolitan police he recognised from a training course in the past. He remembered his name, and recalled being totally unimpressed with him.

'Bill? Bill Wells? Don't say you're taking over,' Gould said.

'Hello, DCI Gould,' Wells said, offering his hand. 'Or should I call you Mr Gould, now you've been suspended? Yes, I'll be taking over the investigation into the Faulkner murder. I understand the Commissioner wants some new blood involved in the case, and that's going to be me.' He smiled mockingly.

Gould could not trust himself to shake his replacement's hand, and brushed past Wells without responding further. From what Wells had said, it was obvious that the Commissioner had planned to replace Gould even before their meeting.

As Gould walked along the corridor, he was surprised he did not experience shock or anger, but merely felt numb. Approaching his desk, he realised he no longer had his warrant card to carry. Was it his imagination or did his pocket really feel lighter? He could not face any sympathetic glances from his close colleagues, so he walked straight out of the police station without emptying his desk.

Gould stood outside on the street and watched the crowds streaming past. For the first time since his student days he realised he had nothing to do. To get his thoughts in order he decided to go to the nearest pub.

He rarely entered a pub during a day, except when on duty. His preconception was that men who drank in pubs in the middle of the afternoon were jobless failures. Looking around the near-empty bar, his prejudice was confirmed. The only man he recognised was an ex-policeman drinking in the corner, who Gould knew had been sacked for alcoholism. Gould could not face talking to the man, so he carefully sat in a corner where he could not be seen. Nursing his pint of bitter, he stared into the brown liquid and wondered what to do next.

All Gould's career had been spent as a police officer. He was too young to give up work, but what other job could he do?

He thought of those former colleagues of his who had jobs in the security industry. They were effectively available for hire to the highest bidder and were universally despised by serving police officers. Gould would rather have almost any other job than that. He looked out of the pub window at the featureless skyscrapers and felt he would hate being at a desk in one of those huge trading rooms. There was only one thing for it, he decided; he would have to fight to be reinstated. But how could he do that?

He thought back over the case. He seethed over the injustice of his suspension. It would be easy to become bitter, but he knew that would not help his case.

The old American maxim 'Don't get mad, get even' came to his mind. It was Sir Giles Palmer who had ruined his career, and Gould told himself somehow there must be a way to solve the case and get even.

Sir Giles's behaviour, combined with the allegations published in *Dirty Money*, convinced Gould the businessman was guilty of something: if not of murder, then of some other major crime. Even off duty, there had to be some way Gould could bring Sir Giles to justice. He decided to set out the available information to himself.

Gould was sure there was something suspicious about Sir Giles's regular trips to Los Angeles. Sir Giles was a money man and it was believable that he would visit Wall Street, but why Los Angeles? What was Los Angeles famous for: Hollywood studios, Disneyland, aerospace, freeways, a huge harbour? Gould decided it must be something to do with films. He had been there a few years before on an official visit and had formed a good relationship with Jeff Zug, and there might be a way of seeking his help. A visit to Los Angeles might help him to get his job back.

Gould had to be there when Sir Giles paid a visit. But how could he find out when Sir Giles would be there? He concluded that Heather was the only source who would still speak to him. He knew she no longer worked at Palmer Associates, but she might still have contacts in the company.

Gould resolved to find out exactly what Sir Giles was up to on these visits. He picked up his mobile phone to speak to Heather.

'Heather,' he said, as soon as she answered. 'I need your help. Can you meet me? I'm in a pub close to Snow Hill police station.'

*

Half an hour later, Gould carried a glass of white wine from the bar over to the table where Heather was sitting.

'I was so surprised to receive your call, David,' Heather said. 'It's quite like old times, meeting like this.'

'Yes, I think I ordered the correct drink. It's what you used to have.'

'It's fine. Now, what's this about? Should I have a solicitor with me?'

'No, I'm not on duty now. In fact, we're in the same boat,' Gould said. 'We've both been sacked by Giles Palmer.'

'What do you mean?' Heather asked. She listened wide-eyed as Gould told her of his suspension from the City police force. 'My God, that's terrible news. You've lost your career, and I've lost the only detective on my side in that interview. If Philippa were put in charge, she'd arrest me tomorrow. If your replacement believes her, I could go to jail.'

'You could be right. That's why I want you to help me. You know you said you were worried about Palmer's visits to Los Angeles?'

Heather nodded.

'Well, you've convinced me whatever is behind this comes from there,' Gould said. 'I need to know when Palmer next goes to California.'

'How could I find out? I've been sacked and banned from the office.'

'You're still friends with Margaret Prestwood, aren't you?'

'Yes, I would say so,' Heather replied.

'Can you ask her when Palmer will make his next visit to Los Angeles?'

Heather stared at Gould. 'Yes, I suppose I could ask her, but she might find it very strange. She would be bound to wonder why I wanted to know.'

'You once said the two of you were both rebels in the organisation. From what you've said, I am sure she would help you.'

Heather sipped her wine thoughtfully. 'Very well, David. I will do my best.'

*

Sir Giles Palmer looked out of the window of the boardroom at the office workers streaming by below. Alison was laying out the papers for the extraordinary general meeting that Derek had agreed to hold.

'It's good the police let us have this room back,' Sir Giles said. 'I suppose we don't know how many people are coming to this meeting, do we?'

'I don't believe so, Sir Giles. Mr Ringer has gone down to meet whoever turns up. He's asked me to take minutes.'

'Yes, very well. I'm looking forward to this meeting, you know. If it goes as well as the one I had yesterday at the Commissioner's office, I shall be pleased. I wonder where DCI Gould is now – probably at the labour exchange, looking for a new job.' He chuckled.

'Yes, Sir Giles. That sounds like Mr Ringer now.'

Derek entered the boardroom, followed by Alf Coates. Alf and Alison took care to appear not to know each other.

'This is Alfred Coates, Sir Giles,' Derek said. 'He says he's acquired the shares that Fretwell used to own.'

Sir Giles stretched out his hand to shake Alf's. 'How do you do, Mr Coates? I gather we will be working together.'

'Oh, you can call me Alf, Sir Giles. Yes, that's right. I've been admiring your company from afar, and I decided I would like a piece of the action.'

'Yes, well, I hope we can cooperate. So, let's start this meeting. Is anyone else likely to appear, Derek?'

Derek checked the clock. 'Well, it's after the time scheduled for the meeting, so legally we can start. Please, everyone, take your seats.'

Sir Giles and Alf sat down, while Sir Giles indicated for Alison to sit next to him.

'Could you tell us your name for the records, Mr Coates?' Derek asked.

'I'm Alfred Coates,' Alf said.

'I used to know you as Alf Jones,' Derek said.

'Yes, well, I think there are lots of things we would like to forget about past transactions, don't you, Sir Giles?'

'I don't know what you mean by that, Mr Coates,' Sir Giles

said. 'I will keep this formal, if you don't mind. Perhaps you can tell the meeting what your plans are for your minority shareholding in Palmer Associates.'

'Are you so sure it's a minority shareholding, Sir Giles?'

'Mr Fretwell owned some 33 per cent of the shares,' Derek said, as Alison took notes. 'Sir Giles owns 40 per cent. The remainder are with various institutional holders. I'm sure they won't want to sell to someone like you, Mr Coates.'

'That used to be the case, Mr Ringer. I have increased my shareholding recently. The price was quite low. It looks as if some investors don't like the publicity your company has been receiving lately.'

'What do you know about the publicity we've been receiving, Mr Coates?' Sir Giles asked sharply. 'You're not behind it, are you?'

'I'd rather not say, Sir Giles,' Alf replied, with a smile. 'Let's just say I've been happy to take advantage of it.'

'And are you seriously saying that you have a majority shareholding?'

'I have a large shareholding. Let's stick to that. I'm happy for you to keep running the company as you have done. I will be sure to let you know when I want changes.' Alf looked around at Sir Giles and Derek and smiled. 'I'm confident we can work together in the short term.'

'What do you mean, the short term?'

'I'll be sure to let you know, Sir Giles. Now, is this the exact place where that poor man was killed?'

'What do you know about the murder, Mr Coates?'

'You seem to be asking a lot of questions, Sir Giles. Shall we just concentrate on the matters on the agenda? Could you read them out, Miss Coates?'

Sir Giles exchanged a horrified glance with Derek, the implications of the shared surname filling their minds. 'Are you related to this man, Alison?'

Alison glanced at Alf, who nodded. 'Yes, Sir Giles. Mr Coates is my grandfather.'

Sir Giles's face went white as thoughts of what Alison might have told her grandfather passed through his head. 'Miss Coates, you're dismissed from the end of the week.'

Alison stood up. 'You can't do that. I haven't done nothing wrong.'

Sir Giles glared at her. 'That's what Heather Morgan said, and it didn't do her any good.'

Alf came to stand by Alison. 'Don't do anything hasty. Alison's a good girl.'

'That goes for you too, Mr Coates. As far as I'm concerned, you and your family can go hang,' Sir Giles said, as he strode out of the office.

There was an embarrassed silence after Sir Giles left the boardroom. Then Alf stood up. 'I take it this meeting is at an end. I am prepared to ignore Sir Giles's rudeness for the time being, but not for very much longer. Goodbye, Mr Ringer. I will be in touch.'

Alf Coates whistled cheerfully to himself as he left the building.

PART 4

CAN GOULD
RETURN TO FAVOUR?

Chapter 27

Later that day, Heather sat in her usual coffee bar near Liverpool Street station and waited for Margaret to join her. She recognised a few old colleagues from Palmer Associates whom she used to regard as friends, but she noticed they all pretended not to have seen her. After a while, she kept her own eyes down to avoid any more hurt. Losing her job and being a murder suspect was bad enough, but, in some strange way, being snubbed by people she had thought were her friends seemed to be even more upsetting. Then she heard a friendly greeting.

'Heather, how are you?' Margaret stood before her.

Heather had never been so pleased to see her friend. Margaret's hippy-style persona sometimes used to annoy her, but now she could not stop herself from jumping up and hugging Margaret.

'Thank God you could come. It's so long since I've seen someone I know from work,' Heather said.

'That's fine. We're still friends, whatever happens. How is the job hunting going?'

'I've applied for hundreds of jobs, but I'm as popular around the City as the plague was four hundred years ago. Companies don't want to employ murder suspects. Men think I might suddenly stab them in some fit of anger. The women in personnel see me as some sort of mad tart. So I've stopped looking for work now.'

Margaret held Heather's hand. 'You poor thing. But what can I do? I'd love to see you return to the office, but you know old Palmer won't have you back.'

'It's about him. I wanted your help.' Heather paused. 'You remember those trips that Palmer made to LA?'

Margaret nodded.

'Well, I want to know when his next one is,' Heather said.

'Why should you care? I know you were always suspicious of them, but you don't work for Palmer Associates anymore.'

'Well, I saw David Gould yesterday, and Palmer's had him suspended from the City police. David thinks if I can give him this information it will help him somehow.'

'Why should David Gould want to know about Sir Giles's business trips?'

'I don't know, but he said it was important. It might clear me. You will find out when he's visiting California, won't you?'

Margaret paused. 'Well, I know he's got a trip there lined up next Tuesday, but don't tell anyone I told you. He usually takes the overnight BA flight from Heathrow.'

'Thank you, Margaret. You're a true friend.' Heather smiled, feeling happy for the first time since her fiancé's murder.

*

Later that day, Margaret knocked on Sir Giles Palmer's office. Hearing a muffled 'Come in,' she entered nervously.

'Yes?' Sir Giles said when he saw Margaret.

'I'm sorry to bother you, Sir Giles,' she said. 'But it's about Heather Morgan.'

'Oh, that woman I sacked. I thought I'd heard the last of her. What about her?'

'We had lunch today, and Heather asked me an interesting question.'

'What do you mean?'

'Apparently, her old boyfriend David Gould wanted to find out when you're next visiting Los Angeles.'

'Gould? Why does he want to know? I had him sacked as well.'

'I don't think Heather knew all the details, but he told her he was trying to make sure she's not convicted for James's murder. Everyone knows she and Gould used to be an item. If Gould finds out who's really guilty of James's murder, then ...' Margaret's voice tailed off.

'What do you mean?'

'I don't need to spell it out, but I suggest you take steps to stop Gould.'

'What did you tell this Morgan woman anyway?'

'I said you had a trip to LA on Tuesday.'

'But I'm not going there any time soon.'

'I suggest you change your plans, then.'

Sir Giles stared at Margaret with astonishment for a long time, then smiled. 'Well done, Margaret. Perhaps on consideration a trip to LA on Tuesday would be useful after all. I have to dispose of some . . . investments.'

Margaret nodded and left Sir Giles's office. Neither of them was aware that Alison Coates, seated outside Sir Giles's office, had been listening to their conversation through her intercom. Once Margaret had left, Alison picked up the internal phone.

'Hello, darling,' she began. 'You know you asked me about old Palmer's overseas trips? He's off to California on Tuesday.'

'Thanks, honey,' Linus replied, keeping his voice down. 'That's very interesting. I just might follow him there.'

Chapter 28

A few hours later, Philippa Cottrell was looking dejectedly at the files on the Faulkner murder, spread out before her. She had been told that Gould had been suspended and realised that she was temporarily the senior investigating officer. She was pondering the next steps for the inquiry when she saw the Commissioner walking towards her, followed by a man in his mid-fifties. Instinctively she stood up to greet them.

'Ah, DS Cottrell,' the Commissioner said. 'I have someone for you to meet. Philippa, this is DCI Wells – Bill Wells. He's been temporarily transferred from the Met. He'll be leading on the Faulkner murder while David Gould's suspended.'

Cottrell politely shook the man's hand. 'Welcome to the City force, sir,' she said.

'I'm sure you will support Bill as much as possible,' the Commissioner continued. 'I'm worried the Faulkner case has not been solved yet. From what I've been told, there is a very strong suspect in the frame, and, if the evidence is there, I expect her to be charged as soon as possible. Do I make myself clear?'

'I am sure Philippa and I will be able to work together, sir,' Wells said. 'I aim to act as a fresh pair of eyes on this case. From what I hear, you were also worried about Gould's approach to the case.'

'DCI Gould was – is – a fine officer, sir, but I am happy to support DCI Wells as much as possible,' Cottrell said.

She tried to analyse her initial reaction to Wells. She was pleased to have a senior officer to take the pressure off her, but, like all City police officers, she had an unspoken animosity to staff being transferred from the larger Metropolitan force and taking over investigations. Trying to put any prejudice to one side, she concluded she still found Wells unimpressive as a man.

She instinctively regarded him as an officer serving out his time until retirement.

She felt the Commissioner's cold glance on her and reminded herself that, while she had respected her old lover David Gould as a person and a detective, it was her duty to support any senior officer that the Commissioner decided to place over her.

'I'm pleased to have your support ... Philippa,' Wells began. 'I'm looking forward to taking the Faulkner case forward. From what I've heard, this Heather Morgan woman is lucky not to have been arrested. What do you think?'

'Well, DCI Gould wanted to look at every other suspect first, sir,' Cottrell said. She blushed as she felt herself defending her old friend.

'Yes, well, you know how I feel about Gould's friendship with Heather Morgan. I've decided we need a fresh approach,' the Commissioner said. 'I'll leave you to it, then, Bill.'

'Thank you, sir,' Wells said, as the Commissioner slapped him on the shoulder and left. 'Well, DS Cottrell, the Commissioner has said it all. I'm the senior investigating officer and I trust I can rely on your full support.'

'Of course, sir,' Cottrell replied.

'Very good. There's no time for idle chatter. First, let's go through the suspects in the Faulkner murder,' Wells said, sitting next to Cottrell.

For the next twenty minutes, Cottrell ran through the various suspects as set out in the Faulkner case files in front of her. Finally, Wells turned to Cottrell to ask the question she had been dreading. 'So, have you found any reason not to charge the obvious suspect, who is Heather Morgan, the woman who was found alone with the body?'

Cottrell tried to think of anything to say to defend Gould's reluctance to charge Heather. 'To be honest, no, sir, I haven't. DCI Gould said we knew she had ketamine in her bloodstream, and so she must have been drugged and framed by some other person.'

'And you don't agree?'

'He might be right, but Morgan could have taken it herself for some strange reason – or it could be totally irrelevant. We'd still have to tell the defence team about it. She could make a case for self-defence if Faulkner had been trying to rape her – but only if she admitted killing him, which she hasn't done yet. She had motive, means and opportunity, and she's the only suspect we could probably get a conviction for.'

Wells slammed his fists on the desk. 'I think you're right. The Commissioner has brought me in to secure a conviction, and that's what I intend to do. Let's bring Heather Morgan in for questioning under caution.'

'Yes, sir. I will arrange that as soon as I can.'

*

Cottrell entered a wine bar in Greenwich that evening, close to where she lived, and bought a drink. She looked around to make sure no one had spotted her. She saw Gould holding a drink in a secluded corner of the bar and went over to speak to him. 'I was surprised to get your call, David. I shouldn't be talking to you, now you're suspended.'

'Yes, I know, and I appreciate it,' Gould said. He reached out to touch her hand, trying to reassure her, but she moved it away. 'But I've got to try to get my job back. It's my whole life.'

'David, I know you're a good cop – a great cop, in fact – and I'm sorry you can't do the job you love any more. What are you going to do? You're far too young to retire.'

'I can't give up, Philippa,' Gould said. 'I'm a detective, and a damned good one. If the City of London police won't employ me, I'll have to go private.'

'I can't see you as a private detective, following up seedy divorce cases. You're worth more than that.'

'I believe you're right. That's why I am going to do my best to solve this case. I need to find out who really killed James

Faulkner, so I can clear Heather's name and get my job back.'

'You're not going to obstruct the police investigation, are you? I have a new boss now, DCI Wells, and it is my duty to support him as much as I can. You won't be difficult, will you, David? I'd hate to ruin your reputation by arresting you for getting in our way – but I would do it, if I had to.'

'I don't want to put you in a difficult position, Philippa, but I need to know what is happening in this case. We both know Heather's not guilty, and we can't see her charged with murder when she's innocent.'

Cottrell reached out her hand to touch Gould's shoulder. 'But, David, I don't know she's innocent. It's the police's duty to go where the evidence leads us, and it keeps pointing us to Heather Morgan. Your past affair with this woman has ruined your career, and you can't see it, can you? You must forget you ever knew her. You should have passed her call on to the uniformed officers as soon as it came in and stood down. You have to leave the case to Bill Wells now.'

'I've met Wells before. He's just a paper pusher. He's more concerned with ticking all the right boxes than finding the real murderer.'

'The Commissioner has decided we need an SIO who follows the rules, and he's probably right. I'm sorry, David, but I can't meet you like this any more. I can't give you any privileged information. Good luck with everything. I must be going.'

'Don't worry. I won't cause any difficulties for you. Good luck with the career, Philippa.'

'I don't need luck. I had a good role model: the old David Gould. I'll try to do what he would do. You should do what he would do as well. Goodbye, David.'

Ex-DCI Gould gazed thoughtfully at Cottrell as she left the wine bar.

Chapter 29

Michael Dawson sipped his gin and tonic in a bar close to the Monument. He looked with distaste around at the twenty-something dealers talking to each other in loud voices. The disco music sounded like a tuneless racket to him.

He thought back fondly to his days in the officers' mess at the various army bases he had served in. His army days were the high point of his life so far. He reflected on how much he had enjoyed working with military men who understood the meaning of discipline. He knew his military colleagues would lay down their lives to help him, and they knew that he would do the same for them.

His childhood, too, had been in army boarding schools, as his family followed his sergeant-major father around the world. He knew his late father would have been proud that he, Michael, had become an officer in the SAS. He was glad his father had not lived to see him leaving the services in disgrace. Since then, Michael's experiences in civilian life had generally not been successful.

Suddenly he saw a reflection of himself in a pub mirror dressed in a suit, with short hair and wearing his regimental tie. It suddenly struck him how he must appear to the people around him. He was a bit older than most of the others in his office and he felt out of touch with the latest fashions, music and mores. He would have liked to see some of his younger colleagues facing the discipline of army training. His father had always said he regretted the ending of national service in the fifties. Michael Dawson was too young to remember those days, but he instinctively felt he would have been more at home then.

He told himself that his old-fashioned views might be the reason he had had no recent successes with women. But he felt that Heather Morgan might be different. His father would have called her a fine figure of a woman, and Michael felt the same. Yes, he decided he would invite her out and see how he got on. He felt he was ten times the man that James Faulkner had been, and, with his rival dead, there should now be no barrier to pursuing Heather.

Just then, he saw a familiar figure from his office in front of him.

'Hi, Mike,' Linus said in his American accent.

Michael hated having his first name shortened. 'Michael, to be precise. What can I do for you, Linus?'

'I've been meaning to talk to you ... Michael. What can we do to help Heather?'

'What do you mean?'

'I've been asking around and I think she's innocent. We can't let her be charged with murder.'

'I don't think Heather needs your help, Linus. Why don't we leave the case to the police? If you've found anything out, you should tell them.'

'The police aren't always right. I know that more than most.'

'What are you talking about? Who are you, anyway?'

'Just someone who wants to see justice done.'

'Heather's a friend of mine, and I'll give her all the support she needs.'

'OK, then. I'll see you around, Mike.' Linus sauntered off with his easy athletic gait, as Michael stared at him open-mouthed.

Michael felt upset by Linus, who did not fit the stereotype of a City worker. He was becoming ever more convinced that the City of London was full of people he regarded as wasters. James – a typical example – was now dead, but there was still a lot of disorder, which Michael felt his duty to put right.

Michael looked down at the carpet in the bar. Its dark red colour reminded him of the blood that he had seen often in the past: gallons of blood pouring out of dead bodies in a desert far away and a long time ago. *Yet who would have thought the old man to have so much blood in him?* He remembered this as a quote from *Macbeth*, which he had been forced to study at school. He had hated the play then. Since he had seen so much blood in Afghanistan, he could understand the sentiment better, which made him hate the play even more.

Michael looked around at the young girls in skimpy clothes, and the young City traders who were chatting them up in their smart suits, with contempt. He resented the fact he had to compete with these people in the job market. He had seen so much more of the darker side of life than they had, and he knew he could do a better job than them. Nevertheless, he had to face the fact that employers in the City seemed to prefer young candidates, no matter how lacking in experience they were.

That young man who had been killed, James Faulkner, was one of the worst of them. He had wormed his way into the affections of Heather Morgan, the woman Michael loved. Michael admitted to himself he was jealous of the dead man. He was not sorry James had died and saw no reason to pretend otherwise.

Michael expected the police to arrest someone soon. He knew Gould was suspicious of him. Michael thought of his military training, and he unconsciously studied his hands. He had been trained to kill quickly and painlessly, and he could see why he was a suspect.

Michael decided the only way to clear his name was to help the police find someone to put in the dock for James's murder. Yes, he told himself, he and Heather could make quite a team. If he did find someone for the police to charge to clear both their names, Heather should be grateful to him. He had a vision of Heather in bed waiting for him, then shook his head to get the thought out of his mind, telling himself that, unless he took some decisive action, he would never see that sight in reality.

He decided he would talk to Heather and plan an alternative investigation. There would be no need to tell the police until it was successfully concluded.

Chapter 30

Heather was startled to hear the front doorbell in her flat. Since James's death, it was an unusual event for it to ring. She had developed a taste for trashy daytime television and was at first annoyed to have her favourite programme interrupted. She then reminded herself that she had to try to re-establish herself in the world of work and among her friends. Heather felt these conflicting emotions as she pressed the intercom. It was with mixed feelings that she recognised Michael Dawson through the security glass.

'Hello, Heather, it's Michael. Can I come in?' he said.

'I guess so,' Heather replied as she buzzed to allow Michael in. She wondered if she was wise to allow this man into her flat, but she was curious to learn more about how things were in her old office. Michael had always been kind to her, especially since James had been killed, and he was an attractive man. Perhaps it was time to launch herself into the world of dating.

'Michael, come in,' she said, as she unlocked her door. 'How are you enjoying my old job?'

'I don't want to talk about work, love,' Michael said. 'I just came around to see how you are.'

'Not too good, to be honest.'

'Why don't we have lunch today? It might cheer you up.'

'That's all right. You don't have to invite me out of my flat. I'm not quite a charity case yet.'

'No, I'm inviting you out because you are an attractive woman.'

Heather stared at Michael to see if she believed him. 'Very well, then,' she said, nodding. 'Wait there and I'll be ready in ten minutes.'

'Sure, I'll wait for you,' Michael said.

While Heather changed in the bedroom, Michael sat in an armchair. He idly looked through a few of the photographs on her coffee table, wondering which of the men were old boyfriends and which family members. He was startled when he recognised David Gould in one photo.

He jumped when Heather appeared, looking much more glamorous than he had seen her before.

'You look great, love. I mean, Heather,' Michael said. 'Let's have a meal in that Italian place I spotted on the corner.'

'Very well. I don't go out much nowadays, but I've heard good reports of it.'

A few minutes later, Michael was holding the chair for Heather in the restaurant.

'You can hold back on the charm offensive, Michael,' Heather said. 'That's your officer background coming into play, is it?'

'No, I'm just being polite,' Michael said. 'What do you fancy to eat, Heather? I'm paying, of course.'

After a few minutes of polite conversation, Heather asked the question that really concerned her. 'Why have you asked me out, Michael?'

Michael sighed. 'Why can't you believe I find you attractive?' He paused as he caught Heather's glance. 'Well, apart from the obvious, I thought we could work together to find out who really killed James.'

'That's what I'd like to know, but that's the police's job. In any case, how do you know it wasn't me? Come to think of it, how do I know it wasn't you?'

'Because I know you and I think you know me. Neither of us is really the killer type. Except in the forces, in my case, but that's different.'

'Did you really kill people when you were in the SAS?'

'Yes, but don't worry; I didn't kill James and I won't suddenly attack you.'

Heather thought for a while as the waiter delivered their meals.

'Oh, very well, I'll take part in your investigation. I don't have much to lose, but let's keep our meetings in public.'

'As you wish. I won't force you to do anything you're not comfortable with.'

'So, let's get down to business,' Heather said. 'What do we know about Palmer Associates' accounts? We can both agree it's something to do with them. Thinking about it, perhaps we're better placed than the police to find out what's really happening.'

'Well, the investments are in small offshore companies – some in Luxembourg, some in the British Virgin Islands. The registrars won't tell us anything about them. They will only talk to Palmer or Ringer. I think James must have thought they were up to something illegal, and somebody had him killed.'

'So, if that's a dead end, let's approach it from the other side,' Heather said. 'Where do we suspect they were invested?'

'Well, if everything is legitimate, the investments should be recorded eventually in the books of Hollywood film companies. But the returns look too large and regular to be based on those.'

'OK, shall one of us check the shareholdings of the big Hollywood film companies and see if the name of Palmer Associates appears?'

'That sounds like a plan.'

'Also,' Heather said, 'we should talk to Robin Lynch.'

Michael looked surprised. 'Who's he?'

'Lynch is the editor of *Dirty Money* – you know, that magazine everyone in the City is talking about,' Heather said. 'He published vague stuff about Palmer Associates' accounts being dodgy – not specific enough to be sued. James said he knew Lynch from school, and apparently phoned him up just before he was killed. James denied leaking anything to Lynch before the article was published. Lynch came to see me not long ago. He says he's doing some sleuthing himself. Perhaps we could share resources with him.'

'Can we trust Lynch?' Michael asked.

'I don't know. He has a reputation for being honest, which is unusual in the City. Shall we see him together?'

'That might work. I wonder if he's found anything out already. Why don't you give me his phone number and address, and I'll contact him to say we'll talk to him?'

'That sounds like a plan,' Heather said, taking Lynch's business card from her handbag and passing it to Michael.

'Now, our strong point is that I'm still working for Palmer Associates,' Michael said. 'What can I do from within the company?'

'Find out more about Palmer's visits to LA,' Heather said. She saw no reason to tell Michael that David Gould had already suggested this to her. 'I'm sure the answer's out there somehow. If you and Margaret work together, you should be able to find out some useful information.'

Michael waited for a moment before he replied. 'I'm not sure about Margaret Prestwood, Heather. How far can we trust her?'

Heather looked surprised. 'She's my best friend in the company. I always felt we were on the same wavelength.'

'Humour me. Let's say Margaret's really working for Palmer or some other dodgy investor, then that Earth Mother image would be a perfect cover.'

'I know you don't like her, but she's not a killer.'

'We'll see about that,' Michael said shortly. 'She has to be a suspect, in any case. And, if we're reviewing the suspects, let's go through who else was at the party. There's Linus Murray. What do we really know about him?'

'All I know is he came over from the company's LA office.'

'Who recruited him in the first place? Who then suggested he come to London?'

'The only person who could tell us that would be Alison Coates, who keeps all the company's personnel files – which presents us with an obvious problem.'

Michael winced. 'I see what you mean. Alison is his girlfriend and would be sure to tell him if I started asking questions like that.'

'Exactly. Let's leave Linus for the moment. How about Fretwell? Could he really be as stupid as everyone says?'

'I don't know,' Michael said. 'I remember him talking to James at the party. He seemed to be interested in any suspicions James had about the accounts. I can't see what motive Fretwell would have to kill James. He had the opportunity, though.'

'But that brings it back to us. The police know we danced together that night, and that you hated James and fancied me.'

'And still do.'

'And still do,' Heather echoed, 'which is why you invited me out. That is the only reason, isn't it? Why are you so keen to prove me innocent, Michael? Do you know something I don't? Like you're really the murderer, for instance.'

'No, I just want to see justice. Call it my sense of fair play, or perhaps I am an old-fashioned gentleman; I like to help a damsel in distress. And we both know you're in distress now.'

'You could be right. It's no fun being everyone's favourite murder suspect,' Heather replied with a rueful smile. Suddenly, she noticed a middle-aged man standing in front of her. She glanced at Michael, but he seemed as surprised as she was. Then she noticed Philippa Cottrell standing behind the man.

'Who the hell are you?' Michael asked.

'Miss Heather Morgan? We've been to your flat, then we saw you coming in here. My name is DCI Bill Wells, on loan to the City of London police,' said the stranger, flashing a warrant card.

'And I'm Michael Dawson,' Michael said, standing up. 'I don't recognise you. What's happened to DCI Gould?'

'I am now the senior investigating officer into the murder of James Faulkner,' Wells said. 'Miss Morgan, please come with me. I have a warrant for your arrest for murder. You do not have to say anything, but it may harm your defence if you do not mention when questioned something which you later rely on in court.

Anything you do say may be given in evidence.'

'Don't say anything, Heather. They can't have any evidence against you,' Michael said.

'And who are you, sir?' Wells asked.

'This is Michael Dawson, sir,' Cottrell said. 'You'll have seen his name on our files.'

'Ah, yes, I remember, and what is this matter to do with you, Mr Dawson?' Wells asked, with a sneer.

'I'm just a friend of Miss Morgan, and I intend to stand up for her,' Michael said.

'Please stand aside, Mr Dawson. Creating a scene won't help the situation, and we don't want to arrest you as well,' Cottrell said. 'Now if you'll take a few changes of clothes from your flat, Miss Morgan, we'll carry on this conversation at Snow Hill station.'

'Give me the name of your solicitor, Heather,' Michael said. 'I'll phone him for you.'

'And people may wonder why you are so interested in Miss Morgan's welfare, Mr Dawson,' Wells said.

Heather turned to Michael. 'Don't annoy them any more, Michael. My solicitor's name is on this letter.' She handed him an envelope. 'Call him for me. I think I need some help, now David's no longer in charge.'

Michael stood up as Heather was led out of the restaurant by Wells and Cottrell. He pulled his mobile out of his case and dialled the number Heather had left. 'Mr Bradshaw,' he said. 'My name's Michael Dawson. Your client, Heather Morgan, has been arrested on a murder charge. She needs your help.'

Michael then dialled the number for Robin Lynch that Heather had also given him.

*

A few minutes later, Heather sat in the back of a police car next to Wells, and directed the driver to her flat.

'We have a warrant to search your property, Miss Morgan,' Wells said. 'You are entitled to be there, but if you attempt to interfere in any way, you will be forcibly removed.'

'I understand, but I could help you if you tell me what you are looking for.'

'I am not obliged to tell you that,' Wells said. As they entered the flat, he told Heather, 'You may choose two changes of clothes, but no more.'

Heather nodded and sat disconsolately on her settee as Wells, Cottrell and DS Fox searched all the cupboards and drawers in the flat. She blushed as her underwear was rummaged through by Fox's gloved hands. The only time the police officers spoke to her was when they found the photograph of David Gould that Heather kept at the back of the sideboard drawer.

'We'll leave this behind, Miss Morgan,' Wells said, 'but DCI Gould can't help you now.' He laughed to himself as Cottrell led Heather back to the car on the way to the prison cells at Snow Hill police station. Wells obviously felt his day was going well.

*

The next day, Robin Lynch was sitting in his office, typing his latest article into his terminal. He cursed as he heard a knock, then rose to go to the door.

'Yes?' Lynch demanded, keeping the door only slightly open. When he recognised his visitor, he tried to close it, but the man pushed his way in.

'What do you want? I told you I didn't want to see you again,' Lynch shouted.

The man did not speak but pulled out an automatic rifle. A single shot entered Lynch's heart. Lynch's mouth opened in surprise as he slumped over his desk. Blood flooded out over the papers as the killer walked unhurriedly away.

Chapter 31

At about the time Lynch was being murdered, Gould stood in the long customs queue at Los Angeles International Airport. A long way ahead of him, Gould could see Sir Giles Palmer in the line to pass through customs. As a first-class passenger, Sir Giles had been allowed to leave the plane first.

Gould was confident he had not been spotted, but moved behind a pillar to be safe. He looked around to gain a feel for the surroundings, as his police training had drilled into him.

He had been in the city three years previously on a fraud investigation, which had been successfully concluded due to cooperation between the City of London police and the LAPD. Although it was easy to make jokes about the smog and artificiality of the city, he had enjoyed his previous visit, which had given him a reasonable knowledge of the area. One particularly useful outcome was his professional friendship with Lieutenant Jeff Zug of the LA police department.

Gould had recently e-mailed Zug from his home address, asking for his help on a personal basis. Gould had not volunteered the information that he was suspended from duty, and he was not sure how much weight his personal request for help would carry.

Looking around at the various officials, Gould was delighted to see Zug standing at the side of the queue. The American detective seemed to be casting a professional eye over the long line of tourists waiting for approval to enter the United States. Gould could tell Zug had spotted him but was too professional to give any sign of recognition.

Gould idly watched as a couple of dogs sniffed the arriving luggage, looking for drugs or explosives. A moment later, he was startled by a dark-skinned Latino police officer touching his elbow.

'Hey, bud, move out of the line. We want a word with you,' the policeman said in a hostile tone. The passengers near Gould instinctively moved away and looked at him with distaste, no doubt assuming he was some sort of criminal. Gould had not noticed that Linus Murray was among those in the line behind him, and was watching him with interest.

'Through that door. Move,' the police officer said, pushing Gould in the back.

Gould considered protesting, but he silently picked up his bag and followed the police officer into a small room nearby. The man slammed the door behind him.

'Is there some sort of trouble, officer?' Gould asked, looking around nervously.

Just then, through the two-way mirror on one side of the room, he saw a face he recognised approaching.

'Hi there, Dave, good to see you,' Lieutenant Zug said, once the door had shut behind him. 'It must have been three years since you were here. How are you doing?' He shook Gould's hand.

'Jeff, I'm really glad to see you. I thought I was under arrest for something,' Gould said, indicating the Latino officer.

'I thought it would be better this way. This is my sergeant, Martinez. He's a nice guy, really.'

Martinez's teeth gleamed white as he shook Gould's hand. 'Pleased to meet you, sir. No hard feelings, I hope. People tell me I can be pretty scary when I want to.'

'You played it just right,' Gould said, with a wry smile. 'You certainly convinced me. It's a good learning experience, thinking one's on the wrong side of the law for once.'

'Well, good to meet you, sir, and welcome to the United States,' Martinez said, as he watched the arriving tourists through the two-way mirror.

'Have a seat, Dave,' Zug said. 'It's good to see you again. It would be great to talk about old times, but I guess this is a business trip.'

'That's right. I sent you the details of a character called Sir Giles Palmer. He runs an outfit called Palmer Associates in the City of London. There was a murder there recently.'

'Palmer's in the line ahead of you. I've got two men tailing him.' Zug paused. 'Your message didn't tell me what you suspect him of doing.'

'That's what we don't know. He visits LA once a month and we're sure he must be involved in something illegal. There's a good chance the murder in London is part of it.'

'Something illegal, you say. That doesn't give us much to go on, does it?'

'I know, but it's the only line of inquiry we have at the moment.' Gould's voice faded away lamely.

Zug sighed. 'I was surprised to get an e-mail from your personal address, David. Is there anything you want to tell me?'

Gould, embarrassed, decided to confess what his position was. 'Well, Jeff, you may as well know I've been suspended from duty. I had to pay for my flight here myself. This is an unofficial visit. I'm suspended because of this murder case. They say I bent the rules to help an old girlfriend, who's a suspect.'

'And did you?' Zug asked, keeping his eyes fixed on Gould's face.

'In a way. But you'd have done the same thing. I just know she's innocent of murder and I want to clear her. If she is proved guilty, I'd be the first one to arrest her and put her away for life.'

Zug waited a few seconds before replying. 'You're certainly asking a big favour, Dave. I'm trying to track down some pervert who's been shooting innocent actresses just so he can video them. Then he's selling the videos on the internet. It makes your skin crawl. One of my best men has been undercover over in London, trying to pin him down. That has to be my top priority. How's it going to look if my boss finds out I'm using official LAPD staff to help some limey cop who's been suspended?'

'Yes, I know how much I'm asking,' Gould replied. 'It's up to you if you want to help. I wouldn't blame you if you played by the rules and wouldn't have anything to do with me.'

Zug thought for a long time. Gould felt himself starting to sweat in the airless office despite the noisy air conditioning. He looked vacantly out at the line of tourists through the reflective glass window and wondered what he would do if Zug turned him down.

Finally, Zug gave a rueful smile. 'I suppose I'm just a sucker for a hard luck story. I have a week's leave due and I'm not doing anything special. I'll lend you a hand, but it'd better be good. If it doesn't look promising, you're on your own.'

For the first time since he had been suspended, Gould gave an unforced smile. He had an insane wish to hug the hard-bitten cop in front of him.

'Thanks, Jeff. You won't regret it,' was all Gould said.

'I'm not sure about that. I'm getting cold feet already, Dave,' Zug said, as he led Gould out of the office.

Chapter 32

While Gould waited in Los Angeles International Airport, Cottrell looked out of her office window at the freezing rain falling on the City of London office blocks outside. She riffled through the papers on the Faulkner murder, to see if there was anything the inquiry had missed.

The only minor recent item of progress was that it seemed no one had seen any member of James's family at the party, and it appeared James's father and brother would have to be eliminated from the inquiry. While Robin Lynch, the editor of *Dirty Money*, had been seen by several people outside Palmer Associates' offices on the evening of the fateful party, there was no evidence that he had ventured beyond the lobby. These two lines of inquiry had never been very promising, but it was reassuring for the detectives to see them eliminated. The police were still suspicious of Lynch's motives, but Cottrell concluded that he did not seem to have had the opportunity to kill James.

Cottrell told herself she agreed with Gould that Heather did not seem to be the murdering kind, and the drug in her system needed explaining. Cottrell would genuinely have liked to find some way of clearing Gould's ex-girlfriend, but she could see nothing to work on.

As an exercise, she pretended she was defence counsel, trying to rebut the prosecution's case that Heather had killed James. There was no doubt Heather Morgan had been in the right place at the right time to have committed the murder. She had motive, means and opportunity. Her fingerprints were all over the murder weapon. Heather was in the cells right now, which logic told Cottrell was the right place for her. Cottrell felt loyal enough to Gould to continue to look at other suspects, but she knew Wells was convinced of Heather's guilt, and, although Cottrell had a low opinion of Wells as a detective, she felt he was probably correct.

Cottrell shrugged her shoulders and continued to look through the file papers. Gould had told her in confidence of his trip to Los Angeles, and she hoped he was being successful in the Californian sunshine. She looked again at the London rain and wondered what Gould could come up with.

Just then, the phone rang. After Cottrell had identified herself, there was a long pause before she spoke again. 'I'll be right over.'

She walked over to the desk of Bill Wells, who was writing a self-congratulatory report to the Commissioner describing Heather Morgan's arrest.

'Gov,' Cottrell said. 'There's a report come in of a killing that could be concerned with our case. It looks as if Robin Lynch has been shot dead in his office.'

Wells looked at her in shock. He did not want anything to interfere with his case against Heather Morgan and had a feeling this latest incident would complicate things. 'I'll come with you,' he said, standing up.

The two officers took a police car and sped through the City streets to the scene of the murder.

Chapter 33

A few minutes after their meeting in the customs hall, Gould and Zug were outside Los Angeles International Airport, watching the Avis car rental booth. A man in an Avis jacket was showing Sir Giles to the car he had just hired. Sir Giles was obviously berating the man for being late with the car, but it was too far away for the police officers to hear his words.

'I don't think Palmer's a satisfied customer,' Gould said. 'It's lucky for us Avis were slow getting him his car.'

'Luck had nothing to do with it. I told the Avis guy to delay things until we're ready,' Zug replied. 'He owed me a favour. OK, we're off now.'

Zug moved his car across the road and followed Sir Giles's red Pontiac into the freeway traffic towards downtown LA. The sun shone brightly in the California sky. For a moment, Gould felt his mind move into holiday mode. The exotic surroundings seemed to induce a relaxed frame of mind. Then Gould recalled the weak light he was used to in London, slipped on his sunglasses and reminded himself of his aim to work hard to be reinstated as detective chief inspector in the City of London police.

*

All the next day, Gould kept an eye on Sir Giles's motel room from a hired car parked on the opposite side of the road, but there was no sign of Sir Giles leaving. He checked his watch and realised he soon had to be back at his hotel room to meet Zug. Gould found it hard to keep awake, and he was about to call the stakeout off when he saw Sir Giles come to the door, yawning. Gould smiled to himself as he reflected that both the suspended policeman and the suspect seemed to be suffering the same jetlag.

Sir Giles walked to his hire car and sped off.

Gould followed Sir Giles's car as it sped on the freeway through the valleys surrounding Los Angeles. After forty minutes, Sir Giles stopped at a rundown studio in a seedy part of Hollywood, close to the unfashionable end of Sunset Boulevard. Japanese tourists wandered around, vainly seeking the Hollywood glamour that they had seen in the movies. Outside there were ancient portraits of stars of many years before, but, as Gould looked around, it was obvious that the area had come down in the fashion stakes, and none of today's stars would ever be seen nearby.

As Gould watched, Sir Giles parked his car in a parking spot close to the front door of the studio and disappeared inside. He walked with an air of confidence and familiarity, and it was obvious that he had visited the studio many times before.

After waiting five minutes, Gould got out of his car and started to walk around the outside walls of the studio. He had reached the corner of the building when he suddenly felt a gun at the back of his neck.

A rough voice sounded in Gould's ear. 'Move quickly, buddy, or you're dead.'

Gould cursed himself for his carelessness. He tried to look around, but could only see the blue jacket of a security man's uniform. Gould looked towards the passing traffic for help, but there were only a few cars on the freeway. He knew America well enough to realise that the sight of a gun was commonplace, and if any passer-by even noticed the two men, they would assume that Gould was being detained legitimately by the security guard. Gould had no doubt that any attempt to flee would be met by a bullet from the man's gun.

'Walk straight ahead. Keep your hands on your head,' the guard's voice said.

Gould walked slowly forward to the front of the building, and was pushed into the reception area of the studio. To his horror, Sir Giles was waiting inside.

'Well, what do we have here?' Sir Giles asked, with a sneer. 'A policeman who is a long way from home, unless I'm mistaken.'

'You know me, Palmer,' Gould said, trying to assert an air of authority. 'I'm Detective Chief Inspector Gould of the City of London police. I order you to let me go.'

Sir Giles laughed. 'Ex-Detective Chief Inspector, I think. I had you suspended. The Commissioner is a member of the same golf club as me. It looks as if you've decided to follow me on your own initiative. I doubt that your ex-superiors know you are here at all. And I don't think the City of London police, in any case, have any authority in the state of California.'

Gould quickly thought of a convenient lie. 'I'm still on duty; that suspension was just for show. The Commissioner doesn't take kindly to being told what to do. Your pressure simply made him keener for the force to investigate you further. I've been ordered here to investigate your activities. If you've nothing to hide, simply let me go now.'

Sir Giles sneered again. 'That's not what I heard, is it, Martinez?'

For the first time, Gould noticed a Latino man standing behind Sir Giles.

'He told my boss that he'd been suspended and he wants to prove his girlfriend innocent. Very touching, it was,' the man said.

With a sickening sense of impending death, Gould recognised the officer who had picked him out at the airport.

'Martinez, is that you?' Gould asked. 'I don't believe it. You're supposed to be a cop. Why would you throw your career away working for a man like Palmer?'

'Just money, Mr Gould,' Martinez said, keeping his gun trained on Gould's heart. 'The LAPD doesn't pay as well as the crooks do. I've always found Mr Palmer more than generous.'

'Let's have no more interruptions, shall we, Gould?' Sir Giles asked, prodding Gould in the chest, while Martinez went behind Gould to grab his arms behind his back. 'You say you want to know what I'm doing here. I'm happy to give you the most direct demonstration you could ever have. Bring him into the studio.'

Martinez pushed Gould from behind along a corridor, still holding his arms. After a few feet, Sir Giles opened a pair of metallic swing doors and Gould found himself shoved into a large film set.

'Have you ever fancied being in the movies, inspector?' Sir Giles asked. 'Our victims are usually young and female. But our customers have many different tastes; there should be quite a market for seeing a real-life detective inspector being killed. If I were you, I might want to start saying a few prayers.'

Gould tried to sound confident, despite feeling terrified. 'You'd better release me straight away. The LAPD know I'm out here. If I don't report in, they'll be bound to find me soon.'

Sir Giles smiled. 'I don't think Lieutenant Zug will be willing to risk his career too much to look for some suspended limey cop. Isn't that what he called you? Now, to satisfy your curiosity, what we make here are called snuff videos. I'm sure you know what they are. People die for real; the fun for our select band of viewers is that all the deaths are different. Pretty girls being killed are always popular, but, as I said, I expect there will be some people who will pay good money to see a man of mature years die before their eyes. So now you're going to be the star of our latest snuff video. It should sell very well.'

Gould looked around for some way of escape. His eyes must have betrayed his growing panic. Sir Giles's smile broadened.

'You've had enough explanation, Mr Gould. You heard what the gentleman said. Walk forward, hands above your head,' Martinez said, indicating with his gun.

There were three movie cameras trained on an unmade bed.

'This is our set. It's seen lots of snuff killings,' Sir Giles said. 'The only expense is we must destroy the sheets to get rid of the blood each time. But the profits are huge. We usually have beautiful young actresses. Sometimes we have porn stars dressed as cops, but you're the first real policeman we've had here. There should be a whole new market for this video. We'll fit a convincing story around this scene. Within a few minutes, we'll have cleared your body away, and it will be clean as new. You know, detective chief inspector, you should be honoured your death's being filmed – it'll ensure you're not forgotten after you're dead.' Sir Giles laughed to himself.

Gould sat on the bed while Martinez held a gun to his head. Gould looked around the locked film set and tried to think of what plans he could make to escape. To his horror, no ideas at all came to his mind.

He wondered how widely Sir Giles's criminal network extended. How did Linus Murray fit into this? Was he on Sir Giles's side or in some other criminal conspiracy?

Gould's mind was in a whirl. He hoped that Zug would realise Gould was in trouble when he missed their appointment and find some way to rescue him. But inwardly he knew he had to prepare for his imminent death.

Chapter 34

As Gould was seated on the bed in the film studio, Zug was waiting impatiently for his English colleague to answer his phone. It was unlike Gould to miss a prearranged appointment, and Zug was concerned about his welfare.

Eventually, Zug tried Martinez's number, as he was the only other person involved in arranging Gould's visit. After a minute or so without response, Zug hung up. He found it annoying both men working on this unofficial assignment should be out of contact. Either it was unprofessional or they were both in some sort of danger.

Zug shrugged his shoulders and decided he had risked so much already; he might as well risk everything. He punched the office number of his best friend at LAPD headquarters into his phone.

'Hi, Fritz, Jeff here. Can you do me a favour?'

'Hi, Jeff,' came the voice of Lieutenant Cuomo. 'I thought you were on leave.'

'Yes, I am, but can you put out an APB for a hired Firebird and a hired Dodge?'

'An all-points bulletin? This is official, I take it? Why did you phone me on your cell phone?'

'That's right, Fritz. I'll take full responsibility.' Zug read out the registrations of both Sir Giles and Gould's hire cars.

'OK, Jeff, I've put them both on the computer, but you owe me one.'

'Sure thing.' Zug ended the call. He had forced himself to sound confident, but he knew that if his superiors knew he had been using official resources to help some suspended English police officer, his own career would be in ruins. He decided to call on a resource that even Gould did not know he had.

Zug walked over to the next room, where several detectives were relaxing between duties. He went up to one of them. 'Hey,' he called.

The man Gould knew as Linus Murray turned around.

'Hi, Jeff,' Linus said. 'What can I do for you?'

'I've not had the call we expected from Gould. It sounds as if he's in trouble. I'm going to try the studio that you suspect Palmer might own.'

'OK, I'll come with you. Gould's a good guy,' Linus said. 'If Palmer has him, his life is in danger. We can't let him die.'

*

Gould looked vacantly at the floodlights in front of him. At this moment, he knew he did not have long to live. The only remote chance of survival was to keep Sir Giles talking and hope Zug would arrive in time to save him. He wondered if, perhaps, an appeal to Sir Giles's vanity might work.

'Killing me won't solve anything, you know, Palmer,' Gould shouted. 'I could help you if you let me live.'

'Killing you will solve at least one of my immediate problems, DCI Gould,' Sir Giles replied, with a wry smile. 'It will solve one of the Commissioner's problems too. He won't have the worry of whether to sack you or not. He'll save on the cost of your pension as well. I'll discuss it with him next time we play golf. He's always telling me his force is looking for ways to save money. My method should be very effective; perhaps he will employ it more. Besides, I will enjoy watching you die.'

Gould's mind raced in search of arguments he could use to persuade Sir Giles to spare his life. 'We know Heather didn't kill James Faulkner. It won't take long for DS Cottrell to pin the murder on you. I phoned her today to tell her where I was going. People will come looking for me very soon.'

For a moment, Sir Giles looked puzzled. 'I didn't kill James. What made you think I did?'

197

Gould tried to keep Sir Giles talking. 'Of course it was you, Palmer. Heather was asking too many questions. Faulkner was shooting his mouth off as well. What more effective way of silencing them both than to kill Faulkner, then frame Heather for the murder?'

'If I was going to kill an employee, Mr Gould, I wouldn't do it in my own office. If that's the extent of your detecting skills, I doubt that the City of London police will miss you very much after we shoot this video.' Sir Giles paused and looked at Martinez. 'OK. Let's roll them. I'll fire the gun myself. I'll enjoy this.'

Gould looked at Sir Giles aiming the gun at him, and braced himself for the fatal gunshots. He instinctively closed his eyes just before he heard gunfire.

After a moment, he opened his eyes again, surprised to find he was still alive. He looked around in amazement to see Sir Giles stagger forward, with blood running from his mouth onto his shirt front. Sir Giles seemed to be trying to say something, but he collapsed on the floor, obviously dead. Gould looked around to see where the shots had come from.

A familiar voice came from behind Gould. 'Your friend Palmer won't be making any more snuff videos now,' Jeff Zug said, as he put his gun away in its holster and came forward to release Gould from his handcuffs.

Gould took three deep breaths. 'Thanks, Jeff. That was too close for comfort. How did you find me?'

'I managed to get a signal from your cell phone. It was close to one from my ex-friend Martinez.' Zug indicated Martinez, who was lying unconscious in the corner. 'I can't stand a crooked cop. I enjoyed giving him a pistol whipping. We've had suspicions about Martinez for some time. I've heard enough to put him in a federal jail for many years. Crooked cops have it worst of everyone in there. The inmates and the guards both hate them and give them a hard time.' He paused. 'I guess this closes the case on Palmer, now he's dead, huh?'

Gould shook his head, as he tried to get circulation back into his hands. 'We've certainly put a stop to the snuff videos. You should have enough to put any of his accomplices away for a long time. I'm still not sure who stabbed James Faulkner back in London, though.'

Zug pulled out a photo of Suzy Flanagan from his pocket. 'This is a photo of one of Palmer's victims. She disappeared just before Christmas. We've been trying to find out what happened to her. At least I can tell her parents the main man behind the racket has been killed. He won't be murdering any more innocent girls like her. I suppose as an LA cop I've seen most things, but I still can't believe a rich man like him could kill a complete stranger just to make even more money.'

'I'm pleased your case is solved, but we must find out who was spreading the videos in London. And I still need to solve Faulkner's murder.'

'I may be able to help you there.' Zug picked up his radio. 'Send in that man who's sitting in our car.'

'What's this?' Gould asked.

'I think you know my colleague,' Zug said. 'You know him as Linus Murray. His real first name is, in fact, Linus, but his surname I'd like to keep secret.'

Gould stared open-mouthed as the man he knew as Linus Murray came into the room.

'I'm pleased to meet you again, sir. Welcome to the United States,' Linus said, offering his hand to Gould. 'I'm glad we managed to save you from being shot.'

'You. What are you doing here?'

'I'm in the LAPD. I've been working undercover here, and then transferred to London. You were right about me. I've never been near Harvard in my life. Sorry I couldn't tell you the truth before now.'

'We'd been aware of some of Palmer's activities for a while,' Zug said. 'Linus started off undercover here in LA, then he was offered a transfer to the London office. It seemed too good an opportunity to waste, and we thought it best to carry on with the investigation at the London end. There were reasons to suspect that there was a corrupt cop involved somewhere along the line, but we weren't sure where. We thought Palmer could have had the police in London under his thumb. So we decided to keep the operation secret. We suspected him of producing snuff videos, and it turned out we were right. But it seems the corrupt policeman was in LA, not London.' He indicated Martinez. 'I'm sorry that I lied to you when you phoned, Dave. But at least, now Palmer's dead, Linus could be a useful witness for you.'

'I don't know how I feel about it,' Gould said. 'We were quite sure Linus was some sort of criminal. It would have saved a lot of time if I had known he was a cop before now. I always hoped our police forces could work together, so I'm disappointed you felt you couldn't trust me.' He paused. 'But I guess I can forgive someone who just saved my life,' he added. 'Now we have to see who else in London was involved in the snuff video racket. Palmer must have had a ready market back in the UK for them. Let's check if he had any papers on him that will help us.'

Zug put on a pair of plastic gloves and rifled through the dead man's pockets. He pulled out a wallet and carefully removed the contents. 'Money ... dollars and pounds ... credit cards ... a few business cards ... some of his own ... now that's an interesting name ... I think that means something to you and Linus.' He passed a business card with an extra phone number written on it to Linus and Gould, who exchanged glances.

'That name looks familiar to me,' Gould said. 'I know it does to you too, Linus.'

'Alf Coates,' Linus said, reading the card. 'It sure does, I'm sad to say. It looks as if Coates must be involved with Palmer Associates in some way. I think it's best if I come back to London with you. I wonder if there's some way I can save Alison from falling into her family business. I suppose you want to put her away in prison with the rest of her family, do you, Mr Gould?'

'If I have to charge her, I will, but there might be some way of saving Alison. Be careful when you see her, won't you, Linus? It won't look good for either of our forces if the public find out you were sleeping with a suspect.'

'I didn't know she was a suspect then, but I don't guess anyone will believe that.' Linus paused. 'Try to let her off easily, Mr Gould. She's a good kid, really.'

'I'll do what I can, Linus,' Gould said, 'but I have to go where the evidence leads. I have a plan that might keep both of us happy, though.'

Chapter 35

Earlier, in London, Wells and Cottrell waited outside the door of Robin Lynch's office at *Dirty Money*. The forensics staff in their white boiler suits were dusting for fingerprints, while their photographic colleagues were taking pictures from every conceivable angle. Lynch's body lay on the floor at the edge of the desk. Blood lay all over the papers on the desk and on the carpet under his body.

'What do you think, gov?' Cottrell asked. 'I'd guess he was shot standing up, then he fell onto the desk first; that's why all the papers are covered with blood. His body then fell off the desk onto the carpet.'

'I'll let the facts speak for themselves, DS Cottrell,' Wells replied. 'I'll wait for the forensic evidence before I make any wild guesses. Unlike Gould, I prefer to follow correct police procedure.'

'Yes, sir,' Cottrell replied. She felt like telling Wells that, unlike him, David Gould encouraged discussion of a case under investigation among all grades. He had often said that speculating among all available possibilities was the only way to reach the truth. She recalled Gould's remark that Wells was an untalented paper pusher, and she agreed. She also remembered her earlier thought that it was her duty to support Wells as much as possible.

She received a nod from the sergeant in charge of the forensics squad that they were finished. She and Wells put on their own white boiler suits and walked into the office, as carefully as they could, so as not to contaminate the scene.

'Let's go through what we have, shall we, DS Cottrell?' Wells said. 'What do you think? It looks like a professional assassin's work.'

'Could be, gov,' Cottrell said. 'It was a very efficient shot straight into the heart. Either professional or lucky, from the perpetrator's point of view. The uniforms said a witness heard a shot about two hours ago. One thing's for sure.'

'What's that?'

'It wasn't Heather Morgan. She's been in custody since last night. We'll have to let her go, unless we think there are two killers involved in this case.'

'Maybe we will, or maybe we won't,' Wells said grumpily. 'I'd like to know how she reacts to news of Lynch's killing, and find out what she knows about it.'

Cottrell opened her mouth to object, but, seeing Wells's stubborn expression, decided to maintain her silence.

'Any fingerprints?' Wells asked the forensic officer, who was finishing off his notes.

'No, I'm afraid not,' the forensic officer said. 'At first sight, there is only the victim's blood too, so there are no DNA clues. Whoever did this knew what they were doing.'

*

Three hours later, once Wells and Cottrell had completed their review of the crime scene at Robin Lynch's office, they held an interview with Heather Morgan and Mr Bradshaw, her solicitor.

'We've had some news that may interest you, Miss Morgan,' Wells said. He paused to assess her reaction.

'I'm listening, inspector,' Heather said eventually.

'There was another killing in the City of London earlier today. It's unusual to have two murders so close together, especially as they are likely to be involved in the same case.'

'And is my client suspected of involvement in the latest murder, detective chief inspector?' Mr Bradshaw asked. 'I think even you will acknowledge, since Miss Morgan has been in custody since last night, she was in no position to go around killing people earlier today.'

'I know where your client was, thank you,' Wells said, making a poor job of hiding his hostility. He turned to address Heather. 'But, as you may know the victim, I would like to see how you react when I tell you that Robin Lynch was shot dead in his office this morning.'

Heather gasped. 'Robin Lynch – he was the journalist who wrote those stories about the company. He came to see me not long ago. He said he used to know James from way back in Scotland.'

'That's the man. He was the editor of *Dirty Money*. He had many enemies in the City from his other inquiries, but we are working on the assumption that someone involved in this case shot him. Do you have any ideas who that may be, Miss Morgan?'

'No, I have no idea,' Heather said, then uttered a small scream. 'Oh, I've just remembered. I was discussing our plans with Michael – Michael Dawson, just before you brought me in. We agreed he would go and have a word with Lynch, and see what he knew. Michael's lucky he wasn't there when the killer visited Lynch. He could have been shot as well.'

Cottrell gasped. 'Let's be clear. You're saying you and Michael Dawson agreed Dawson would visit Robin Lynch, as part of some private investigation,' she said. 'And now Lynch has been shot. That's very suspicious. You should leave investigating crime to the police.'

'I'm sorry, but we had to do something. Is Michael all right?'

'As far as I know, but we will certainly be having a formal word with Mr Dawson,' Wells said. 'At the very least, he seems to have been interfering with our inquiry.'

'I'm so relieved Michael wasn't killed as a witness to Lynch's murder. If he happened to be there when the killer arrived – they would both be dead,' Heather said.

'There is another possibility, Miss Morgan,' Cottrell said. 'I think we all know what that is.'

Heather looked puzzled, then a thought struck her, as she stared at the police officers' sceptical faces. 'You mean ... no, that's too horrible. You think Michael killed Lynch, which must mean he also killed James. Oh, no.' Heather started to cry. 'I thought Michael was just being friendly when he asked me out for a meal in that restaurant. That means I've had a lucky escape, doesn't it? If you're right, he could just as easily have killed me.'

'When we arrested you, Mr Dawson seemed very keen to convince me you were innocent of killing Faulkner,' Wells said. 'Perhaps this is some lunatic attempt on his part to confuse us and make us release you. I'll terminate the interview now, Miss Morgan.' He indicated for Cottrell to turn off the tape. 'Thank you. We must have a word with Mr Dawson – or Captain Dawson, as he used to be – and see how his story tallies with yours. You can return to the cells, Miss Morgan.'

Bradshaw interrupted. 'On what grounds are you continuing to hold my client, detective chief inspector? You admit Miss Morgan couldn't have killed this Robin Lynch, as she was in custody at the time.'

'I'm still investigating the murder of James Faulkner, and your client had motive, means and opportunity for that killing. I am not releasing her until I've had some answers from Michael Dawson,' Wells said. 'For all I know, the two of them could be accomplices in both these murders. Even if they're not, I've a good mind to arrest both of them for interfering in a police investigation. Have Miss Morgan taken back to the cells, DS Cottrell.'

*

The next morning, Michael Dawson was sitting in the same interview room where Heather had been. An angry Bill Wells harangued him. 'I understand from Heather Morgan that you two decided to conduct your own investigation into James Faulkner's death. Is that right?'

'Yes, we thought we would do all we could to clear Heather's name, as the police weren't doing anything,' Michael replied, in a calm voice. 'We were both worried that she can't find a job while

205

this investigation is dragging on. I offered to help her as much as I could.'

'And helping as much as you could included interviewing Robin Lynch, did it?'

'That was the first step,' Michael said. 'I thought we could see where he was getting his information from.'

'And what did you find out from Mr Lynch?'

'I went to his office yesterday and spoke to him, but he wouldn't tell me anything,' Michael said.

'So I'm guessing you lost your temper and shot him,' Wells said. 'You are a dangerous man to annoy. We know that from your SAS history.'

'No, I left quietly. Robin Lynch was alive and well when I left him,' Michael said. 'I did learn one thing that might be of interest to the police.'

'What's that?'

'When I saw Lynch, I realised I'd seen him talking to James Faulkner in a pub the night before James was killed. Lynch denied it, but I'm sure it was him.'

'It sounds like you were following James Faulkner even before the murder,' Wells said. 'It seems you started your private detective business very early on in this inquiry, Mr Dawson. I don't think even Sherlock Holmes would try to solve a crime before it happened. It makes us even more suspicious. The only person who knew Faulkner's life was in danger at that stage was the murderer. Did you kill James Faulkner, Mr Dawson?'

Michael looked around, exasperated. 'No, I did not. I saw Lynch and James together by chance while I was out drinking, for God's sake. I was not following either of them. Is this all the thanks I get for doing the police's job for them?'

'It looks as if Robin Lynch was killed by an expert, Mr Dawson. We're looking for someone with firearms experience for this murder. I see you qualified as a sharpshooter while you were in the SAS.'

'I don't know why you and DCI Gould have this obsession with my history in the forces,' Michael said. 'Yes, I was in the army and was trained to shoot. I am proud of my military career, despite the way it ended. As I have said, I have left my SAS days behind. I am a civilian now. I don't go around the City of London killing people.'

'I'd like to believe you,' Wells said, his voice rising. 'But you must admit death has a habit of following you around, doesn't it, Mr Dawson? You were at a party on the 16th of December, where your girlfriend's fiancé was murdered. Then a man you met with yesterday was shot by an expert marksman the same day. If you are not a killer, then you seem very unlucky.'

'Heather is not my girlfriend – not yet, at any rate. I only spoke to Robin Lynch once, and had no reason to kill him.'

'We'll be investigating your movements further,' Cottrell said. 'In the meantime, we wish to take fingerprints and a sample of your hair for DNA testing against the crime scene, Mr Dawson. Do you object?'

'Not at all. I am always happy to help the police.'

'Very well; the interview is terminated,' Wells said, turning the tape recorder off.

Once the samples had been taken and Michael had left, Wells turned to Cottrell. 'What do you think? He sounds convincing, but I'm suspicious of him.'

'He was very cooperative. He admitted visiting Lynch yesterday, but denied killing him. He didn't object to giving his fingerprints and DNA sample. Most guilty men refuse to help the police at all.'

'That's true as far as it goes,' Wells said. 'Mind you, if he was such a damned expert and killed Lynch in cold blood, he would realise we don't in fact have any fingerprints and DNA from the scene to compare his samples with.'

Chapter 36

After a tiring overnight flight from Los Angeles, Gould went to bed in his Barbican flat at five o'clock in the morning. He had an appointment with the Commissioner at 2pm and only managed to snatch a few hours' sleep before he reported for the interview at Snow Hill police station in the City. He had faxed a report on Palmer's death and was anxious to hear his superior's views.

Gould was worried about how he would be received, but, when he entered the room, he was relieved to see the Commissioner looking embarrassed.

'I read your report, David. It's very interesting. Lieutenant Zug sent a report too. He was pleased you helped to expose that snuff video racket Palmer was running. It seems I owe you an apology for suspending you from duty.' The Commissioner's voice faltered. 'Giles Palmer seems to have fooled a great many people for a very long time, but that's no excuse for me.'

Gould remained silent. He saw no reason why he should make the Commissioner's apology any easier.

'You'll be reinstated immediately, of course, with full back pay. It was a splendid initiative of yours to follow Palmer to Hollywood. He won't be distributing any more of his snuff videos. It's ironic he was shot dead in front of the cameras himself. I'll make sure the force pays for your expenses, of course.'

Gould felt he had to make some acknowledgement of the Commissioner's attempt to make amends. 'Thank you, sir. I was just doing my duty.'

'Now, we must get the Faulkner murder solved,' the Commissioner said. 'It took place in Palmer's offices and, in view of what we know now about his criminal activities, he must be the prime suspect, don't you think?'

'I don't believe so, sir,' Gould said. 'Palmer denied he killed Faulkner when he was talking in the studio before he died. He seemed genuinely surprised when I suggested it. He thought he was going to kill me, so there was no reason for him to lie. I think he'd have been happy to boast about murdering Faulkner if he was the killer.'

'Are you sure, David? We could make a strong case against Palmer, if he was still alive to be charged.'

'Palmer may have been involved, sir,' Gould said, 'but he wouldn't have the guts to put a knife into Faulkner. Whoever did that is still out there.'

'It could still be that Morgan woman killed Faulkner for some domestic reason. Do you think you are still the right person to handle the case, bearing in mind your relationship with one of the main suspects? I can put you on compassionate leave for a while if you want time to recover from your ordeal with Palmer.'

'I believe I am the right person to solve this case, sir. I am certain Heather is innocent, and I can use my friendship with her to our advantage.'

'Well, I'll leave it up to you to carry on,' the Commissioner said, standing up to shake Gould's hand. Gould, still resentful about his suspension, hesitated, but respect for the other man's rank made him shake the offered hand. 'Do you have any new lines of inquiry?'

Gould finally smiled with relief at the prospect of completing the Faulkner investigation. 'Yes, I'm fairly sure I know now who killed Faulkner. It's just a question of uncovering the proof. Can I still have DS Cottrell on the case, sir?'

'Yes, she'll be back working with you. I'm sending Bill Wells back to Scotland Yard. He didn't make much progress. Perhaps the Met aren't so brilliant after all. It's good to have one of my own men back in charge of the case.'

Gould stood to attention. 'I'll go back to my office, then, sir.'

*

After leaving the Commissioner's office, Gould walked back through the open-plan rooms of the police station, acknowledging the friendly greetings from his colleagues, many of whom he had worked with on several inquiries. Eventually, he arrived at his own office. He saw Bill Wells at his old desk, tidying up some papers. It was obvious that he had been told about Gould's reinstatement and was preparing to return to Scotland Yard.

'How are you, Bill?' Gould said, his voice icy.

'Ah, DCI Gould. The Commissioner told me you were back,' Wells said, his voice as cold as Gould's. 'I've tightened things up quite a lot while you've been away. I feel I've made a good deal of progress. For some reason, the Commissioner wants you to take over the case again. So be it.' He smiled cruelly. 'But you should know I arrested your ex-girlfriend for the murder of her fiancé. She's down in the cells now.'

'You've arrested Heather? You must be joking. That's terrible. She could never kill anyone.'

'I'm perfectly serious. The evidence against her was overwhelming – motive, means and opportunity. I'm sure I would be able to convince a jury she's guilty, if I were still in charge.'

'Thank God you're not, then. I gather there was a further murder while you were obsessed with building a case against Heather. Do you think she was guilty of that killing as well?'

'Yes, indeed, there was a second murder,' Wells said, pompously. 'A journalist called Robin Lynch, who you interviewed, was shot. Morgan and Michael Dawson were pursuing some unofficial inquiry of their own and were planning to meet up with Lynch, before I arrested Morgan. Dawson is the front runner for Lynch's murder. Dawson is known to have a terrible temper – perhaps he killed Lynch in a rage, or perhaps he was trying to persuade us Miss Morgan was an innocent flower. I tell you, that woman's as harmless as deadly nightshade.'

'Well, I'll review the fresh evidence you have and decide whether to release her.'

'There hasn't been much fresh evidence. The case notes I inherited from you pointed to Heather Morgan's guilt. I was surprised you hadn't arrested her before; so was the Commissioner,' Wells said, with a mocking smile.

'Well, thank you for your views. I won't keep you, Bill. I'm sure the Met is missing you.'

'I won't be sorry to return to the Met,' Wells said, looking around the station with obvious contempt. 'I've always thought the City force was an absurd relic. I know you've been going longer than the Met, but I prefer to do things properly – the Met's way.' He nodded to Gould, and walked out of the room, holding his head high.

Gould sat down at his desk, and made a mental note to remove any changes Wells had made to his office.

Hearing a familiar voice, Gould entered the room next door quietly, and smiled to himself as he saw Cottrell putting papers into a filing cabinet. She was singing softly to herself in a way he had heard many times before. She only sang when she thought she was on her own, and it was obvious she had not seen Gould arrive.

'Hello, Philippa,' he called, and smiled as Cottrell jumped in shock.

'David ... I mean, DCI Gould,' Cottrell stammered. 'What are you doing here? Don't let anyone see you. You're supposed to be suspended.'

'It's all right,' Gould replied. 'The Commissioner has given me my job back. I thought of throwing my warrant card back at him, after the way he treated me. In the end, I've decided to forgive him for the way he let old Palmer have me suspended.'

'If you're sure, then I'm glad to see you back,' Cottrell said. She moved forward to hug him, but the move ended in an awkward half-embrace. 'I thought you were still tailing Palmer around Hollywood.'

'Jeff Zug shot him dead. If he hadn't, Palmer was going to star me as a corpse in one of his snuff videos. If he was still alive, we could be charging him with all sorts of offences, but murdering Faulkner isn't one of them.'

'What do you mean?' Cottrell asked. 'Palmer must be the main suspect, knowing what we know about him now.'

'Just before Palmer was going to kill me, he denied murdering Faulkner. He seemed genuinely surprised we suspected him.'

'Can we believe anything a man like Palmer says?'

'I think so in this case,' Gould said. 'He was boasting of all his crimes. I can't see why he would keep quiet if he had murdered Faulkner. Now bring me up to speed on the Lynch case. All I know is what was in the *Evening Standard* I picked up on the way in, and what Wells has just told me.'

'Well, we know Lynch was killed by a high-calibre rifle from a few feet away. The aim was perfect, so it's either an expert or a lucky amateur. There are no fingerprints or DNA at all, so my guess it's an expert.'

'Are there any suspects? Wells said Dawson is in the frame for it.'

'We know Michael Dawson arranged to meet Lynch. Apparently, for some reason, Dawson and Heather Morgan had set themselves up as budding amateur detectives. Dawson says he only met Lynch once – earlier on the day he was killed. Lynch denied any knowledge of Faulkner's murder and was alive when Dawson left him, according to Dawson's story. We've confirmed Dawson was at work that day, but he could have slipped out without anyone knowing. The only certain thing is that the killer of Robin Lynch wasn't Heather Morgan. She was in our cells at the time, under arrest for the murder of James Faulkner.'

'Wells told me that,' Gould said, with a pained expression. 'How could he arrest Heather in the first place? There was never enough evidence against her. Bill Wells ought to go back to issuing parking tickets – that's all he's good for.'

'No matter what you think about Wells, the position is that Heather Morgan is in custody. She comes up to the magistrates' court again tomorrow. Her solicitor said she should be released, as she obviously could not have murdered Lynch, who was probably killed by the same person who killed Faulkner. Wells argued Lynch's death doesn't change the position on the earlier murder, and perhaps someone – Dawson, say – killed Lynch to make Heather look innocent. So Wells wanted to oppose bail, but you can change the police position if you want to.' Cottrell started to blush, as she felt the need to defend Wells. 'I know Heather's a friend of yours, David, but you have to admit the evidence is strong against her. Can't you persuade her to admit she killed Faulkner? She should get off if she pleaded provocation or self-defence.'

'Heather has always claimed she's innocent, and I believe her,' Gould said, in a firm tone. 'I'm going to release her now. I'm sure someone else killed Faulkner and framed Heather for the crime. Someone put ketamine in her drink and left her in the room with the body, and I have a good idea who it was. I've thought of a plan that should work, if I can persuade Heather to help us find out who the real murderer is.'

Gould left Cottrell behind as he walked down into the cells below the station. The temperature seemed a few degrees colder in the basement as he approached the custody sergeant.

'Ah, DCI Gould. Good to see you back, sir,' the sergeant said.

'Thanks, I'm glad to be back. I've come to release Heather Morgan from custody.'

'Very good. I don't think she belongs here. She's a cut above most of our other prisoners. Just sign these papers, sir.'

Gould signed a few documents and then followed the sergeant to one of the cells reserved for female prisoners. The sergeant pulled out his set of keys and inserted one into the door of the cell.

'You're free, Miss Morgan,' the sergeant said as he opened the door, and Heather gave a short shout of relief.

Gould entered the cell, and was shocked to see how gaunt his former girlfriend appeared. 'Yes, Heather, it's true,' he said. 'I've signed the papers.'

Heather's eyes brightened as she saw Gould. 'David, you're back,' she said, rushing forward to hug him. 'Has that awful Wells man gone?'

Gould put his arms out to stop Heather from hugging him. 'Yes, I'm back in charge. Don't be too effusive, Heather,' he said. 'All the other prisoners will start talking. Come over to the desk, and the sergeant can give you your possessions back.'

'Oh, I'm sorry to embarrass you, but it's such good news. The other women in here are terrible. They are all ... well, you can imagine what they are.'

'I can see you've had a tough time, Heather,' Gould said, with a half-smile. 'I've had a terrifying experience in LA, but I've been reinstated now. With your help, the two of us are going to solve the Faulkner case.'

'Oh, that would be great. Then I can start my life again without those horrible suspicions hanging over me.'

'Well, it's not that easy. You see, as I said, I need your help. First of all, after the last time I saw you, did you tell anyone else about my trip to LA?'

'No ...' Heather thought for a while. 'Oh, I had to tell Margaret, to get the information, but she wouldn't tell anyone.'

'I thought you might have told her,' Gould said, thoughtfully. 'Come on, I'll drive you home.'

Later, as they arrived outside Heather's flat, Gould turned to her. 'I gather Wells told you about the murder of Robin Lynch.'

'Yes, he did,' Heather said. 'Wells seemed to suspect Michael Dawson. At first, I couldn't believe what he was saying. I like Michael and hope he's innocent, but I don't know what to think now.'

'Yes, well, Dawson is one suspect at the moment. He's an expert shot from his army days, but to nail him, we need your help.'

'So you think Michael's a killer, just like Wells did.'

Gould paused before giving an answer. 'I can make a very good case against him for James's murder. But, as I say, I need you to help us. I'll tell you about it tomorrow.'

*

The following afternoon, Gould and Cottrell waited outside the door of Heather's flat.

'I'm still not sure about your plan, David,' Cottrell said. 'It sounds very irregular to me. If it goes wrong, you might be suspended again.'

'You're getting to sound like Bill Wells,' Gould said, with a half-smile. 'You don't want to end up like him. We have to think laterally if we're to find out who killed James Faulkner.'

'I don't mind taking some risks to get a conviction, but I don't like having to rely on Heather Morgan's cooperation. It still looks as if she's a killer. We could make a good case that she killed Faulkner, even if she only faces a manslaughter charge. We know she didn't murder Lynch, but that doesn't make her innocent of her fiancé's murder.'

'It will be useful if you put your case for Heather's guilt when we see her. It might convince her to cooperate in my plan.'

The detectives' discussion was interrupted when they heard a series of bolts being pushed open.

'Hello, Heather,' Gould said. 'May we come in? I'm back investigating the Faulkner murder. It's an official visit, I'm afraid.'

Heather's face, which at first expressed delight at seeing Gould, darkened as she saw his serious expression and took in the presence of Cottrell. Their body language made it obvious the antipathy between the two women was undimmed.

'Yes, you'd better come in, David, or Detective Chief Inspector Gould, should I say? And it's always a pleasure to see Detective Sergeant Cottrell, of course,' Heather said, her voice steeped in sarcasm, as she stood aside to let her visitors in. 'I apologise for the mess. The police search left the place untidy. I haven't had time to tidy up since I came home from prison.'

Gould and Cottrell entered the flat and sat on a sofa while Heather sat in an armchair. Gould looked around to see the flat was far less clean than he remembered it.

'I apologise for the way Bill Wells treated you, and I'm glad you're free again. Now, I have some news for you, Heather,' Gould began. 'I'm not sure if it's good or bad. That's for you to say.'

'If you mean that Sir Giles Palmer's dead, I already knew. I saw it in the papers.'

'An American police officer shot Palmer just in time to stop him shooting me.' Heather's eyes opened wide with sympathetic fear as Gould described the scene in the Hollywood studio. 'Palmer was running a network to distribute snuff videos. I'm very lucky I didn't star in one.'

'That must be why he was making all those visits to Los Angeles,' Heather said excitedly. 'I bet he was worried when James got drunk and asked him all those questions. I'm sure Palmer killed James to shut him up. At least that means I am in the clear.'

'No, we don't believe Palmer killed James Faulkner,' Gould said. 'Palmer denied it when I suggested it, and he had no reason to lie at that point. He thought he was about to kill me, and he was boasting about all his crimes. Even if he ordered the murder, the person who actually stabbed your fiancé is still free. It's our job to put that guilty person behind bars. The inquiry into James Faulkner's murder is still very much open. We are interviewing many of the original suspects.'

Heather looked shocked as she took in what Gould had said. 'If you don't think Palmer killed James, who do you think did it? You don't still think I killed James, do you? You're as bad as that Wells man. He didn't believe a word I said. Is that why you're here? Do you seriously think I would ever murder James?'

Gould instinctively put out his arms to comfort Heather. 'Calm down, Heather. We think we know who killed James Faulkner, and it wasn't you.'

'Why don't you arrest them, then?' Heather asked, looking tearful.

'Because we don't have enough evidence against them. Knowing someone's guilty is one thing. We need to have proof to put them behind bars.'

'If you don't make an arrest, everyone I meet's going to carry on looking at me as if I'm Jill the Ripper. Can you imagine what it's like? I can't get a job and I hardly go out in case people start pointing at me.'

'It's up to you if you want to put your life together again, Miss Morgan.' Cottrell spoke for the first time. Her cool voice had the effect of calming Heather down. 'We're giving you the chance to help us convict the killer, if you are as innocent as you say.'

'What do you mean?' Heather asked.

'The police could still make a strong case against you for killing your fiancé,' Cottrell said. 'We look for motive, means and opportunity. You have all three. You'd broken up with him that evening – a perfect motive. You were found in the same room as him with your fingerprints all over the murder weapon. Do you want that hanging over you for the rest of your life? Why don't you admit you killed him in self-defence?'

Heather looked at the two officers in panic. 'But you can't still think I did it – not after all that's come out about Palmer.'

Gould spoke. 'To be honest, Heather, I believe you're innocent, but as you can see my sergeant is more sceptical. Some day, a different investigating officer may come along, believe her, and arrest you again. Why not help us to put the real murderer behind bars?'

'That's right. We can't get the evidence, but you may be able to,' Cottrell said.

Heather turned to Gould. 'What's she talking about?'

'We want you to meet the killer and get a confession from them,' Gould said. 'You could invite them here for a meal. We'd be listening next door.'

'You want me to invite a killer to my flat? But he could become violent again,' Heather said in a horrified tone. 'What have I done to you? First the police think I'm a killer, and now you want me to be killed myself.'

'We can't force you, of course,' Cottrell said. 'You have a choice. You can go on living like this, with everyone thinking you're a murderer, or you can help us to help you. This is the quickest way to find the real killer.'

Heather looked helplessly from Cottrell to Gould. 'You want me to do the police's job for you? I have had enough of the police to last me a lifetime.'

'I understand how you feel, but I think this is the best course for you,' Gould said. 'We'll be here to make sure you don't come to any harm. If all goes well, as I expect, you can live life as usual, before all this happened.'

Heather paused as she weighed the options in her head. 'Oh, very well, I'll do it. I have nothing to lose – apart from my life, of course. Who do you want me to trap?'

'At the moment, Michael Dawson is in the frame. We know he was keen on you. He admitted he despised James Faulkner. With his army training, it was simple for him to kill James. I think if you tackle him about it, he'll admit it.'

'But I've been alone with Michael lots of times,' Heather said, her voice rising in panic. 'You're saying he could have killed me at any time. And now you want me to invite him alone for dinner? What if he decides to kill me in my flat? He's a very strong man, and I would never be able to escape.'

'I won't pretend you're not in some danger, Heather,' Cottrell said. 'Michael Dawson was a trained killer in the army, and it looks as if he's carried on in civilian life. We'll be here, but I think it would be good for you to have a chaperone to protect you. Who could you invite to the dinner that would seem natural – someone you both know?'

'That would be Margaret Prestwood,' Heather said, after a pause. 'I suppose I owe her a meal. She stood by me while I was in trouble with you lot.'

'That's exactly the person I was thinking of, Heather,' Gould said.

'Could you phone them now, Miss Morgan?' Cottrell said. 'Don't tell them who else you've invited. We want it to be a surprise.'

'Oh, it will be a surprise, all right. They hate each other,' Heather said.

'So it's best all round if neither knows the other is coming,' Gould said. 'Can you phone them straight away?'

Heather shrugged. 'I suppose so,' she said, picking up the phone and dialling the first number. 'Michael, it's me ... Yes, I'm out of jail now ... David Gould's back in charge, and he says he realises I'm innocent ... Yes, it's great news ... I wondered if you'd like to come for a meal – perhaps on Friday evening to celebrate – about eight o'clock ... See you then ...'

Heather put the phone down. 'Well, that's one of them. I feel like a right tart inviting a man for dinner under false pretences.' She looked at Cottrell. 'I suppose you do this all the time, do you?'

Gould interrupted. 'Now, can you invite Margaret?'

Heather picked up the phone again and dialled. 'Margaret, it's Heather ... Yes, I'm out now ... I wondered if you'd like to come around for a meal on Friday evening ... Yes, that's right ... Only a few special friends ... Great, see you then ...'

She put the phone down. 'Well, there you are. I've invited two of my friends and colleagues under false pretences. Is there anything else I can do for the City police?'

'No, you've done well,' Gould said. 'As long as neither of them suspects, that's great.' He stood up and indicated for Cottrell to go with him. 'We have to deal with some other aspects of the case now, but we will be back here early on Friday evening.'

Chapter 37

The following evening, Cottrell switched on the ignition in the police car in the garage beneath Snow Hill police station, and turned to Gould, who was sitting beside her. 'Are you sure about this arrest, David?' she asked. 'Do we need backup? I can't see our suspect coming quietly.'

'Yes, I've arranged for Fox to bring in another suspect who might help us,' Gould said. 'Now, stop at the next corner; there's someone I want to give a lift to.'

Cottrell was about to ask what Gould meant, but noticed his expression in the rear-view mirror did not encourage questions. She stopped as instructed and was amazed to see Linus Murray standing there.

'Come in, Linus,' Gould said. 'We've not far to go.'

'What's going on?' Cottrell asked. 'I thought this man was a suspect.'

'Good evening, ma'am,' Linus said. 'I don't think DCI Gould told you my little secret. Here's my badge. I'm in the LAPD, so we're on the same side.'

'You're in the police?' Cottrell echoed, inspecting the LAPD badge. She turned to Gould. 'Why wasn't I told about this?'

'Believe me, I was as surprised as you are when they told me in LA. I was pretty angry about being kept in the dark. Then Zug saved my life, with help from Linus, so I decided to forgive them. At least that removes one suspect from our list.' Gould glanced at Cottrell, who looked furious.

'Shall we be friends, then, Philippa?' Linus asked.

'We may be colleagues. It'll take a long time before we're friends,' Cottrell said. 'I've wasted many hours investigating you, when you could have come clean before now.'

'So you still think I'm a suspect, then?' Linus asked. 'Even now you know I'm in the police?'

Cottrell scowled in response. 'I've met some dodgy policemen in my time. I'm keeping an eye on you in case you're one.'

'You can see Philippa has a suspicious nature, Linus,' Gould called to Linus, who was seated in the back.

'If you mean I'm a detective, then I'm proud to say I am,' Cottrell said. 'Tell me, Linus, was sleeping with Alison Coates a perk of the job?'

'No, it just happened,' Linus replied, turning serious, 'but I guess I'm not proud of it.'

'And I gather there was a corrupt colleague of yours called Martinez, who was involved with Palmer. How do we know you're not working with him?'

'Wow, you don't like me, do you? No, honey, I'm not corrupt. I'm glad at least Dave trusts me.'

'Are you going to let Alison know you're an undercover cop?' Cottrell asked. 'I'm looking forward to seeing that.'

'Yes, I'll tell her,' Linus said, in a more thoughtful tone. 'I know I owe her that much. I'm hoping we'll be able to keep her out of trouble – that is, if what your boss and I have planned works out.'

Cottrell turned to Gould. 'Are you planning something with this man, David? How do you know you can trust him?'

'Let's just wait, shall we? We're nearly there.'

*

As the police car approached its destination, Alf Coates peered through the tobacco smoke in the East End pub he owned, to see if his expected visitor had arrived yet. Very few people realised he was in fact the owner of the pub, which displayed the name of a well-known chain outside. Alf felt he was very adept at hiding the money he had built up from many years of thuggish violence behind a façade of legitimate businesses. This evening he was feeling particularly pleased with himself, as he looked forward to expanding his reach into film finance.

'Mr Coates, sir.' The voice he was expecting came through the doors.

'Ah, Linus,' Alf said, standing up to shake Linus's hand. 'It's good of you to come. Come and have a pint of English bitter. You might get a taste for it.'

'That's very kind, sir. I'm just back from LA. You probably heard that Palmer was killed? I was there, but they say you've been busy while I've been away.'

'What do you mean?'

'Distributing snuff videos, running down the share price of Palmer Associates and killing Robin Lynch. That seems pretty busy to me.'

Alf chuckled to himself. 'Yes, well, it's all part of business. Your business as well, so I understand.'

'In a way that's true, sir,' Linus replied. He paused. 'But I'm afraid I have some very bad news for you, Mr Coates. I'm not who you think I am. I've brought someone you know very well to see you.'

Just then David Gould and Philippa Cottrell came into the pub.

'DCI Gould, what the hell are you doing here?' Alf asked, looking around for some imaginary source of help.

'Alfred Coates,' Gould began, 'I'm arresting you for the murder of Robin Lynch in the City of London on the 4th of January. You do not have to say anything, but it may harm your defence if you do not mention when questioned something which you later rely on in court. Anything you do say may be given in evidence.'

Alf looked at Linus with reproach. 'Are you behind this? I thought you were on our side. Are you working with the filth? If you are, you'd better spend the rest of your life looking behind you. I don't like traitors.'

'Sorry to disappoint you, Mr Coates, but I'm with the Los

Angeles police department,' Linus said, showing his police badge.

'You're a sodding pig. I might have known,' Alf said, as he looked around for some means of escape.

'I can see you're surprised, Alf,' Gould said, walking around to slip handcuffs onto Alf's wrists. 'But not as surprised as I was when I found out.'

'You mean you didn't know he was a cop either? I suppose that's sort of funny,' Alf said. 'But if you arrest me, you'll be wasting your time. I'll deny everything. With the lawyers I can afford, I'll run rings around you.'

'You might be right, of course, but I should say we're also arresting your granddaughter, Alison Coates, as part of the conspiracy. We believe she passed privileged data to you. In turn, you passed the information to Robin Lynch, who published it in *Dirty Money*. That drove the share price down and you bought control of the company for a song. You two quarrelled with Lynch for some reason, and you killed him, either yourself or using a hitman. How does that sound?'

'Alison didn't know anything about it,' Alf said, looking genuinely baffled. 'She was just bringing me the latest office gossip – she didn't know I was angling for information. You've got to leave Alison out of it.'

Gould looked at Alf. 'Alf, you know what, I believe you, but I don't think a jury would, and I have to follow the evidence. I've sent a team to arrest your granddaughter.' He glanced out of the pub window and saw Alison Coates in the back of a police car, handcuffed to DS Fox. 'She's outside now. Of course, it's in your hands if you want me to send her home uncharged. I think you've bought a shedload of shares in Palmer Associates. Who's going to run the company while you're in prison? If your granddaughter is a free woman, I'm sure she would do a marvellous job in charge of your investments. It would be difficult if she's in some women's prison somewhere.'

Alf stood up and peered through the pub window at Alison.

'You can't do this. She doesn't belong in prison. I want her to have a better life than me.'

'Yes, it would be a pity for her to end up in a cell. She's young and pretty. I hate to think what the older women would do to her. Of course, there is one way to leave her out of it. It's up to you.'

Alf stared at Gould, then realisation came to him. 'I get it. You're saying if I cooperate and plead guilty to murder, you'll let Alison off. Is that the position?'

'You know I can't negotiate with criminals. I couldn't possibly agree to blackmail of that kind, Alf,' Gould said, with a smile.

'I'll take that as a yes, then,' Alf said, looking around his pub as if he were seeing it for the last time. 'Very well, I'll cooperate. I'll confess to killing Lynch, just as long as you keep Alison out of it.'

Gould took a mobile phone from his pocket and dialled a number. 'Foxy? Gould here. Take the suspect back to her flat. She can go free.'

He made sure Alf could see Alison being driven back home.

Gould looked at the old man in handcuffs in front of him. Most of Alf's previous liveliness had seeped away. Gould knew better than most how hardened a criminal Alf Coates had been, and how much pain he had caused this part of London in his seventy-odd years. Yet Gould could not help being moved by Alf's downfall. He reflected that police and criminals had a strange relationship, with contempt mixed with a grudging respect for a worthy opponent. Alf's one saving grace did seem to be that he loved his granddaughter, and Gould knew he had relied on that slight weakness to bring Alf down.

Gould shook Linus's hand as two uniformed officers took charge of Alf. 'Thanks, Linus. I don't think we need to bother Alison anymore. There's just one last problem to solve. To do that, we must keep Coates in custody for forty-eight hours before we formally charge him for murder. I've given orders to keep everything secret from the public until then, and I'll apply to hold him without charge past the one-day limit. That should give us time to make an arrest for the murder of James Faulkner.'

As the constables led Alf away, the old man shouted, 'You're a bastard, Gould.'

'I'll see you at the station, Alf,' Gould said.

Cottrell turned to Gould. 'Sometimes I'm not sure I really know you, David,' she said. 'You're not much better than the criminals we try to put away, are you?'

'What do you mean?'

'You realised that old man only had one weakness – he loved his granddaughter – and you used it to get him to confess. You've destroyed him now. How could you do that?'

'That old man has been a professional criminal all his life,' Gould replied, with a shrug. 'It's our job to put him away for however much longer he has to live. I'm proud of doing just that.'

Cottrell sighed. 'I don't agree, David. We have to follow the rules. I think we should be better than the criminals. Not go down to their level and use blackmail.'

'Perhaps that's the difference between you and me,' Gould replied. 'I just want to get results. Come on, we still have to make an arrest for the murder of James Faulkner.'

*

Alison stood in the front room of the flat she shared with Linus Murray, and pondered her reflection in a mirror. She was in a contemplative mood. She knew she was reasonably attractive, but she asked herself what she had to show for her life so far. She was unemployed since Sir Giles had sacked her and she would have liked to be able to talk over her feelings with a friend, but she had no one to talk to. She understood Linus was still out in Los Angeles, doing God knows what, and she had few friends from school days. All the other girls had been scared away by her grandfather's reputation. Alison could still recall the mothers of her school friends ushering them away from her as she walked home from school.

Alison asked herself what she had gained from trying to make her own legitimate living in the City, and concluded that it had not worked out. She did not know why the police had taken her to her grandfather's pub the previous day, but, in any event, it seemed that she could not escape the reach and reputation of Alf Coates. So, she wondered, what should she do now? Was it worth trying to find another legitimate job in the City, or should she go into her grandfather's crime business?

As she pondered the answers to her own questions, she heard a sudden knock on the door. She walked into the hall and pulled the door open. She saw Linus standing there, gave a delighted laugh and hugged him.

'Linus, honey,' she said. 'You're back. How was LA? You should have phoned me as soon as you arrived. Have you lost your key?'

'No, I have it here. But let's go for a walk. I have some things to tell you.'

Alison was surprised, but she nodded. 'Yes, sure, why not? It's a nice day for a walk.'

After strolling a few hundred yards into the local park, Linus indicated that they sit down on a bench.

'What's this about, Linus?' Alison asked. 'When did you get back from LA? There have been lots going on while you were away. The police arrested me and took me to my granddad's pub, then released me. What do you think was going on? Granddad's not returning any of my calls.'

'Honey, I had some business to take care of while I was in LA, but it wasn't the kind of business you think I'm in. Alison, I'm a detective in the Los Angeles police department,' Linus said, pulling out his LAPD badge.

Alison looked around in fear. 'What? You're in the police? Are you going to arrest me?'

'No, don't panic. David Gould and I have made sure you're not in any trouble. But your grandfather is. He's under arrest for the murder of Robin Lynch and he's admitting it. I'm sorry you've had to go through all this, but at least you can carry on with your own life now.'

'So our life together was a complete lie, was it?' Alison asked, with tears in her eyes.

'No, I loved being with you.' Linus caught her expression. 'But yes, I guess it was all based on a lie. I was sent here to London on an assignment, and am returning to LA tomorrow. Forget about me now. You must look forward, Alison. You're a decent person. Are you going to make a good life for yourself? Or are you going to let your grandfather drag you down into his family business? I know he loves you, but you've got to keep your distance from him.'

'I don't think you're in a position to give me advice, are you, Linus – if that is your name?'

'Yes, it is. That's one thing I told the truth about.'

'I've got to try to get Granddad out of prison,' Alison said, standing up. 'He's an old man.'

'He may be old, but you know he's a wicked man, and he doesn't deserve your support.'

'He's still my family. Goodbye, Linus. I think we'll meet on opposite sides of the law from now on. I have a family business to run.' Alison turned to hurry away.

Linus looked after her sadly. He wanted to tell her to stick to the right side of the law, but it seemed likely the lure of her family business would be too strong for her.

He took an airline ticket from his pocket and studied it. He would soon be flying home, to deal with a new batch of criminals. Before then, he needed to help Gould make a second arrest.

*

Alf Coates sat slumped in the interview room at Snow Hill police station. Gould was seated opposite with DS Fox beside him. Gould was summarising Alf's statement for the benefit of the tape recording. 'So, Alf Coates, you admit to the murder of Robin

Lynch in the City of London on the 4th of January this year.'

Alf looked at Gould with contempt. 'I just said that, didn't I?'

'Yes, you did, Alf, but please tell my colleague why. You'd like to know, wouldn't you, Foxy?'

'Oh, I would, but an old lag like Alf isn't clever enough to have reasons,' Fox said, fulfilling his rehearsed role as the sceptical young cop. 'He's too stupid to tell us why.'

Alf looked at Fox. 'That's what you think, is it, you young tyke?'

Fox shrugged his disbelief. As the two officers had planned, they could tell Alf was torn between a desire to show off and a more sensible wish to avoid incriminating himself.

'Come on, Alf, put DS Fox right,' Gould said. 'He just thinks you're an old fool. We both know better than that, don't we?'

Alf's eyes lit up at the prospect of displaying his cleverness. 'I'll tell you how it happened. I'd had some dealings with Palmer Associates – dodgy videos, that sort of thing – before, and I decided the company would be a useful addition to my – what do you call it? – business empire. The only trouble was the share price was too high, so I persuaded Alison – my granddaughter – to work there, but I didn't tell her my plans, so she didn't know anything.'

'Go on, Alf,' Gould said.

'Alison liked to visit my pub and tell me all the news about where she worked – she's a good girl, always comes around to see me. I knew if I spread the gossip she told me about Palmer Associates, it would drive the share price down, and I could buy the company cheaply.' Alf glared at Fox. 'Sure, I may be old, but I ain't stupid, no matter what you think.'

Fox made notes as Alf continued.

'I knew about this scandal rag called *Dirty Money*, and I phoned the editor, a bloke called Robin Lynch, and fed him with lots of gossip that I picked up from Alison. I knew a lot about the porn side, but I only hinted at that, because I didn't want you lot to close it down. It worked a treat, and the share price collapsed. It fell even further after the murder at their Christmas party. I didn't have anything to do with it, but it was lucky from my point of view. I've bought the company now.'

'So why kill Lynch, if he was doing what you wanted?' Gould asked, leaning forward.

'He was getting greedy, and cheeky. He threatened to tell the City authorities about me. I felt it was easier to get rid of him permanently.'

'And what can you tell us about the murder of James Faulkner?'

'Nothing at all,' Alf said. 'You have to believe me. You've got me for killing Lynch. Isn't that enough for you?'

'We're after the truth, Alf. If you say you didn't kill Faulkner, then I'll believe you until we can prove otherwise. And you say Alison Coates is innocent of involvement in any of your crimes?'

'Yes, I brought her up to go straight. You said you would go easy on her if I cooperated with the police, and I have, haven't I?' Alf looked at Gould pleadingly.

'Unless I receive any evidence of her guilt, Alison can go free. She can even run the company, as far as I'm concerned. Just one thing: tell us about these dodgy videos. What was on them, and who sold them to you?'

'The man gave me some made-up name, but I found out who he was when I followed him to his office once. He's Derek Ringer – he's managing director of Palmer Associates. That's when I decided the company was worth buying. I expect Alison will enjoy firing him. I don't know what was on the videos. The usual stuff, I expect. I just sell them. I don't watch them.'

'Thank you. We'll be interviewing Mr Ringer, and your evidence will be useful. But it wasn't the usual stuff,' Gould said, his voice rising in anger. 'They were snuff videos – young girls were killed making them. There are lots of grieving mothers of girls who were filmed in them. You're lucky we don't charge you with conspiracy to murder one of those models, but we've got enough to fill the rest of your time. You're seventy-two years old, aren't you? I don't expect you'll see that pub of yours again. You'll probably get at least twenty-five years inside.'

'Twenty-five years? With my health? That's a laugh.'

'You probably won't manage to do the full term, but don't worry.'

'Don't worry?' Alf echoed.

'You won't be able to complete the sentence, Alf,' Gould said, then smiled. 'Just do as much as you can.'

Fox laughed, and Alf swore at the police officers as he was led out of the interview room.

*

The next day, Alison waited outside Brixton prison for the start of visiting hours. The other people in the queue seemed to be middle-aged women, obviously prisoners' wives, some of whom were holding babies or leading children in school uniforms. Alison remembered being one of those children when her mother would bring her to visit her grandfather during one of his many spells in prison. She knew that many of these same women around her would have been in the queue all those years ago, as their husbands were serving long sentences.

She had hoped never to be waiting in one of these queues again, but now that her grandfather was imprisoned again, probably for the rest of his life, she realised visiting Alf Coates in prison would again be a regular occurrence.

Alison's head was still teeming with thoughts following Linus's revelation that he was a cop. She told herself that she had put all her efforts into her job at Palmer Associates, and it had done her little good. She knew that her grandfather would support her in some less legitimate business. But was that what she really wanted for herself?

After passing through several security checks, Alison followed the other visitors into the seedy visiting room. She noticed her

230

grandfather sitting at a corner table, and reflected on how his old air of authority had vanished from him. She forced herself to smile as she joined him at the table.

'Granddad, this is like the old days. I never thought I'd be visiting you in prison again,' she said as she hugged him, ignoring the protests from the nearby guard.

'Yeah, well, nor did I, I suppose,' Alf said, with a sigh. 'Still, it's what you might call an occupational hazard. It gives me a chance to catch up with some old friends and colleagues.'

'It doesn't help my career, though, does it? Having a granddad in prison doesn't go down well with employers in the City.'

'I'm not so sure about that, kid,' Alf said, smiling. 'I'll bet you've been wondering who controls the company you used to work for, now Palmer's dead.'

'I should say I have, even if I've been sacked. I've started looking at the job adverts. There must be some company in the City that needs a new secretary.'

'How about being more than a secretary?' Alf asked.

'What do you mean? If you're suggesting something criminal, I don't want to end up like you. No offence, Granddad.'

'None taken. I mean how would you like to sit on the other side of the managing director's desk? I'm the owner of Palmer Associates, and I'm asking you to run it for me.'

Alison stared at the old man. 'If that's a joke, Granddad, it's not funny.'

'It's no joke. I own the majority of the shares. You know more about the business than anyone else I know, and I'm offering you the job of managing director.'

Alison went pale. She pondered turning her grandfather's offer down, knowing the source of his money. Then she imagined herself the next day, walking into the office and seeing the shocked faces of all the executives who used to look down at her.

'It would be fun bossing all those City types around,' Alison said. 'We could change the name to Coates Associates.'

'It's not just for fun, Alison, love,' Alf said. 'I wouldn't ask you to do it if I didn't think you were the best person. You'd have a free hand to run the company how you like. Just come along and see me every week and tell me about it. I'd like that.'

Alison paused as she mulled her grandfather's proposal over. 'All right, granddad, I'll do it.' She hugged her grandfather, before being separated from him by the nearby prison officer.

As Alf was led back to his cell, Alison smiled to herself. She walked out of the prison with a new confidence, inwardly pondering her future plans for Palmer Associates. She looked forward to returning to the office the next day, but no longer as secretary.

*

While Alison was visiting her grandfather in prison, Derek Ringer eyed up his putt on the eighteenth green at Hindhead golf course. He knew that if he holed this putt, he would win the club competition for this month. The prize would be some two hundred pounds: a trivial amount compared to his large salary from Palmer Associates, but Derek felt this was a sign that he had finally arrived.

Derek pulled his putter back and hit it eighteen inches straight into the hole. He cheered in delight, then nodded an apology in response to the glares from the players on the nearby first tee. He shook his opponent's hand, and signed for the score that his opponent had recorded.

All things considered, life was good. Now that Sir Giles was dead, Derek would be in an ideal position to take over the reins of the company. After all, he was the only one who knew many of the company's secrets.

He walked off the green and walked towards the clubhouse, talking excitedly about his performance to his opponent. Just then, he saw a familiar figure standing in front of him.

'Derek Ringer,' David Gould began, 'you are under arrest for conspiring to murder Susan Flanagan in the state of California.'

Derek stared at Gould as if he were mad. 'Who? I've never been to California.'

'I know, but your boss Palmer went many times, and made some illegal films, which you distributed.'

Derek looked around and saw his golfing companion edging away. 'You're arresting me for selling some mild pornography. Haven't the police got better things to do?'

'Indeed we have. Tell Mr Ringer about it, why don't you, Linus?'

Derek stared as the man he knew as Linus Murray climbed out of Gould's official car.

'I'm a police officer in the Los Angeles police department, Mr Ringer,' Linus said, drawing out his police shield. 'I've been working undercover in your company to investigate the sale of snuff videos. These have involved several deaths in California, and I am assisting DCI Gould to track down the customers in the UK. You are top of the list.'

'I'm going to fight this,' Derek said.

'You do that, Mr Ringer,' Gould said. 'And I should say I'm still investigating the murder of James Faulkner.'

'You can't stick that on me,' Derek yelled, as he was led away to Gould's waiting police car.

'What do you think, Dave?' Linus asked, once Derek was secured inside the car. 'Did Ringer have anything to do with James Faulkner's murder?'

'Not with his own hands, but I'm hoping to arrest the hands-on perpetrator. Then we'll see how far Derek Ringer was involved.'

Chapter 38

Later that day, Heather made the finishing touches to her dining table. It was set for three people: herself and the two guests she was expecting. She was always nervous when having to cook for visitors, but that was trivial compared with the realisation that the outcome of tonight's meal would affect her whole life. If she was lucky, this would put a criminal behind bars and allow her to start her career – and her whole life – again.

Heather was standing back to admire her handiwork when she heard a knock on her door. When she opened it, she saw Gould, Cottrell and a third detective she did not recognise, who was carrying a case that seemed full of electronic apparatus.

'Hello, David,' Heather said. 'As you wanted, I've got my flat ready for the visitors.' She glared at Cottrell. 'I see DS Cottrell is here too.'

'Hello, Heather. May we come in?' Gould asked, already leading his colleagues in. 'I see you have the table set. Good, that means we can put our plan in action. I have all the tape equipment ready. Philippa and I will wait in your bedroom. DS Fox will be outside to stop anyone leaving. I'll set this up now.'

Gould indicated for Fox to wait outside. Then he placed a small microphone behind some books on the bookcase, as Cottrell entered the bedroom.

'Can you talk now, Miss Morgan?' Cottrell called. 'I need to test for sound levels.'

Heather took a breath. 'Welcome to my home, police officers,' she said. 'I hope you can hear me. I've never knowingly invited a murderer to my flat before, and I'm scared – totally terrified, in fact. So I hope you will find time to protect me, if anyone attacks. How's that? Did you manage to record what I said?'

'The sound level's fine,' Cottrell called back. 'Try not to worry,

Miss Morgan. You can trust us. We'll be able to protect you if there's any incident,' she added, as she returned to the main room.

Heather looked at Cottrell with resentment. 'You were the one who treated me like a criminal and locked me up. And now you want me to trust you. Very well, I suppose I have no choice.'

'Yes, we're ready to go,' Gould interrupted, checking his phone. 'Now, are you still expecting the two people we discussed?'

'Yes, I am. Michael's coming and Margaret is acting as a chaperone. I think Michael thought his luck had changed. He's always been inviting me out since James was killed. He doesn't know I've invited Margaret as well; that should cramp his style a bit.'

Gould checked his radio. 'Foxy's told me your first guest is arriving. We'll leave you to it. Try to remember everything I told you to ask. And scream for help and run like hell if there's any violence.'

'Don't worry about that. I'll be sure to scream the place down,' Heather replied. She was about to say more, but she went quiet as she heard the doorbell ring.

She checked the bedroom door was closed and the detectives could not be seen. Then she walked across to open the front door, wondering which of her two guests would arrive first. She was not sure whether she was pleased or disappointed to see Michael Dawson standing there, clutching a bottle of wine.

'Heather, love. How kind of you to invite me,' Michael said. 'I never told you what a lovely flat you have.' He leant down to kiss Heather on her lips.

'Michael,' Heather said, moving her head to one side, so that his lips only touched her cheek. 'It's good of you to come. I thought a few of us would have a party to celebrate old Palmer's death and my release from prison.'

'That sounds great, but did you say a *few* of us?' Michael's face fell. 'I thought it was just us two. Who the hell else is coming?'

'Margaret Prestwood,' Heather mumbled, embarrassed.

'Oh, God, the earth goddess. She always looks like a tramp. Why did you invite her?' Michael asked, instinctively moving away from Heather.

'She's a good friend. Oh, this meal should be fun. You know we all hated Palmer. We can talk about the old days and drink to my release,' Heather said, forcing herself to maintain the tone of a carefree hostess.

'Oh, well,' Michael replied, shrugging his shoulders. 'It's your flat. You can invite whoever you like. I'll be polite to her for your sake.' He sat on the sofa, sipped his wine, and then clumsily tried to change the subject. 'What's going to happen to you now, Heather?'

'I don't know, to be honest. I'm a free woman now, but I can't find another job while everyone still thinks I murdered my fiancé. The men in charge of companies think I'm going to use them for target practice, and the women in personnel all look at me as if I'm some sort of murdering harpy.'

'No one who knows you thinks you're like that. I know you couldn't hurt a ...' Michael's voice trailed away as the doorbell rang.

Heather mumbled an apology as she went over to the door. Margaret Prestwood stood there, holding a bunch of flowers that looked several days old.

Heather bent forward to kiss her guest as she ushered Margaret in. 'Margaret, so good of you to come. I'll put these flowers in some water to revive them.'

'Hello, Heather,' Margaret said. 'I can't tell you how much I've been looking forward to this meal. It's great to see you free. You look surprised to see me, Michael,' she added, noticing Michael. 'I wasn't expecting to see you either. I'm sorry if I've disrupted your plans for tonight.'

'Hello, Margaret. I won't pretend I'm pleased to see you, but I'll be polite for Heather's sake.'

'Won't you take your seats? I'm ready to serve starters,' Heather called, walking into the kitchen. Michael and Margaret silently took their places at the table, while Heather brought out the first course.

*

Heather waited until the end of the meal before broaching the subject that Gould had primed her to raise. She had managed to fulfil her job as a hostess and provided a meal she was proud of. She had persuaded her guests to make light conversation, despite their mutual dislike, and the mood of the group had mellowed. She now brought out a jug of coffee and passed the cups around.

'That was a fabulous meal, Heather,' Michael said. 'Thank you for inviting me.'

'Yes,' Margaret said. 'I've always said you are a great cook.'

'I'm glad you enjoyed it, and it's great you could both come. But, to be honest, I had an ulterior motive for bringing you two here. I'd like to talk about who really killed James,' Heather said, moving her eyes from Michael to Margaret. Her remark was met with a stunned silence.

'What do you mean? It must have been Palmer, mustn't it?' Michael asked after a moment's pause. 'Everyone now knows what a crook he was. It must have been some crime deal that went wrong.'

'I saw David Gould the other day, and he doesn't think Palmer did it – not on his own, anyway. Apparently, he was boasting about his crimes, but seemed genuinely surprised when David suggested he had killed James.'

'Well, let's leave it to the police to consider,' Michael said. 'They're the professionals.'

'Oh, they aren't doing anything,' Heather said. 'They told me they aren't looking for anyone. They can't carry the investigation forward unless there's more evidence. Meanwhile I am stuck here with no job and no future. I may be free, but half of London still thinks I murdered my fiancé. When I go out, all the women in the shops look at me as if I'm Jill the Ripper brought back to life.'

'I know it's tough for you,' Margaret said, 'but the police can't have any evidence against you if you're still free. I don't think I've ever agreed with Michael before, but I'm sure it's safest to leave it to the police. I expect they'll make an arrest before too long.'

'But they're not doing anything,' Heather said. 'It leaves me in limbo, with everyone I meet thinking I'm some sort of monster. I'm sure the three of us can come up with something if we put our minds together. What harm can it do to at least try?'

'OK, I'll play along. I've always wanted to be a detective,' Michael said. 'We'll see what we can come up with. Let's go back to that party. You said you were locked in the boardroom when you woke up and saw James's body. Let's pretend this is the boardroom. Relive that day. You open your eyes. Now what do you see?'

Heather stood in the middle of the room, then closed and opened her eyes. 'Going back to earlier in the evening, there were lots of people from the company; you two were there, of course. There were hideous Christmas decorations all around. I was upset James was flirting with other girls, especially Alison. I'd just broken off our engagement, and was about to go home. I finished up my drink and everything went blank. A long time later – it must have been the next day – I opened my eyes. I recognised the boardroom. I looked out of the window and realised it was Sunday morning – that was why it was so quiet. Then I saw James on the floor, covered in blood. It was horrible. I called out, but nobody came. Then I phoned David Gould and the police came.'

'How were you feeling inside?' Margaret asked.

'Well, shocked, obviously, but a bit woozy. Everything seemed unreal. I've never felt like that before, even when I've had too much to drink. But I told all this to the police before. How does it help us now?'

'What else can you remember before you blacked out?' Michael asked.

'I'd just told James that we were through. I didn't want to see him again. I was really upset. Then that Fretwell man was pestering me, so I passed him on to James, out of spite, I suppose. I got hold of a glass of white wine – then everything went black.'

'You should tell the police to look at whoever had most to gain from James's death,' Margaret said. 'They must be the murderer. Michael, for instance, you had a motive,' she continued, turning to face Michael. 'You've been lusting after Heather for ages. It was very convenient when James was killed and you had a free hand with her. You know how to kill – you're always telling us about your time in the SAS. You said you thought James was a waste of space. You could easily have killed him.'

'What are you talking about?' Michael demanded. 'Yes, I was in the SAS – I'm proud of it – so what? It was my job. I had to kill then, but I didn't kill James Faulkner. You don't have any evidence against me.' He turned to Heather. 'Tell me you don't believe this, Heather.'

Heather's voice suddenly turned cold. 'Michael, the police have told me you're the number one suspect for killing James. To make it worse, you made it look as if I were guilty. Then you must have killed Robin Lynch as well, after we had that chat. To think I trusted you. How could you do it?'

'I didn't do it. I didn't kill either of them,' Michael said, his eyes turning from one woman to another in helpless appeal.

Margaret yelled at him. 'Yes, you must have killed James. It all hangs together. You put ketamine into Heather's drink and murdered James Faulkner in the boardroom. You put the knife into Heather's hand and left the key on the floor, then locked the door behind you with a copy. By the time she woke up, you were far away.'

'I'm not going to stand for any more of this,' Michael said, standing up. 'I thought we were friends, Heather, so I'm disappointed. I was hoping we could work together to solve James's killing, but, if you think I'm the killer, let's call it a day. I won't bother you again. Goodbye.' He walked across the room and tried to open the door, but it was locked. 'What's wrong with this door?' he asked, pulling on the handle.

'My colleague locked the door, Mr Dawson,' Gould said, entering from the bedroom.

Michael jumped with surprise when he saw Gould standing there. 'DCI Gould, what are you doing here? Have you set this whole farce up?'

'Yes, I have. Please take your seat,' Gould said. 'Don't try to break down the door, Mr Dawson. Even if you did, my colleague wouldn't let you out. He's very tough and has a terrible temper.'

'I'm glad you're here, David, but it didn't work. I couldn't get Michael to admit anything,' Heather said.

'That's all right, Heather,' Gould said, ushering Michael back to his seat. 'We have it all on tape. I'm able to make an arrest now.'

'Are you behind all this, chief inspector?' Michael said furiously. 'Is this some sort of trick? You want me out of the way, don't you? You just want to make an arrest – you don't care who really killed James. I tell you I didn't kill anyone.'

'I never thought you did, Mr Dawson. I believe you're an innocent man. You can leave now.' Gould waited until Michael had left the flat. 'I'm sorry, Heather, I lied to you. It's Margaret Prestwood I've come to arrest.'

Gould put a pair of handcuffs on Margaret's wrists. 'Margaret Prestwood. You are under arrest for the murder of James Faulkner in the City of London on the night of the 16th of December. You do not have to say anything, but it may harm your defence if you do not mention when questioned something which you later rely on in court. Anything you do say may be given in evidence.'

'You're arresting me? But Heather said you thought Michael did it,' Margaret protested.

'My little lie, I'm afraid. You've just explained how it was all done,' Gould said. He played back Margaret's shouted response to Michael. '"Ketamine into Heather's drink," you said. That's the exact drug we found in Heather's blood, but we kept it secret. Not even Heather knew that.'

Margaret looked around as if she had entered a parallel universe. 'I just suggested that's how Michael could have done it.'

'Yes, but why did you mention that particular drug? You were very specific it was ketamine. Why that drug and not another date rape drug? Caught with her fingerprints on the knife. Key on the floor, too. You've just supplied lots of details only the police knew about. Except the murderer, of course.'

'It's not true, is it, Margaret?' Heather asked. 'I thought you were my friend.'

Margaret looked wildly at Gould and Heather. Something about Heather's horrified expression seemed to make Margaret lose her customary calm.

'Oh, what's the use?' Margaret said. 'Yes, Heather, of course it's true. It was nothing personal. I was just obeying orders. Ringer knew James was getting too close to the truth about Palmer's snuff videos, and told me to sort it out. As far as I know, Palmer didn't know anything about it.

'I planned the murder very skilfully, I must say. It was all as DCI Gould said. A few drops of ketamine in your drink and you went out like a light. I left it in a glass near that old fool Fretwell, as I knew he would offer it to you. I persuaded James to come into the boardroom. I implied we could have a bit of a fling there. I may not look much, but I knew James would do anything for the promise of sex. Then I stabbed him to death wearing gloves. I put the knife in your hand to get your fingerprints on it. I left the key by you and locked the boardroom up, using a spare key that I had made,' Margaret concluded, in the tone of a craftsman proud of his work. 'It all went to plan.'

'But why did you do it?' Heather asked. 'I thought you liked James, and I trusted you. I thought we were friends. Don't you remember you used to say we were always on the same side in the company?'

'No, Heather, we were never friends. Ringer paid me to keep an eye on any traitors in the company, and I knew you weren't a company woman. So it was all to help my career. Ringer promised me a promotion.' Margaret stopped resisting the handcuffs and smiled to herself. 'But to be honest, Heather, it was just a little bit personal. It was my idea to frame you. You always pitied me, didn't you? To you, I was a frumpy bag you had lunch with because no one else would. Maybe I am, but James was happy at the thought of having sex with me, so I pulled one over on you, didn't I? You ought to pick your friends better in the future, Heather.'

Cottrell came out of the bedroom and led the killer out to the waiting police car, while Gould turned to Heather. 'We'll process Margaret Prestwood's arrest for murder. We've already brought Derek Ringer in for interview under caution. He's the only one of the ringleaders left alive in the snuff video plot, now Palmer's dead. We've arrested him for that. We should be able to charge him with murdering Faulkner as well if Margaret gives evidence against him, but we'll leave that to the courts.

'This all means you can start your life again, Heather. I hope it all goes well with you. I hope you'll always think of us as friends, but it's time for both of us to move on. Good luck,' Gould said, touching Heather's shoulder. 'We're not really compatible. We both know I'm too wedded to my work. It may be none of my business now, but you could do worse than give Michael Dawson a chance. He's been through hell in the forces, and now we've treated him like a criminal. Go easy on him. I have a feeling he is a good man, really.'

'But what will happen to Margaret?' Heather asked, following Gould to the front door.

'We'll be charging her with murder, of course. She's incriminated herself too much now, and we have it all on tape.'

'Do you think it all happened the way she said? How could she hate me so much?'

'I don't pretend to know what was going on in her mind, but it's police business now, Heather. Thank you for your help in preparing the trap. But you shouldn't worry about this case any more,' Gould said, giving Heather a chaste hug.

Heather looked out of the window as Gould joined Cottrell outside the police car. Margaret was in the back seat, and was now calmer. Heather flinched as she saw Margaret glare at her with contempt. Gould gave Cottrell a smile of congratulation before they took their seats in the police car and drove away.

Heather looked after the vehicle until it was out of sight. Suddenly, she realised she could never be part of a policeman's life and that any relationship with Gould was at an end. As he had said, he was wedded to his police job: a world he shared with Philippa Cottrell, but never with Heather.

Chapter 39

Around nine o'clock the following morning, Heather staggered to her front door. 'Who is it?' she called through the intercom.

'It's Michael,' the voice said. 'I've come to take you to work.'

'Work? What are you talking about? I haven't had a job for ages.'

'Will you let me in? It's cold outside,' Michael called.

Heather let him into the hall. 'I'm still in a state of shock, Michael. I wasn't expecting any visitors. Last night was terrifying, wasn't it? After you left, Margaret confessed to murdering James, and they've arrested her. To think she could kill someone I thought I loved like that, and frame me for it.' Heather instinctively moved towards Michael for comfort. 'Thank God it's over, Michael. Why did Margaret despise me so much?' she asked, tearfully. 'I've never had someone look at me with such hatred. I thought we were friends. I never did her any harm.'

'The Chinese have a saying: "Why do you hate me? I've never done you a favour",' Michael said. 'Don't worry about that awful woman any more, love. She was jealous of you; you have beauty, and you have a heart, which are two things she'll never have. The reason I came round is that Palmer Associates – whatever it is going to be called – needs its staff back. I had a call from Alison Coates last night. She seems to be in charge and says I can continue in my previous job.'

'I'm pleased for you, Michael, I really am,' Heather said. 'But I still don't know why you're here.'

'I'm going to tell Alison to reinstate you. If she wants me, she will have to take you as well. If you want your job back, I'll wait here while you get dressed.'

Heather nodded agreement as she left Michael in the hall.

'Come on, you can do it,' Michael called to Heather an hour later, as they stood outside the office block where she used to work.

Heather looked up at the building and shivered. 'I never thought I would come here again,' she said. 'There are too many painful memories. I can't face being thrown out again. And that morning after the party when I found James's body ...'

'No, don't worry. I'll make sure there's a position for you,' Michael said. He took Heather's hand and coaxed her into the foyer. Suddenly they heard a young female Cockney voice behind them.

'I'm glad you could join us, Michael,' Alison Coates said. 'I'm surprised you brought a friend with you.'

'Yes, I knew we could use Heather's experience.' Michael paused when he saw Alison's sceptical expression. 'Let me put it this way. If you want me, you'll have to take Heather back as well.'

Alison looked at Heather. 'Are you sure you want to come back? It'll be different now. You used to treat me as a skivvy. Now I'm the new managing director. Can you deal with that?'

'Yes, I think so,' Heather said. 'I really need this job, Alison.'

'All right, I'll take you back,' Alison said, before walking away.

Heather smiled for the first time in weeks as she walked into the office.

*

At lunchtime, Michael came over to Heather's desk. 'How are you managing?' he asked.

'I think I'm getting the hang of the job again. It's good to be back at work after all this time.' Heather paused and turned to face Michael. 'Thank you for persuading Alison to give me my job back. I suppose I do owe you an apology for thinking you were a murderer, Michael, but let's not move forward too quickly.' She smiled. 'Why don't I treat you to lunch? We never finished that last meal, did we? That one was cut short a bit too dramatically for comfort.'

Michael Dawson put his arm around Heather's shoulders to reassure her. 'Yes, let's do that. We both have memories we want to forget. Let's hope you're not arrested this time.'

Heather touched his hand and gave him a friendly smile.

*

After a short walk, Michael and Heather sat down for a meal at a familiar restaurant at Broadgate shopping centre.

'I can't forget all those meals Margaret and I used to have here. Do you think she was planning her crimes even then?' Heather asked, once they had been served. 'It makes me shiver to think how much she must have hated me.'

'You must forget about Margaret,' Michael said. 'We're in a new company, starting from scratch. Let's look forward.'

Suddenly, Heather saw Gould and Cottrell eating in a far corner of the restaurant. She gave Gould a small wave and he came over to talk to her.

'Hello there, and you, Mr Dawson,' Gould said. 'It's good to meet in a less stressful way. How are you settling down, Heather?'

'I have my old job back, thanks to Michael. I'm working for Alison Coates now, so everything is very different.'

'Margaret Prestwood appears before the magistrates this afternoon,' Gould said. 'The Crown Prosecution Service are still deciding what to charge Derek Ringer with, but he should face a long prison sentence.'

Gould seemed about to continue talking when Cottrell came up to him, holding her mobile phone. 'Excuse me, Miss Morgan.' Cottrell gave Heather and Michael the briefest of acknowledgements. 'Gov, we have a shout. It looks like a murder.'

'I'll be there. There's no rest in the police, as you know. Have a good meal together. Look after Heather, won't you, Mr Dawson?' Gould said as he left.

'I'll do my best,' Michael said. He looked over to Heather, who, for the first time in their relationship, was looking at him with respect and affection.